IF HEMINGWAY HAD WRITTEN A RACING NOVEL

The Best of Motor Racing Fiction: 1950-2000

Edited by Richard Nisley

Trademarks
All trademarks used herein are for identification purposes only.

Copyrights

Acknowledgments
Editor: Richard Nisley
Publisher: Stephen Glenn
Production: Allison Reed
Cover Art: Paul de Jean of Bohemian Dinosaur

Published by
VelocePress
1260 Patrick Ave
Reno, NV 89509
Tel: 775.786.8298
contact@velocepress.com
www.VelocePress.com

ISBN 1-58850-048-9

**To Scott and Bill,
my two sons**

particular thanks to
Stephen Glenn, Bill Nolan, John Tomerlin, and Jim Sitz.

Foreword

"There are only three sports: bullfighting, motor racing
and mountaineering; all the rest are merely games."
   Is that *so* Hemingway or what? And any of us who ever
ventured on a racing circuit wearing one set of goggles with
another dangling around our necks were inclined to think of
it from time to time if not actually slip it into conversation
in mixed (racing, non-racing) company.
   So why didn't Hemingway, standing at his mantelpiece,
write about motor racing? Or why didn't Faulkner? *Pylon*
dealt with air racing; a few feet lower and it would have
been recognizable as a 1950s SCCA National.
   Or maybe motor racing doesn't lend itself all that well
to fiction because its reality is so precise. It has a printed
history and it lives in meticulous memories (whose owners
will let you know if you transpose the figures citing Stirling's
qualifying time at Monaco in a decades-old Grand Prix.)
   If an author puts the hero in a Ferrari or a D-type, a
reader's lip might curl: "That guy was never on the factory
team." Or if a name is invented for a race car ("Hopkins" or
"Goretti") some picky voice whispers: "That's not real," even
though the reader thinks himself willing to suspend disbelief in pursuit of a good story.
   Aye, there's the rub. Good stories, great stories, live in
the *reality* of motor racing. How can anyone make up
anything that would embroider the truth of Nuvolari's
exploits in his out-classed Alfa? Or enhance the reality of
Fangio's 1957 performance at the Nurburgring beating
Hawthorn and Collins? Or improve the facts of the Moss/
Jenkinson Mille Miglia record run in the Mercedes SLR?
Why put legs on snakes?
   Ah, but time can smooth stark facts like sucked candy;
the ridges of "was" wear to "must have been." Now all, *all*, is
perceived as make believe. And here's where the fiction
writer enters with his loom to weave a fabric of "might have
been" with threads of memory and possibility. Here's a
chance to interlace some deeper truths.
   Maybe a moldering trunk in a Ketchum cellar or a viney
Cuban shed holds an undiscovered Hemingway racing
novel. In the meantime what follows here can lead all of us
down the lane where memory and imagination motor wheel
to wheel. I've already begun to seek the wholes from which
these parts are chosen.
   See you there. - *Denise McCluggage*

CONTENTS

INTRODUCTION

If Hemingway Had Written A Racing Novel
by Richard Nisley

It seems ironic that Ernest Hemingway—champion of all things male—should never have written a motor racing novel. He revelled in writing about toughness and self-reliance, cruel misfortune, defeat, and death, and what glorified them: war, bullfighting, big-game hunting, boxing. Why not motor racing?

One reason perhaps is that he didn't have a connection with the sport. As a journalist, he never covered motor racing as he did, say, the Spanish Civil War. Nor did he participate as he did big-game hunting in Africa and deep-sea fishing in the Caribbean. If he wasn't involved with a subject on some personal level, he didn't write about it.

Hemingway was never one to watch from the sidelines. Born in Illinois in 1899, he began his writing career at age 18 working for the <u>Kansas City Star</u>. During the First World War, he volunteered as an ambulance driver on the Italian front—a very dangerous job —suffered a wound and was sent home. In the 1920s, he settled in Paris as a free-lance writer and became part of the expatriate circle of Gertrude Stein, F. Scott Fitzgerald, Ezra Pound, and Ford Madox Ford. He wrote in the morning, hit the bars and cafes in the afternoon, and when he could get away, hunted and fished in the Ardennes, skied in the Alps, attended bullfights in Spain. The higher the risks, the more dangerous the game, the more it attracted him.

His first book, <u>Three Stories and Ten Poems</u>, was published in Paris in 1923 and was followed by the short story collection <u>In Our Time</u>, that marked his American debut in 1925. With the publication of <u>The Sun Also Rises</u> in 1926, Hemingway found himself hailed as the preeminent writer of his time. In the 1930s, he settled in Key West, and later in Cuba, and traveled widely—to Spain, Italy, and Africa—and wrote about his experiences in <u>Death in the Afternoon</u> (1932), his treatise on bullfighting, and <u>Green Hills of Africa</u> (1935), an account of big-game hunting in Africa. His reporting on the Spanish Civil War provided the background for his novel <u>For Whom the Bell Tolls</u> (1940). In 1953, Hemingway was awarded the Pulitzer prize for <u>The Old</u>

<u>Man and the Sea</u>. A year later, he won the Nobel Prize in Literature "for his powerful, style-forming mastery of the art of narration."

What Hemingway did was remodel the English sentence, purging it of adjectives—which he didn't trust—and any hint of sentiment. Like Mark Twain before him, his writing was simple and direct. According to writer/editor Clifton Fadiman, he taught language honesty.

One can only imagine what stories might have resulted had Hemingway spent a summer following motor racing. Grand Prix racing in the 1930s—the so-called Age of Titans— would have made the perfect setting for a Hemingwayesque story, and Tazio Nuvolari the ideal character model—tough, resilient, dogged. With supercharged engines delivering 650 horsepower to tires no wider than a man's palm, Mercedes Benz and Auto Union were perhaps the most difficult racecars to drive ever conceived. They often competed on tree-lined country roads winding through hills, past houses and over bridges, giving real meaning to Stirling Moss's oft-quoted remark: "To go flat-out through a bend that is sur-rounded by level lawn is one thing, but to go flat-out through a bend that has a stone wall on one side and a precipice on the other—that's an achievement!" In the 1930s, it was common-place.

After World War II, the Titans were gone but the story possibilities were no less intriguing. In the United States, motor racing was growing as never before and in several different directions at once. In the Southeastern United States, moonshine runners were emerging from the Appala-chian back country giving rise to NASCAR. In the Northeast, sports car racing was advancing outside its clubby confines into the brave new world of professionalism. In the Midwest and on the West Coast, midget and jalopy racing were producing the next generation of Indianapolis 500 drivers.

Hemingway wasn't alone among authors failing to take notice. When American publisher Ian Ballantine became smitten with racing and went looking for a realistic motor racing story to publish, what he found was typical of sports fiction of the day: novels written for juveniles, often with a message about good sportsmanship and doing the right thing. Undeterred, Ballantine turned to Europe and eventu-ally a book was found, a literary novel with adult themes, written in German and published in Switzerland, by an ex-racer named Hans Ruesch.

Ruesch proved the perfect stand-in for Hemingway, a talented writer who raced and wrote about it. He had drafted much of his novel in the pits between practice sessions. No slouch behind the wheel, he set fastest lap and won the 1936 Donington Grand Prix with Richard Seaman as co-driver. Eventually he might have signed with Mercedes Benz or Auto Union had an accident not interrupted his racing career. Fluent in three languages, Ruesch learned a fourth language—English—in order to do the translation himself. As he did, he made several changes, and the Hemingway style—lean, tough English prose and bare-bones dialogue—was clearly influential. The result was the best racing novel Hemingway never wrote, the story of a super-ambitious Grand Prix driver who claws his way to the top and in the process loses everything he values including his wife and the friends who helped advance his career.

The Racer by Hans Ruesch proved hugely successful in the United States, with paperback printings of 350,000 in 1953 and a movie based on the book in 1955, The Racers, starring Kirk Douglas.

Ruesch's stunning success proved to be an anomaly, however, and few writers followed his lead. Instead, novels about teens, cars and racing were published in greater number than ever before in what became a golden age of juvenile fiction that lasted into the mid-1970s. Authors such as Henry Gregor Felsen, William C. Gault, and Patrick O'Connor wrote not one but a series of juvenile car and racing novels. Juvenile novels proved to be evergreen sellers that often didn't go out of print for several years. Felsen's Hot Rod (1951), for example, stayed in print a remarkable 27 years.

Inspired by Ruesch perhaps, Felsen turned his back on juvenile fiction long enough to write one adult racing novel, Fever Heat (1954), under the pseudonym of Angus Vicker. Set against the bust-knuckle world of jalopy racing; Felsen knew this world well. Minutes from the door of his Des Moines home was a quarter-mile oval of blackened clay where stovebolt Chevies and flathead Fords regularly crunched fenders on Saturday nights and where Felsen could be found in the pits or in the stands watching the race with his son and daughter. A Hemingwayesque line on the novel's dust jacket reads: "Why do they do it? Maybe because it's a world where a man can be beaten, but never defeated...."

A few adult racing novels did get published, some

pulpishly written, some literary, including Speed Triumphant (1953) by Pierre Fisson, The Streak (1953) by Paul Darcy Boles, Passion Road (1955) by Richard Glendinning, My Mistress Death (1956) by Robert Spafford, and two by John Bentley, The Faster They Go (1957) and The Perilous Path (1961). None stayed in print very long.

After Fever Heat, Bentley's two novels packed the most convincing drama and realism. Like Ruesch, Bentley raced as an amateur, competing at the Le Mans 24-Hour (where he finished eighth overall in 1956), and the Sebring 12-Hour.

In Southern California, three other writer/racers emerged with the publication of Omnibus of Speed (1958), an anthology of motorsports writings two of them had edited. The three were Charles Beaumont, William F. Nolan, and John Tomerlin. Young and hungry, they raced sports cars in club events and sometimes on the streets of an unfinished tract-house development in the San Fernando Valley. Omnibus was their baby, a tribute to the sport they loved, featuring the cream of race reports, driver profiles, and technical analyses, by leading automotive journalists of the day. At heart, they were fiction writers, and riffled in among the articles were a few critically acclaimed short stories, including one each by Beaumont, Nolan, and journalist Ken W. Purdy. It was Tomerlin, however, who would write a full-length racing novel.

Like Hemingway, Tomerlin moved to Europe to broaden his experience. He attended races at Monaco, Monza, the Nurburgring, Le Mans, taking it all in while living on money out of his own pocket. He stayed a year, writing Challenge The Wind (1966). He returned home around the time the motion picture Grand Prix was going into production. For a while it appeared Tomerlin had timed his novel perfectly, publication coinciding with the release of a racing movie with worldwide appeal. Despite good reviews, sales were flat, so Tomerlin turned to writing juvenile racing novels, which paid the bills. One, The Magnificent Jalopy, went into eight printings, a runaway best seller where car stories are concerned.

Writer/club racer Joseph Carter, who later would earn fame and fortune writing Raging Bull, saw his racing novel Death and Four Lovers (1961) suffer the same fate as Challenge the Wind. Erich Maria Remarque, author of All Quiet on the Western Front, did somewhat better with Heaven Has No Favorites (1961), which eventually was made into the

1977 movie <u>Bobby Deerfield</u>.

Englishman Jeffrey Ashford (real name: Roderic Jeffries) wrote adult racing novels that his American publisher released as juvenile fiction. <u>Grand Prix Monaco</u> (1968) and <u>Grand Prix Germany</u> (1970) are two titles of note.

Some writers tried another tactic, spicing up their stories with who-done-it murders and international intrigue. Enter Larry Kenyon and his "Don Miles Adventures." In 1967, he cranked out three such potboilers: <u>Countdown at Monaco</u>, <u>Revenge at Indy</u>, and <u>Challenge at Le Mans</u>. English writer Alistair MacLean, famous for <u>Where Eagles Dare</u> and <u>Guns of Navarone</u>, tried his hand with <u>The Way to Dusty Death</u> (1973). The plot: heroin trafficking, murder, and fixing of races in Formula One.

Englishman Douglas Rutherford had it both ways, writing juvenile novels involving murder and political intrigue. Some telling titles: <u>The Guilt-Edged Cockpit</u> (1969), <u>The Gunshot Grand Prix</u> (1972), and <u>Rally to the Death</u> (1974).

When actor Steve McQueen decided to make a movie about Le Mans, he hired newspaper reporter-turned screenwriter (and one-time Hemingway protege) Denne Petitclerc to write a realistic story for the big screen. Petitclerc duly traveled to France to see the race and take notes. Mesmerized by what he saw, he wrote out a complete novel before beginning work on a screenplay. Unimpressed, McQueen rejected it and several other screenplays that followed (including one by Ken Purdy) and in the end made a quasi-documentary rather than a typical Hollywood movie with plot and character development. Petitclerc's effort wasn't a complete loss however. A publisher purchased the rights to his novel, titled <u>Le Mans 24</u> (1971), and released it around the time McQueen's <u>Le Mans</u> hit the theaters. Neither made much of an impression on the paying public.

<u>The Boondocks</u> (1972) by English screenwriter Desmond Lowden, <u>Out of Control</u> (1974) by racer/poet Dan Gerber, and <u>The Fast One</u> (1978) by journalist/novelist Robert Daley were three more serious efforts that went largely unnoticed. For Daley, who had written two number-one bestsellers and who would write several more, it was particularly frustrating. Readers ate up his novels about good cops/bad cops, but ignored his one novel about good race driver/bad race driver.

There was one happy exception in the 1970s, however unlikely, by a couple of good-old-boy writers who as authors of <u>Stand On It</u> (1973) wished to remain anonymous, despite the novel's instant cult status. Bob Ottum and Bill Neely did not write <u>Stand On It</u> in the traditional sense of the word, but rather told each other the funniest racing anecdotes they could think of, laughed themselves to tears writing them down, and sent the whole thing off to a publisher. The funniest part was the stories were all true.

The one adult racing novel to appear in the 1980s was not written by an ex-racer or journalist, but by the undisputed queen of romance novels—Nora Roberts. In fact, the racing scenes in <u>Heart's Victory</u> (1982) hold up fairly well. It's the rest of the story—the stuff of romance novels—that's hard to swallow. With the juvenile market having dried up, the only other racing novels to appear were in the mystery/ intrigue category. Novelists Andrew Neilson and Bob Judd knew their motor racing, at least. Neilson's <u>Braking Point</u> (1983) and Judd's <u>Formula One</u> (1989) soar when engines are roaring but stall out on tired who-done-it murder plots.

A veteran writer of juvenile racing fiction, Eric Speed, a.k.a. Sylvia Wilkinson, turned to her North Carolina roots to write a convincing story about moonshine running and the early days of stock car racing. Despite winning reviews, <u>On the 7th Day God Created the Chevrolet</u> (1993) didn't crack the best-seller list. Neither did Burt Levy's <u>The Last Open Road</u> (1994). In fact, he couldn't find a publisher for his story about U.S. sports car racing in the early 1950's so he published it himself. And sold it himself, too, like a traveling salesman, going from circuit to circuit, working the crowd on race weekends.

As the twentieth century drew to a close, the genre showed signs of new life as three adult novels appeared in consecutive years: <u>Fine Tune</u> (1998) by Gerald Hammond, <u>The Ragged Edge</u> (1999), by Richard Nisley and <u>The Unfair Advantage</u> (2000) by Michael Breslin. Sales wise, these novels flat-lined. That much hadn't changed.

With the exception of the authors who have passed away, it was my privilege to interview the writers whose stories comprise this book. Without exception, each expressed pride in his story as one would in a son or daughter, and one sensed that each had written his tale not so much to meet a commercial obligation as to fulfill an inner need. Perhaps novelist William Faulker expressed it best when he once wrote:

"The writer's only responsibility is to his art. He will be

completely ruthless if he is a good one. He has a dream. It anguishes him so much he must get rid of it. He has no peace until then. Everything goes by the board: honor, pride, decency, security, happiness, all, to get the book written."

The knock on motor racing fiction is that it doesn't ring true. It seems everyone at one time or another has picked up a racing novel and laughed at the glaring errors. True. But I venture to say in most cases the novel in question was juvenile fiction or a murder mystery dressed up as a racing novel. The pure racing story—the one where the author sets out to tell the truth as he finds it—is rare and quite another matter.

The short stories and excerpts presented here are that—the pure racing story—and some of the best fiction I've come across. If Hemingway had written a racing novel, it would not be that dissimilar from what you are about to read in these pages.

A word about fiction. Fiction is subjective rather than objective writing. It's telling a story from the inside of a character: what he thinks, feels, sees, hears, smells. It's dealing with overworked mechanics, a team owner who won't listen, a competitor who's a tad quicker than you, a heckler in the crowd, a journalist who thinks you're overrated, a vengeful ex-wife perhaps, a temptress probably. It's the answer to the question, "What if?" It's conflict because conflict drives stories and reveals character. It's the opposite of hero worship because it strips the character bare, revealing his strengths and weaknesses, thus making him three-dimensional and believable. You may or may not like him, but if the writer has done his job, the character will be alive for you and you will live his story. After you've finished, it will seem as real to you as if it actually had happened.

Enjoy.

A Death in the Country
a short story by Charles Beaumont

The world was going to hear from Charles Beaumont.

At the time of his death in 1967, readers of horror and science fiction stories were familiar with his writings, and Hollywood producers who had turned his screenplays and teleplays into movies and TV shows knew him personally, and of course gearheads who'd read Omnibus of Speed and When Engines Roar were aware of him as well. It was only a question of time and the larger world would know of him too. Charles Beaumont was just warming up when--rare for a man of his age--he came down with Alzheimer's disease, and passed away. He was 38.

In the 1950s Beaumont and his pals William F. Nolan and John Tomerlin were drawn together by a desire to make it as writers and by a love of motor racing. They started out racing Beaumont's 1954 Volkswagen Beetle, advanced to Porsche Speedsters, and eventually campaigned a home-built special they dubbed "The Nothing Special." Led by Beaumont's unbridled enthusiasm, they sometimes staged their own races on the streets of an unfinished tract-house development. Alas, the racing halted for Beaumont when the first stages of Alzheimers set in.

By then, they were successful writers and core members of "the Group," a loose association of sci-fi, fantasy and horror writers. Members included Ray Bradbury, Richard Matheson, Jerry Sohl, George Clayton Johnson, and Robert Bloch, with writing credits for several motion pictures, classic segments of "Thriller," "Alfred Hitchcock Presents," "One Step Beyond," "Star Trek" and virtually every episode of "The Twilight Zone" other than those not written by series creator Rod Serling.

The busiest of them was Beaumont. So much work was coming his way that he enlisted group members to ghostwrite some of his projects. At the time of his death, Beaumont had written countless teleplays, movie adaptations of Edgar Allan Poe's works, two novels, three anthologies, and four collections of his writings.

As the title suggests, A Death in the Country is unabashedly Hemingwayesque. According to Bill Nolan, that was the intent. Such was Beaumont's talent that, on a whim, he could mimic the style of most writers.

He had been driving for eleven hours and he was hungry and hot and tired, but he couldn't stop, he couldn't pull over to the side of the road and stop under one of those giant pines and rest a little while; no. Because, he thought, if you do that, you'll fall asleep. And you'll sleep all night, you know that, Buck, and you'll get into town late, maybe too late to race; and then what will you do?

So he kept on driving, holding a steady 70 down the long straights, and around the sweeping turns that cut through the fat green mountains. He could climb to 80 and stay there and shorten the agony, except that it had begun to rain; and it was the bad kind that is light, like mist, and puts a slick film on the road. At 80 he would have to work. Besides, you have got to take it easy now, he thought. You have got a pretty old mill under the hood, and she's cranky and just about ready to sour out, but she'd better not sour out tomorrow. If she does, you're in a hell of a shape. You know that, all right. So let her loaf.

Buck Larsen rolled the window down another three inches and sucked the cool, sharp air into his lungs. It was clean stuff, with a wet pine smell, and it killed the heat some and cleared his head, but he hated it, because rain made it that way. And rain was no good. Sure, it was OK sometimes; it made things grow, and all that; and probably people were saying, By God, that's wonderful, that's great-- rain! But they would feel different if they had to race on it, by Christ. It would be another story then. All of a sudden they would look up at the sky and see some dark clouds and their hearts would start pounding then and they'd be scared, you can bet your sweet ass; they'd start praying to God to hold it off just a little while, just a few hours, *please.* But it would come, anyway. It would come. And that nice dirt track would turn to mush and maybe you're lucky and you don't total your car out, and maybe this is not one of your lucky days and the money is gone and you don't have a goddamn thing except your car and you make a bid, only the rain has softened the track and somebody has dug a hole where there wasn't any hole a lap ago, and you hit it, you hit that hole, and the wheel whips out of your hands and you try to hold it, but it's too late, and you're going over. You know that. And nothing can stop you, either, not all the lousy prayers in the world, not all the promises; so you hit the cellar fast and hope that the roll bar will hold, hope the doors won't fly open, hope the yoyos in back won't plow into you -- only they will, they always do. And when it's all over, and maybe you have a broken arm or a cracked melon, then you begin to wonder what's next, because the car is totaled, and they'll insure a blind airplane pilot before they'll insure you. And you can't blame them much, either. You're not much of a risk.

He shook his head hard, and tried to relax. It was another sixty miles to Grange. Sixty little miles. Nothing. You can do it standing up, you have before; plenty of times. (But you were younger then, remember that. You're forty-eight now. You're an old bastard, and you're tired and scared of the rain. That's right. You're scared.)

The hell!

Buck Larsen looked up at the slate-colored sky and frowned; then he peered through the misted windshield. A bend was approaching. He planted his foot on the accelerator and entered the curve at 97 miles per hour. The back end of the car began to slide gently to the left. He nicked the wheel, eased off the throttle, straightened, and fed full power to the wheels. They stuck.

Yeah, he said.

The speedometer needle dipped back to 70 and did not move. It was fine, you're OK, he thought, and you'll put those country fair farmers in your back pocket. You'd better, anyway. Maybe not for a first, but a second; third at worst. Third money ought to be around three hundred. But, he thought, what if the rain spoils the gate? Never mind, it won't. These yokels are wild for blood. A little rain won't stop them.

A sign read: Grange-41 miles.

Buck snapped on his headlights. Traffic was beginning to clutter up the road, and he was glad of it, in a way; you don't get so worried when there are people around you. He just wished they wouldn't look at him that way, like they'd come to the funeral too early. You sons of bitches, he thought. You don't know me, I'm a stranger to you, but you all want to see me get killed tomorrow. That's what you want, that's why you'll go to the race. Well, I'm sorry to disappoint you. I really am. That's why I'm not popular: I stayed alive too long. (And then he thought, no, that isn't why. The reason you're not popular is because you don't go very good. Come on, Larsen, admit it. Face it. You're old and you're getting slow. You're getting cautious. That's why you don't run in the big events no more, because in those you're a tail-ender; maybe not dead last, but back in the back. Nobody sees you. Nobody pays you. And you work just as hard. So you make the jumps out here, in the sticks, running with the local boys, because you used to be pretty good, you used to be, and you've got a hell of a lot of experience behind you, and you can count on finishing in the money. But you're losing it. The coordination's on the way out; you don't think fast any more, you don't move fast: you don't drive fast.)

A big Lincoln, dipping with the ruts, rolled by. The driver stared. I'm sorry, Buck told him. I'd like to die for you, Buddy, but I just ain't up to it; I been kind of sick, you know how it goes. But come to the track anyway; I mean, you never can tell. Maybe I'll go on my head, maybe I'll fall out and the stinking car will roll over on top of me and they'll have to get me up with a rake. It could happen.

Buck steadied the wheel with his elbows and lit the stump of his cigar. It could happen, OK, he thought. But not to me. Not to Buck Larsen. He clamped his teeth down hard on the cigar, and thought, yeah, that's what Carl Beecham always said: you got to believe it'll never happen to you. Except, Carl was wrong; he found that out -- what was it? -- four years ago at Bonelli, when he hit the wall and bounced off and went over ...

He tightened his thick, square fingers on the taped wheel. He pulled down the shutters, fast. Whenever he'd find himself thinking about Carl, or Sandy, or Chick Snyder, or Jim Lonnergan, or any of the others, he would just pull a cord and giant shutters would come down in his mind and he would stop thinking about them. They had all been friends of his. Now they were dead, or retired and in business for themselves, and he didn't have anyone to go out and have a beer with, or maybe play cards or just fool around; he was alone; and you don't want to make a thing like that worse, do you?

So I'm alone. Lots of people are alone. Lots of people don't even have jobs, not even lousy ones like this.

He told himself that he was in plenty good shape, and did not wonder -- as he had once wondered -- why, since he hated it, he had ever become a race driver. It was no great mystery. There'd been a dirt track in the town where he grew up. He'd started hanging around the pits, because he liked to watch the cars and listen to the noise. And he was young, but he was a pretty good mechanic anyway so he helped the drivers work on their machines. Then, he couldn't recall who it was, somebody got sick and asked him to drive. It was a

thrill, and he hadn't had many thrills before. So he tried it
again.

And that was it. He'd been driving ever since; it was the
only thing he knew how to do, for Christ's sake. (No, that
wasn't true, either. He could make a living as a mechanic.)

So why don't I? I will. I'll take a few firsts and salt the
dough away and start a garage and let the other bastards
risk their necks. The hell with it.

The rain grew suddenly fierce, and he rolled up the
window angrily. For almost an hour he thought of nothing
but the car, mentally checking each part and making sure it
was right. God knew he was handicapped enough as it was
with a two-year-old engine; it took all his know-how to find
those extra horses, and still he was short. The other boys
would be in new jobs, most of them. More torque. More top
end. He'd have to fight some.

Buck slowed to 45, then to 25, and pulled up in front of
a gas station. He went to the bathroom, splashed cold water
over his face, wiped away some of the grime.

He went to a restaurant and spent one of his remaining
six dollars on supper.

Then he took the Chevy to a hotel called The Plantation
and locked it up. The rain gleamed on its wrinkled hide,
wrinkled from the many battles it had waged, and made it
look a little less ugly. But it was ugly, anyhow. It had a
tough, weathered appearance, an appearance of great and
disreputable age; and though it bore a certain resemblance
to ordinary passenger cars, it was nothing of the kind. It was
a stripped-down, tight-sprung, lowered, finely-tuned, balanced savage, a wild beast with a fighter's heart and a
fighter's instincts. On the highway, it was a wolf among
lambs; and it was only on the track that it felt free and
happy and at home.

The Chevy was like Buck Larsen himself, and Buck
sensed this. The two of them had been through a lot together.
They had come too close too many times. But they were alive,
somehow, both of them, now, and they were together, and
maybe they were ugly and old and not as fast as the new
jobs, but they knew some things, by God, they knew some
tricks the hot-dogs would never find out.

Buck glanced at the tires, nodded, and went into the
hotel. He left a call for 5:30. The old man at the desk said he
wouldn't fail. Buck went to his room, which was small and
hot but only cost him three dollars, and what can you expect

for that?

He listened to the rain and told it, Look, I'll find second or third tomorrow, you can't stop me, I'm sorry. A man's got to eat. He switched off the light and fell into a dark black sleep.

When he awoke, he went to the window and saw that the rain had stopped; but it had stopped within the hour, and so it didn't matter. He went out and found a place that was open and ate a light breakfast of toast and coffee.

Then he drove the Chevy the 13 miles out of town to the Soltan track. It sat in the middle of a field that would normally have been dusty but now was like a river bank, the surface slimy with black mud. The track itself was like most others: a fence of gray, rotting boards; a creaking round of hard, splintery benches; a heavy wooden crash wall; and a narrow oval of wet dirt. A big roller was busily tamping it down, but this would do no good. A few hot qualifying laps and the mud would loosen. One short heat and it would be a lake again.

Dawn had just broken, and the gray light washed over the sky. It was quiet, the roller making no sound on the dirt, the man behind the roller silent and tired. It was cold, too, but Buck stripped off his cloth jacket. He got his tools out of the trunk and laid them on the ground. He removed the car's mufflers first; then, methodically, jacked up the rear end, took off the back left tire and examined it. He checked it for pressure, fitted it back onto the wheel and did the same with the other tires. Then he checked the wheels. Then the brakes.

Soon more cars arrived, and in a while the pits were full. When Buck had finished with the Chevy, when he was as sure as he could ever be that it was right and ready to go, he wiped his big hands on an oily rag and took a look at the competition.

It was going to be rougher than he'd thought. There were two brand new supercharged Fords, a 1957 fuel-injection Chevrolet, three Dodge D-500s, and a hot-looking Plymouth Fury. The remaining automobiles were more standard, several of them crash jobs, almost jalopies, the sides and tops pounded out crudely.

Nineteen, in all.

And I've got to beat at least seventeen of them, Buck thought. He walked over to a new Pontiac and looked inside. It was a meek job, real meek. But you can't tell. He examined the name printed on the side of the car: Tommy Linden.

Nobody. Buck put the rag away, returned to the Chevy. Several hours had passed, and soon it would be 12 o'clock, qualifying time. He'd better get some rest.

He lay down on a canvas tarpaulin and was about to close his eyes, when he saw a young man walking up to the Pontiac. They apparently hadn't heard of the No Females Allowed rule in Soltan, for a girl was with him. She was young, too; maybe twenty-one, twenty-two. And not hard and mannish, like most of them, but soft and light and clean. Some girls always stay clean, Buck thought. No matter what they do, where they are. If Anna-Lee had been more that way (or even a little) maybe he'd have stuck with her. But she was a dog. Why the hell do you marry a damn sloppy broad like that in the first place? God. He looked at the girl and thought of his ex-wife, then focused on the kid. Twenty-five. Handsome, brawny: he thinks he's got a lot, that one. You can usually tell. Look at his eyes.

Buck half-dozed until a loudspeaker announced time for qualifying; he sat up then and listened to the order of the numbers. 22, first. 91, second. 7, third.

He was ninth.

People started running around in the pits; customers drifted up into the grandstands; the speaker blared; then number 22, a yellow Ford, rolled up to the line.

It roared away at the drop of the flag.

Others followed.

When he was called, Buck patted the Chevy, listened to it, and grunted. The track was getting chewed up, but it was still possible to get around quickest time. He eased off the mark slowly as the flag dropped, got up some steam on the backstretch and came thundering across the line with his foot planted. He grazed the south wall slightly on his second try, but it was nothing, only a scratch.

He went to the pits and removed his helmet in time to hear the announcer's voice: "Car number 6, driven by Buck Larsen -- 26:15."

The crowd murmured approval. Buck decided it would be a decent gate and settled down again. The Fury went through at something over 26:15.

Then it was the Pontiac's turn.

"Car number 14, driven by Tommy Linden, up."

The gray car's pipes growled savagely as it rolled out. The track was bad, now. Really bad. Buck felt better: he had second starting position sewed up. No one could drop a hell of a lot off of 26:15 in this soup.

The Pontiac accelerated so hard at take-off that the rear almost slewed around. Easy, 14, Buck thought. Easy. It'll impress the little girl but your ass'll be at the end of the pack.

Number 14 came through the last turn almost sideways, straightened, and screamed across the line. It stuck high on the track, near the wall, at every curve. Buck saw the kid's face as he went by. It was unsmiling. The eyes were fixed straight ahead.

Then it was over, and the loudspeaker roared: "Tommy Linden, number 14, turns it in 26:13!"

Buck frowned. The other supercharged Ford would probably make it under 26. Sure it would, with that torque.

The kid crawled out of the Pontiac but before he could get his helmet off, the girl in the pink dress jumped from the stack of tires and began to pull awkwardly at the strap. The kid grinned. "Come on, leave it go," he said, and pushed the girl gently aside. Already his face was dirty, no longer quite so young. He looked at his tires and walked over to Buck. "Hey," he said, "I had somebody fooling with my hat, I didn't get the time. You remember what I turned?"

"26:13," Buck said.

"Not too bad, huh?" the kid said, happily. Then, he spat out his gum. "What'd you turn?"

"26:15."

The kid appraised Buck, looked at his age and the worry in his face. "That's all right," he said, "hell, nothing wrong with that. You been around Soltan before?"

"Not for a while," Buck said.

"Well, like, sometimes I steal a little practice; you know?" He paused. "I'm Tommy Linden, live over to Pinetop."

Buck did not put out his hand. "Larsen," he said.

The young man took another piece of gum from his pocket, unwrapped it, folded it, put it into his mouth. "I'll tell you something," he said. "See, like I told you, I practice here once in a while. I got Andy Gammon's garage backing me -- they're in Pinetop? -- see, and the thing is, I'm kind of after 36. You know? The blown Ford?"

"Yeah."

"So, what I mean is, if you can pass me, what the hell, go on, know what I mean? But, uh -- if you can't, I'd appreciate it if you'd stay out of my way." The kid's eyes looked hard and angry. "I mean, I really want me that Ford."

Buck lit his cigar, carefully. "I'll do what I can," he said.

"Thanks a lot," the kid said. Then he winked. "I got the chick along, see. She thinks I'm pretty good. I don't want to let her down; you know?" He slapped Buck's arm and walked back to his car, walked lightly, on the balls of his feet. His jeans were tight and low on his waist and the bottoms were stuffed into a pair of dark boots. He doesn't have a worry, Buck thought. He may be a little scared, but he's not worried. It's better that way.

The sun began to throb and the heat soaked into Buck's clothes and he began to feel the old impatience, the agony of waiting. Why the hell did they always take so damn long? he wondered. No reason for it.

He started to walk across the track, but the plate in his leg was acting up -- it did that whenever it rained -- and he sat down instead. His face was wet; dirt had caked into the shiny scar tissue behind his ear, and perspiration beaded the tips of the black hairs that protruded from his nostrils. He looked over and saw Tommy Linden and the girl in the pink dress. She was whispering something into the kid's ear; he was laughing.

Damn the heat! He wiped his face, turned from Tommy Linden and the girl and rechecked his tires. Then he checked them again. Then it was time for the first race, a five-lap trophy dash. It didn't count for anything.

The race started; the two Fords shot ahead at once; Buck gunned the Chevy and took off after them. Number 14 spent too much time spinning its wheels and had to drop behind. But it stayed there, weaving to the right, then to the left, pushing hard. Buck knew he could hold his position -- anyone could in a five-lapper-- but he decided not to take any chances; it didn't mean a goddamn. So he swung wide and let the Pontiac rush past on the inside. It fishtailed violently with the effort, but remained on the track.

Within a couple of minutes it was over, and Buck's Chevy was the only car that had been passed: he'd had no trouble holding off the Mercs, and they kept daylight between themselves and the Fury.

But of course it meant nothing. The short heats were just to fill up time for the crowd; nobody took them seriously.

A bunch of motorcycles went around for ten laps, softening up the dirt even more; there were two more dashes; and then it was time for the big one-for the 150-lap Main

Event.

Once again Buck pulled into line; it was to be an inverted start. Fast cars to the rear, slow cars in front.

He slipped carefully into the shoulder harness, cinched the safety belt tight across his lap, checked the doors, and put on his helmet. It was hot, but he might as well get used to it; he'd have the damn thing on for a long time.

Number 14 skidded slightly beside him, its engine howling. Tommy Linden fitted his helmet on and stretched theatrically. His eyes met Buck's and held.

"You know what?" Linden yelled. "I don't think them two Fords is exactly stock, you know what I mean?"

Buck smiled. The kid's OK, he thought. A pretty nice kid. "Well, are you?" he shouted.

"Hell, no!" Linden roared with amusement.

"Me either."

"What?"

The loudspeaker crackled. "Red Norris will now introduce the drivers!"

Up ahead, the track was like a rained-on mountain trail; great clots of mud and sticky pools of black surfaced it all the way around; there wasn't a clear hard spot anywhere.

Buck glanced over at number 14 and saw Tommy Linden waving up at the grandstand. A middle-aged man waved back. Buck turned away.

"Gonna let me get him?" The kid was pointing at number 36.

"Don't ask me! Ask him!"

"Yeah, why don't I do that!"

After the introductions, the official starter walked up with a green flag, furled. The drivers all buckled their helmets. The silence lasted a moment, then was torn by the successive explosions that trembled out of the nineteen racing stock cars.

Buck stopped smiling; he stopped thinking of Tommy Linden, of any other human being. He thought only of the moments to come. I'll follow 36, he decided, let it break trail; then I'll hang on. That's all I have to do. Just don't get too damn close to the wall. You don't want to spend time pounding out a door. Be smooth. Hang on to 36 and you're in hardware.

The cars roared like wounded lions for almost a full minute, and some sounded healthy while others coughed enough to show that they were not so healthy; then the man

with the flag waved them off, in a bunch, for the rolling start.
Buck could see the Pontiac straining at the leash, inching
forward, and he kept level. They circulated slowly around,
the starter judged them, he judged they were all right, and
gave them the flag.

It was a race.

Buck immediately cut his wheel for a quick nip inside
the Pontiac, but the kid was quicker; he'd anticipated the
move and edged to the right to hold Buck off. At the first
turn, number 14 threw its rear around viciously, and Buck
knew he'd have to kiss the wall and bull through or drop
back. He dropped back. There was plenty of time.

He followed the Pontiac closely, but he found that it was
not so easy after all. The car cowboyed through every turn,
scaring off the tail-enders, and it was everything he could do
to hang on. Ahead, the Fords were threading their way
through traffic with great ease, leaving a wake of thick mud.

He relaxed some and allowed the long years of his
experience to guide the car. Gradually the Pontiac was
picking off the stragglers; within fifteen minutes it had
passed the fifth-place Mercury, and was drawing up on four.

You better not try it, Buck said. Those boys aren't
working too hard. They can go a lot faster. I hope you know
that.

But the Pontiac didn't settle down, it didn't slacken its
pace any, and Buck knew that he would have to revise his
strategy. He'd planned to wait for number 14 to realize that it
couldn't hope for better than a third; then he was going to
bluff him. You can bluff them when the fever's passed, when
they're not all out and driving hard.

But he could see that he wasn't going to be able to bluff
the Pontiac.

He could only out drive him, nerf him a little, maybe,
shake him up, cause him to bobble that one time, and then
streak by.

Once the decision was made, Buck moved well back in
the seat. They were about halfway through now. Give it seven
more laps; then make the bid.

He started to swing past a beat-up Dodge on the north
turn when the driver lost it. The Dodge went into a frenzied
spin, skimmed across the muddy track and bounded off the
wall. Buck yanked his tape-covered wheel violently to the
left, then to the right, and managed to avoid the car. Damn!
Now number 14 was four up and going like the wind. Well.

Buck put his bumper next to the Merc in front of him and stabbed the accelerator. The Merc wavered, moved over; Buck went by. It worked on the second car, too; and he was in position to catch 14 as it was passing a Ford on the short straight.

He waited another three laps, until they were out of the traffic somewhat, and began to ride the Pontiac's tail. They both hit a deep rut and both fishtailed, but no more than three inches of daylight showed between them.

Buck tried to pass on the west turn by swinging left and going in a little deeper, but the Pontiac saw him and went just as deep; both missed the wall by less than a foot.

Perspiration began to course down Buck's forehead, and when he tried nerfing 14, and found that it wouldn't work, that 14 wasn't going to scare, the thought suddenly brushed his mind that perhaps he would not finish third after all. But if he didn't, then he wouldn't be able to pay for gas to the next town or for a hotel, even, or anything.

His shoulders hunched forward, and Buck Larsen began to drive; not the way he had been driving for the past two years, but as he used to, when he was young and worried about very little, when he had friends and women.

You want to impress your girl friend, he said to the Pontiac.

I just want to go on eating.

He made five more passes during the following six laps, and twice he almost made it, but the track was just a little too short, a little too narrow, and he was forced to drop behind each time.

When he was almost certain that the race was nearing its finish, he realized that other tactics would have to be used. He clung to 14's bumper through the traffic on the straight; then, as they dived into the south turn, he hung back for a fraction of a second -- long enough to put a bit of space between them. Then he pulled down onto the inside and pushed the accelerator flat. The Chevy jumped forward; in a moment it was nearly even with the Pontiac.

Buck considered nothing whatever except keeping his car in control; he knew that the two of them were at that spot, right there, where one would have to give; but he didn't consider any of this.

The two cars entered the turn together, and the crowd screamed and some of the people got to their feet and some closed their eyes. Because neither car was letting off.

Neither car was slowing.

Buck did not move his foot on the pedal; he did not look at the driver to his right; he plunged deeper, and deeper, up to the point where he knew that he would lose control, even under the best of conditions; the edge, the final thin edge of destruction.

He stared straight ahead and fought the wheel through the turn, whipping it back and forth, correcting, correcting.

Then, it was all over.

He was through the turn; and he was through first.

He didn't see much of the accident: only a glimpse, in his rear view mirror, a brief flash of the Pontiac swerving to miss the wall, losing control, going up high on its nose and teetering there . . .

A flag stopped the race. Two other cars had crashed into the Pontiac, and number 14 was on fire. It wasn't really a bad fire, at first, but the automobile had landed on its right side, and the left side was bolted and there were bars on the window, so they had to get it cooled off before they could pull the driver out.

He hadn't broken any bones. But something had happened to the fuel line and the hood had snapped open and the windshield had collapsed and some gasoline had splashed onto Tommy Linden's shirt. The fumes had caught and he'd burned long enough.

He was dead before they got him into the ambulance.

Buck Larsen looked at the girl in the pink dress and tried to think of something to say, but there wasn't anything to say; there never was.

He collected his money for third place -- it amounted to $350 -- and put the mufflers back on the Chevy and drove away from the race track, out onto the long highway.

The wind was hot on his face, and soon he was tired and hungry again; but he didn't stop, because if he stopped he'd sleep, and he didn't want to sleep, not yet. He thought one time of number 14, then he lowered the shutters and didn't think any more.

He drove at a steady 70 miles per hour and listened to the whine of the engine. She would be all right for another couple of runs, he could tell, but then he would have to tear her down.

Maybe not, though.

Maybe not.

The Faster They Go
a novel by John Bentley

John Bentley was the Alistair Cooke of motor racing, a Brit living in the United States writing a weekly column for the folks back home. In Bentley's case, it was "New York Notebook," which appeared in The Autocar *in the 1940s and 1950s. The English writer was known to take a turn at the wheel as well. In 1956, Bentley and American co-driver Ed Hugus finished first in class and eighth overall at Le Mans, driving a 1.1-liter Cooper-Climax sportscar.*

Bentley wrote a couple of mystery novels before joining the Royal Air Force in World War II. After the war, he moved to the U.S and settled in Long Island, New York, where he worked for an import car distributor and wrote for The Autocar *and a number of U.S. publications including* Sports Illustrated, Esquire, Motor Trend *and* Auto Age. *He was among the original group of motoring journalists calling themselves "The Madison Avenue Sports Car Driving and Chowder Society" which began meeting monthly for lunch, beginning in March of 1957.*

When Bentley returned to writing novels, the subject was motor racing. The first was The Faster They Go *(1957), the second* The Perilous Path *(1961). Both received excellent reviews. Bentley's other books, all non-fiction, include* The Cobra Story *(1965) co-authored with Carroll Shelby;* We At Porsche *(1976) co-authored with Dr. Ferry Porsche (1976); and* The Grand Prix Carpetbaggers: the Biography of John Cooper *(1977).*

The excerpt is from chapters one and two of The Faster They Go. *The scene is the Carrera Panamericana Mexico, a five-day race Bentley covered for* Sports Illustrated *in 1954. Journalist and amateur racer Wesley Rich has conned his way into driving a 135 horsepower rear-engine Zust Sierra Coupe (alias Porsche Carrera) and is leading his class. This will soon change.*

So here I was behind the wheel of a seven thousand dollar Zust Sierra coupe — ninety cubic inches of rear-engine dynamite with an output of 135 hp and a top speed of about 140 mph. It was the hottest small car I had ever laid hands on, yet its amazing roadability was what had just saved me. This baby didn't handle anything like the ordinary 1,600 Zust; that much I knew because I owned a 1,600 and it was I who had talked Paul into buying the Sierra.

It took a full minute for the cold, clammy feeling to leave me, but then I got to thinking I wasn't doing so badly, after all. I had left the steaming jungle mud-town of Tuxtla Gutierrez near the Guatemalan border at 6:23 a.m. that morning — twenty-third on the starting grid and last in the small sports car class of a dozen entries. During that first hell-bent 125 miles of winding road — a thousand foot climb out of Tuxtla, followed by a 1,500 foot dive towards the Plain of Tehuantepec — the Zust had shown her mettle. I had overtaken all the cars in my class and three of the big machines, inching up to ninth place over-all. A typed chart taped to the instrument panel showed me that I had aver-aged around 80 mph.

If I could hold the pace; if my tires didn't wear too thin; if the engine withstood the beating; if the brakes didn't play any tricks; if I could stay on the road for another 954 hairpin turns, there was a fighting chance I might scoop the class on that first leg to Oaxaca. And there, at the end of the first leg, my co-driver, Johnny Bates, was waiting to take over.

If Johnny did as well on the second leg to Mexico City, remembering that murderous zigzag skirting the square in Atlixco better than I had remembered the hard right out of Miltepec, then we might win the second leg, too. But after that there would still be Leon, Durango, Parral and Chihua-hua before we zoomed into Ciudad Juarez by the Rio Grande, to collect that $4,000 jackpot, plus some side money and $120 for the class winner of each of the eight legs.

"Quit pipe-dreaming," I said to myself. "All you've done so far is just take a nibble out of this thing."

Ahead lay some easy going along the Isthmus; nearly sixty miles of flat-out driving to Tehuantepec on a wide, almost dead-straight billiard table of a road. This was the place to make time, but it was also a trap to lure the unwary into bursting their engines. I eased up on the throttle so that the tach held a steady 6,200 rpm — about 130 mph. This was plenty fast enough, bearing in mind that the Zust was a shade under-geared for the job in hand. Also, some pretty rough motoring lay between Tehuantepec and Oaxaca. There was the haul up the brutally beautiful Sierra Madre mountains and a writhing, dizzy jaunt to 6,500 feet at Portillo San Dionisio. On the outside of the road's black ribbon — a narrow shelf hewn out of living rock — would yawn precipitous chasms over a thousand feet deep, with eternity at the bottom.

I had driven over every inch of the course as far as Mexico City, and all I knew now was that, for the purposes of a race, I had learned almost nothing about it. Nor was I so lucky as the boys in the Lincolns whose co-drivers were also skilled navigators. They were using ordinance-type strip maps rolled up like photo film which you unwound as you went along so you could tell your driver: "Watch out for that narrow bridge a mile ahead." Or: "Five hundred yards from here there's a tight left bend with nothing on the outside."

Johnny and I, being the world's worst passengers, preferred to drive our shifts alone, relieving each other at the end of each leg, then flying on ahead to the next stop. Paul Hughes, who was a good pilot, was tickled at the prospect of taking some part in the race by ferrying his drivers from point to point in his Piper Apache.

Already it was getting hot. The asphalt of the road shimmered like onyx in the searing rays of the fast-rising sun, but I kept the windows shut for better airflow. Outside, the still air, whipped into a miniature tornado by the speeding car, boomed against the windshield and slid over the roof with a sound like a distant tide. The tires hummed softly; the engine throbbed its steady rhythm. I watched the oil temperature gauge creep steadily up, but at 240 degrees Fahrenheit it stayed pegged. This was a safe limit. In fact it left a pretty good margin because the oil take-off indicated the temperature of the oil coming out of the engine—not going into it.

It took the Zust less than thirty minutes to cross the plain, but that can be a long time when you're just sitting there, holding a featherweight steering wheel and pushing on a throttle. The seat began to feel a bit hard and I slackened my safety belt and wriggled around a bit. I'm long in the leg and quickly get the fidgets if I have to sit down and do nothing for a while. About the fifth time I looked in the mirror, a small dot bobbed up on the road, far behind me.

Profillosa in the two-liter Milano? Not likely. I had passed
him at Los Amates, before the dip into the plain, and he was
taking it easy. Might just be one of the Lincolns—the large
stock cars had left immediately after our group—but somehow it didn't look that kind of a dot. Must be my runner-up
in the class, Louis Varron, that cheerful Frenchman from
Monaco in his Sparta. Varron's machine was geared right for
the job and might be just a little faster on this all-out
straight; perhaps five miles an hour.

Coming down the hills, the superior acceleration of the
Zust had given me the edge over the Sparta through those
endless, twists and turns, until I had lost Varron. But now
the position was reversed. Still, he must be at least two
miles—a full minute —behind. If I had anything to do with it,
that was just the way it was going to stay.

As I neared Tehuantepec, a human picket fence of
green-clad soldiers armed with rifles lined both sides of the
road. They had orders to shoot on sight any animal that
strayed across the road, but from the way some of those boys
held their shooting irons, anything that incurred their
displeasure might stop a bullet. They looked like a trigger-
happy lot.

Zooming past the first houses, I eased my foot off the
throttle and coasted down to about 80. At the end of the
town was a deceptively sharp left curve, its dangers masked
by the unusual width of the road and a slightly banked
surface. It was here, the year before, that two cars had
vaulted the rim and crashed down a hundred-foot embankment into a riverbed, killing seven people.

Suddenly, I forgot all about Varron. The only filling
station in the town stood well off the road to the left, and
there was nothing in its layout to distinguish it from a
thousand others in Mexico, all selling government-controlled
gas of mediocre quality out of bright red pumps; but the
corner of my eye caught something which made me jerk my
head back for another fleeting look. Parked beside one of the
pumps was a low-slung silver machine that could only be
one of the German Protos. Two men standing beside it hid
the number, and I was past before I could recognize the
helmeted, goggled figures. Still, I was curious.

Together with the big three-liter Italian Milanos, the
three Protos were the crack entries of the Mexican road race.
The last of this trio had started fifteen minutes ahead of me. I
should never have set eyes on them. Obviously, the crew was

in some kind of trouble. What had gone wrong? The German team hardly ever experienced mechanical failure. Its cars were too well prepared. "Der system," Herr Mannheim had once told a bunch of reporters, "you cannot beat it!" Mannheim should know. He was the Protos team manager.

No more time to think. A quick stab of the brakes, a downshift into third at seventy, then another brake stab and a flick of the wheel to set the Zust up for a drift through the curve. As usual, the machine responded immediately, and as the tail began crabbing up towards the apex of the bend, I paid off on the steering and gunned the engine.

It would have been fun, except that right on the apex there were hundreds of Mexicans lining the road at its most dangerous point and spilling out into it. They stood rows deep, waving their arms excitedly, with the boldest trying to touch the car as it sped by, not a foot from them. A couple of these maniacs actually made it. I heard the thump of a palm on the roof and another whacking the tail end of the engine compartment.

Right here, where the gendarmes were sorely needed, there wasn't one in sight.

After a while, in the Carrera, you get used to these unruly mobs clearing a path for you at the last penultimate second— if you keep your foot hard on the throttle. That's the unnerving part of it. Ease off a fraction and it's all over— you'll kill a dozen people before you crash. They have to sense that you're going through; then they fall back.

It seemed as if all Mexico was gathered around that curve at Tehuantepec: buxom, leather-skinned women with vivid bandannas, towing broods of barefooted, half-naked children; peons in battered sombreros, patched shirts and wrinkled pants rolled up at the ankles; small gray burros, cruelly laden with pyramids of baskets, pawing the ground and twitching their ears against the incessant irritation of flies. Countless pairs of glittering black eyes following my progress with a fanatical curiosity. This was their biggest fiesta. It cost them nothing to watch, and maybe, if they were lucky, they might see another spectacular smash-up like the one last year. Better than a bullfight, any day. That two or three thousand pounds of plunging machinery traveling at a hundred miles an hour could mow them down like a scythe was an incidental risk to which they gave no thought.

Once, I unclenched my teeth to yell at them, "Get out of the way, you nitwits!" but they mistook my fury for a greet-

ing. Then, in a flash they were gone and the Zust began
nosing up the tortuous curves of the deserted Sierra Madre
foothills. I let go like a pair of bellows with a big sigh of relief
and started playing with the gearbox. Third—second—third—
second—third; high gear for a brief straight, then third again.
Keep the revs up; keep her rolling. With that racing cam-
shaft, anything below 4,000 rpm was useless. It meant a
precious second wasted, dropping down into the next lowest
gear. Whenever the Zust showed less than sixty on the clock,
I had the feeling I was almost standing still.

After a while you find the groove and this shifting and
correcting business becomes a sort of reflex action. I could
hear myself spelling out the curves: sharp left; hard right—
gosh! this one's tight—two more curving rights; a swing to
the left; a short straight one. It was like announcing a prize
fight.

Steep, rocky canyons magnified the boom of the exhaust, throwing its echo back and forth as we cut through a
succession of blind curves. It was kind of lonely, here. An
endlessly rising vista of scrub and cactus, rock and baked
brown earth. No more soldiers, peons, fat women, squirming
brats, mangy dogs or placid burros. Nothing but those giant
buzzards, volplaning in circles as they cast minatory shadows over the parched landscape. By this time the Sparta
must be out of Tehuantepec, chasing me with everything
Varron had to give; but the knowledge didn't bother me
much. As long as the road twisted and writhed, reaching ever
upward, I had the edge on the Sparta because of my gear
ratio; I could even widen the gap some.

And the silver car?

Something made me look in the mirror just in time to
watch the low, down-curved snout of the Protos gain on me
with menacing speed. One moment it was a hundred yards
back; the next it filled the mirror as though the driver was
getting ready to dive under the tail of the Zust.

I caught a glimpse of twin crash hats behind a dirt-
spattered windshield—then a corner came up which kept me
busy placing the car just where I wanted it to go. But that
sudden vision had flustered me a little and I overcorrected
and felt the tail yaw. Then came the high-pitched whistle of a
suddenly accelerated engine, the metallic rasp of a lightning
downshift and the imperious "Beep!" of a horn. I had priority
through the turn and was within my rights in choosing
whatever line suited me best, but the Protos was getting

impatient, trying to nose me out of the way.

"The devil with you!" I thought. "I'll let you pass when there's room for both of us."

There would be nearly enough room seconds later on a wide left curve, but the Protos driver waited no longer. With a roar, the silver car swung out and edged by me not six inches away, its left wheels churning the dust on the narrow shoulder. Then, fishtailing with a vicious burst of power, it shot clear and vanished at tremendous speed around the next bend. It was an ill-mannered but brilliant exhibition of absolutely fearless driving, by none other than Protos Number Eleven— two bold black strokes on a big white disc. That was Hans Delius, ace driver of the German team, and Walter Knecht, his "co-piloto." Obviously in a hurry and running about twenty minutes late.

You may be doing all right in a very hot, one-and-a-half liter car, but something like this can deflate you fast, at least for a moment. Here I was, burning up the road with every trick I knew, when that Protos bombed past me on the hair-trigger of poise and gave me the feeling I was tied to a pole.

Some quick figuring told me the Germans had less than two and a half hours to cover the remaining 140 miles to Oaxaca, including that mad roller coaster over the Sierra Madre and a pit stop for tires and gas further up at Portillo de Nejapa where their depot was set up. That was the maximum time allowance they could count on to check in just inside the time limit set for the big sports cars. The toughest part of the drive still lay ahead.

I began to feel hungry. Breakfast at the Hotel Bonampack —one of the only two habitable hostelries in Tuxtla—had been a sketchy, hurried, pre-dawn meal with more black coffee and cigarettes than food. Milk and butter are likely to be mildly poisonous, down near the Guatemalan border. The Lincoln team had brought with them not only a mobile kitchen but every scrap of the crew's chow and every drop of drinking water.

Water. That was what I needed. A nice, long, cool drink. I'd brought some bottled Coke along with me, but it had been jouncing around in the warm air of the car for a week, and probably was flatter than the Plain of Tehuantepec by now. Even laced with brandy from my hip flask, it wasn't the right kind of medicine for thirst.

A cigarette might help, but not in a closed car with the windows tight shut. It was a short cut to a headache. Besides, I had both hands full cranking the steering wheel back and forth and shifting gears every other minute. So I settled for some chewing gum. During the brief prelude to the next upward surge into the Sierras, I managed to coax ninety out of the Zust in a couple of spots. This was really twisting the devil's tail. One bad skid and that would be the finish. There was no place to go except rocks or the void.

What kept spurring me on, I guess, was the rear-end view of that beautiful silver Protos shooting ahead like a lightning bolt. Delius must be miles ahead already, chasing his teammates and the Milanos and Astra Romanas. I would have traded every cent I owned for a chance to drive one of those superb machines. Especially the Protos, with its three-hundred horsepower, fuel-injection engine, fabulous disc brakes and leechlike roadability. That was the car. Along the plain I figured Delius must have been doing a hundred and seventy or better. And there were the deserts north of Mexico City where the road ran like an unswerving scar for a hundred miles at a stretch. Given the right ratio, two hundred might be possible under those conditions. That was real motoring.

What happened next brought me back to reality with the same kind of shock you get when someone shakes you violently awake out of a deep sleep. Coming out of a sweeping right-hand bend I found myself suddenly on top of black tire marks ground into the road's surface by tortured rubber. The marks veered crazily to the right, going no place. I was past the spot before my brakes took hold, but in that instant I had seen enough. A thin wisp of smoke curled ominously upward through the underbrush camouflaging the steep drop at the right. A couple of Indians were making frantic signs as they ran down a hill on the opposite side of the road.

I had my safety belt unhooked before the Zust came to a screeching halt half on the shoulder of the road, and I was sprinting back to where the tire marks clawed off the asphalt and disappeared in a dense jungle of cactus and sagebrush. The Mexicans were shouting something unintelligible, but I didn't wait for them. I started down the steep slope, floundering through the underbrush and fighting off the barbed grasp of the cactus on my coveralls and hands. Hooked darts pierced the thin leather of my driving gloves and ripped at my skin. Twice I slipped and fell, collecting the torment of a hundred needlelike stabs. I could see it now—a flattened trail of shrub where a car had ploughed its way down the embankment at high speed.

Then I spotted the silver machine lying upside down at the bottom of the ravine, its bent wheels pointing drunkenly skywards. It was Protos Number Eleven.

Partly enveloped in acrid smoke, a figure struggled with desperate urgency to lift the wreck a little—to drag the other man out from underneath. The German car, built of aluminum and featherweight magnesium alloys, scaled under twenty-two hundred pounds, but he might just as well have been trying to move the Rock of Gibraltar.

The Mexicans were still at my heels. They had found a less painful way down. Oblivious of danger, they were uttering strings of slurred syllables, few of which seemed to belong to any dictionary.

"Come on!" I waved to them. "Give us a hand with this thing."

They got the idea at once and the four of us, straining and heaving like crazy, somehow managed to lever the wreck up on its side. There was a fire smoldering somewhere at the back and the gas tank was leaking. At any moment it might blow up in our faces.

The driver was still wedged behind the smashed steering wheel; his helmet was very little dented, but the lenses of his goggles had splintered into milky opaqueness. You couldn't see any blood, yet I didn't have to be a doctor to know at once that he was beyond help. His head was twisted at a queer angle and the rag-doll limpness of his body meant only one thing—a broken neck.

As we fought and tugged to get him out, I suddenly became aware that my heart was pounding like a trip hammer and I had a queasy feeling in my stomach. So this is Delius ... I thought. Hans Delius, one of the world's three greatest drivers; champion of Germany, winner of countless Grand Prix and last year runner-up for the Driver's World Championship. Delius, brilliant stylist, hero of the crowds, little tin god of all aspiring drivers, survivor of some amazing crashes. Sooner or later they all get it in the neck—but this ... in the lonely Mexican shrub . . .

We finally got him clear, the other man and I, and we lifted him by the armpits and carried him, stumbling, as far away from the wreck as we could. The Mexicans had started chattering again, their mahogany faces and beady black eyes highlighted in the glare of the licking flames.

I turned and doubled back, pushing them away with a sudden ungrateful fury. "Run, you bastards! Run!" I shouted at them.

Even thirty feet away from the wreck, where the body lay, the heat was getting unbearable. Flames had set fire to the arid vegetation and the crackle of burning wood made a startling obbligato to the roar of the fire. That the gas tank hadn't blown up was a miracle. The fuel was blazing furiously now, and my eyes were streaming tears from the sharp sting of the billowing smoke.

I got a blurred glimpse of the other German as he straightened up from examining the body and made the sign of the Cross. Then my vision cleared for an instant and I looked at him squarely for the first time. A pair of cerulean-blue eyes framed in a grimy face gazed miserably back at me. Blood ran down his cheek like a rivulet of bright red paint, but he had removed his crash helmet and there was no mistaking the neatly brushed gray hair and the clean-cut features snapped by so many automotive photographers.

"Good God!" I croaked. "*You're* Delius!"

The Fast One
a novel by Robert Daley

"The cruel sport" is a phrase often used in connection with motor racing, but few know it was Dan Gurney who first uttered these words, and fewer still that it was Robert Daley who heard Gurney utter them. Daley used them as the title of his book.

The Cruel Sport (1963) was Daley's valedictory to a sport he had been writing about since 1956 and would soon leave. At the time, the book's candid appraisal of drivers and its frank discussion of accidents and death was controversial and in some quarters unwelcome. Yet, it reflected only what most drivers had been telling him. Today, Daley's book wouldn't turn a head, but in 1963 reporting of this sort just wasn't done by motoring journalists.

After this, Daley turned his reporting skills to corruption within the New York City police department and in doing so launched a second career writing a series of best-selling cop books including Target Blue (1973), To Kill A Cop (1976), Prince of the City (1979), and more recently Tainted Evidence (1993) and Wall of Brass (1994).

Somewhere in between Daley found time to finish a racing novel he'd started several years earlier, The Fast One (1978). About motor racing Daley says: "It's such a rich subject for literature. It's really underestimated as a possibility for art and everything else."

Set in 1959-60, The Fast One is about a rivalry between drivers—on track and off. One is impulsive, the other tightly controlled. Each bears a striking resemblance to drivers Daley interviewed several times: Alex Cavelli to the late Alfonso de Portago, and Jack Blakemore to America's first world champion, Phil Hill. The excerpt is from chapter 48. It's early Sunday morning at Le Mans. Cavelli has wrested the girl from Blakemore and won the race. Now he's out to further humiliate his rival.

Fifteen hour, dawn: Above the trench that is the road, the incandescent Ferris wheel still staggers like a drunk. Sometimes the bottom of the wheel is sunk in fog, which it whips like cream. Sometimes it stops and seems to stand on end, like an egg with a dented shell. Its benches are as empty as the vanes of a paddle steamer—now that the romantic hours are over, who wants to ride a Ferris wheel ever again?

Race headlights probe the uncertain light. In every place where grandstands bestride the road, fog lies like a lover over the valley. At the esses, sandwiched between the embankments, the fog is as thick as mayonnaise but Cavelli, who leads the race, does not even slow down. He places his machine. He noses through at great speed. He is man: lustful, vengeful, brave. He is in love with female flesh and with himself and with danger. He feels himself the fastest driver in the world, and on the long dull straight, his car flirting with two hundred miles an hour, he imagines in advance the headlines which, later today, will scream his new victory at the world. Let people wipe him out of their eyes like dew—if they can. He is in their consciousness to stick. He can bend anything to his will, this car, race, season; this girl, this day, life itself. He is—man.

The light gets stronger and redder. Wisps of fog part to permit the passage of his face.

Suddenly he comes up behind the only green Aston Martin left in the race: Blakemore, three laps behind, and his car only half repaired.

Cavelli trails for a while, curious.

The car moves, he notes, in spurts, like a man with a knife in his back. He must soon pass it, but for the moment its erratic behavior fascinates him—on the straight all its power comes back, and he finds he could not gain if he wanted to. Its braking seems firm. Its power out of the slow turn is adequate—but immediately it stutters and he nearly rams it. It is like a man who can whisper or shout, but whose voice fades out in between.

Cavelli perceives that Blakemore knows he is there. Blakemore is trying to hold him off, and perhaps thinks he is doing so.

Nose to tail, the two cars race toward holocaust.

The shrewd Cavelli, having appraised correctly the condition of Blakemore's machine, concludes, wrongly, that its driver has given up, and so decides to rub defeat in like furniture oil. Make the piece glow so no one can miss it, particularly its owner.

Cavelli decides to pass the Aston Martin in the exact spot he himself was passed earlier, and in the exact way: outside wheels on the grass. He will force Blakemore off the fast line as well. Let the world champion recognize the raw fact: this year, all of it is mine.

But inside Blakemore's helmet the habit of victory has begun to reassert itself. Although he is three laps behind and in fifth place, the race has nine hours still to run. It must be a clogged fuel line, he tells himself. It could clear itself. A single monstrous fart. You might still win, still salvage— whatever is left to salvage out of today. It is entirely possible that he has lost neither the race nor the girl, merely misread the signs.

As they enter the corner at Arnage, Cavelli draws alongside and both heads turn. But the glass in their goggles goes white so that neither can read the message in the other's eyes.

Cavelli's eyes read: Sorry, but inasmuch as you want her, I've decided to keep her this time. You can't have her anymore.

Blakemore's read: That girl is as reversible as a rain-coat. I can't fight her. But in a racing car I'll fight you or anyone else as long as my car goes on running.

In a moment Blakemore's concentration is functioning perfectly. All he sees is the road, his own car, Cavelli's.

Although Blakemore has the line, Cavelli easily stays beside him. Cavelli's tires give their little scared squeals, and the steering goes light in his hands, but he stays where he is as the next turn, with the velocity of death, rushes at both of them.

Again their goggles flash like signals sent with mirrors. Again neither tries to decipher the other's code.

Blakemore's is meant to read: I've had enough of you. Don't push me any farther.

The bottom half of Cavelli's face smirks, which he means to read: I am more man than you are, and can take your title as easily as I took your girl.

But Blakemore is not thinking about the girl anymore, only about the race. As they accelerate into the turn called Maison Blanche, Blakemore's car is functioning perfectly. Their speed has climbed to about a hundred and forty miles per hour. The road bends left, then right. Both aim toward the apex of the second curve; both plan to slice straight across it, straightening the road out.

The cars are almost touching. If a door were swung open it would strike the other car. Between them is a two-foot ribbon of road rushing backward at great speed. The flat planes of goggles flash white across the void. Both drivers are still sending signals that no one receives.

Cavelli decides to bear in on the world champion, forcing him to concede the fast line.

Blakemore thinks: He's taken too much already. It stops here. He gets no more.

Cavelli decides: The world champion must be made to surrender his line, to admit the supremacy of another—me.

He's trying to use his reputation for imprudence, Blakemore realizes coldly, to scare me out of his way.

Cavelli commits himself still further.

Don't hang it out there, Blakemore's blind eyes warn, or I'll cut it off.

But Cavelli is almost overcome by an intoxicating rush of feeling. He is wedded to absolute now. He is again risking everything for the sake of everything else.

He is certain Blakemore's foot will lift—the alternative is an accident involving both of them—the cars will collide: Blakemore hates and fears accidents, and knows Cavelli doesn't particularly. Blakemore has always backed off before and will again, and the instant he does, Cavelli disappears into the distant future.

Just then the glare disappears from the glass and their eyes meet. One goggled face stares at another, an instant— their first and last—of perfect comprehension. Cavelli is not stupid. He reads Blakemore's expression and realizes instantly that Blakemore has been pushed too far, or not far enough.

Cavelli thinks: He looks at me with the detachment of a banker.

Blakemore thinks: My business is driving race cars and you have threatened it; nothing enters into what happens next except profit and loss.

You accept the risk?

You leave me no choice.

Cavelli calculates the distance left him, perceiving with alarm that it is not enough. The road is disappearing and the grass is rushing toward him faster than he can solve the equation.

Blakemore, who holds the mortgage, forecloses: one of us is about to go bankrupt, and I have more resources than you do.

Cavelli runs out of road. His left front wheel bites grass, spitting it out backward and voraciously biting more. He wrenches the car to the right to bounce back onto the road, knowing he will flow directly into Blakemore. The two cars are so close they should bump together at the wheels, straightening Cavelli out, keeping him in the road, arresting his slide and glancing him the way he wants to go. This is what he hopes. What it might do to Blakemore does not concern him. In business, businessmen get hurt. He can project his own life only three or four seconds into the future, and cannot project anyone else's at all.

The turf splits and the earth under it sucks at his tires. For a moment Cavelli can't break the suction, then suddenly does. But when he flows toward the stability represented by Blakemore's car, there is only air. With astounding deftness, Blakemore has avoided the confrontation. His car seems to hover in the same spot, then to come on again, but too late to stop the slide of anyone.

Cavelli's car reels. All four wheels drag in mush as sticky as peanut butter. Breaking loose, the car climbs the embankment. Its nose rears like a horse, then levels. The ride becomes rough. It is like driving over rooftops. He feels the two front wheels bend flat under the car. Then the car is in the air, and he is sailing soundlessly toward the oncoming sun, which at that moment sets fire to the tops of the trees, and to the world, the second time this morning he has seen this happen. Still in the car, he sails half over, half through a fence—the wires twang like banjo strings. There are faces near him. Campers. One or two show fear, others nothing at all. The car carves through arms and legs and heads and bodies. Blunt tires, neat as razor blades, slice open tents.

Never mind these people, thinks Cavelli clearly. They are statistics in tomorrow morning's newspaper. I'm the one who counts here.

He is adrift on a moment in time. There is no sound, and scarcely any movement except the wind past his face below the goggles. There is a wetness on one arm that might be dew or blood, his own or someone's. But he has no time to look, and dew or blood—it's immaterial to him. Rising weightlessly out of his seat, he stands upon the air. Pieces of the car drift back all around him. The sun catches the bonnet of the car—it is scything soundlessly, slowly toward his waist and the sun has turned it molten red. He puts out a hand to stop it, and his hand disappears. He sees it a little ways off and grabs for it—hey, I need that—as the ax edge reaches his midsection, an executioner's sword that slices through him and keeps going. Now it is his hips and legs that float away. He reaches for them with his good hand, but misses.

I've made a mistake here somewhere, he tells himself. Blakemore should have ceded me the turn, he wasn't even a contender, whereas I was leading the race, and the rule is to let faster cars by. I was faster.

Cavelli wants to reverse time. If he can reverse it a single second he can change all this. But with every thought that crowds his head, the moment that needs reversing, the moment that brought all this on, recedes farther out of reach. He can't get either hand on it, even if he still had two.

Still cerebrating, Cavelli is amazed that this has happened. The image crowds his brain of his photo in the race program. Other people will have photos at all ages, but that is the last one of him.

He thinks: But I'm losing only time, right? And what is time without the ability to measure it? At this moment I'm losing everything, but as soon as it ends I'll have lost nothing. In a moment, time won't be important to me at all.

It occurs to him to disavow death. The ultimate anarchy: Fuck death. But the next moment he changes his mind. He is almost overcome by grief. Why has Blakemore killed him? She was only a girl. The world is full of girls, all of them stupid cunts, every one.

He strikes earth headfirst and can smell it. His body somersaults, the briefest somersaults he has ever made. The sun grows dimmer. Night comes on, ending the shortest Sunday of his life. The instant that might have reversed all this is so far out of reach now that he doesn't even think to grab for it.

Can nothing be done?

No.

Church bells toll for outdoor mass. The crowd collects out of the pup tents, out of the parked cars. In Catholic Europe, this is as it should be. The race howls satanically around the perimeter of all those lives, his too. Mass is sacrificed near the bare ground where, only a few minutes ago, Elizabeth sacrificed her real virginity.

Cavelli wants to gather up all he loved and fought for and is losing, and also that bigger pile which contains all he never had time to achieve, and lump them all together so as to impress somebody, but that won't work. His monument will be modest.

He thinks: But I wanted a pyramid.

The clock hand jumps forward on church steeples in every village in France and the world. At this very moment men impregnate women. Human beings begin to exist who have never shared this earth with him.

Life continues. Time continues as before. Imperceptibly, without sound or movement, time extends toward the outer reaches of —nothingness.

Cavelli's last thought comes in fragments:
The world goes on
Without
Me.

Fever Heat
a novel by Henry Gregor Felsen

Henry Gregor Felsen (1916-1995) has the distinction of writ-ing the only million-seller of the genre, albeit juvenile fiction. The book is Hot Rod *(1951) which remained in print well into the 1970s. A prolific writer, Felsen wrote some 60 books. His most popular were those in a car series that included* Street Rod, Crash Club, *and* Boy Gets Car. *About eight million copies were sold. His short stories—numbering in the hundreds—appeared regu-larly in the* Saturday Evening Post.

Fever Heat *(1954), written under the pseudonym of Angus Vicker, was Felsen's rare attempt at writing adult fiction. The author had caught the racing bug and regularly attended races at Pioneer Speedway near his Des Moines home, the story set-ting. Like all good novelists, Felsen captures a time and a place— an attitude, really—that is grassroots stock car/jalopy racing. It's a world where on humid Saturday evenings the air is thick with the smell of spent fuel and the sweat of desperate men spending money they don't have on battered cars that haven't a prayer of winning. The very crucible that produced the likes of Parnelli Jones and Mario Andretti.*

Future historians may very well dispense with record books and race reports and study novels such as Fever Heat *to learn about twentieth-century motor racing, as, for example, today's historians read Charles Dickens' novels to understand the shabby working conditions of child laborers in nineteenth-century En-gland.*

The excerpt (from chapters six and seven) finds Ace Jones with his new best friend and mechanic Toad making his first visit to the local speedway at the edge of town. The cynical ex-racer has seen it all a hundred times before.

Toad and I ate dinner at the counter in the Town Cafe—
Toad called it the Town Cayf—and set out for the track
on foot.

"Fill me in on the track lash-up," I said to Toad.

"It's a simple, but it ain't sweet," Toad said. "It's a one-
man deal. Fella named Herpgruve is the sole owner, proprietor, promoter, and puke-head."

"Don't the owners and drivers have a piece of it? In a
town like this? Don't they have an Association?"

"Hell," Toad said. "You couldn't get any two guys here to
agree on which end of the horse the tail is hung on."

"What about Herpgruve? He run any cars?"

"He don't run nothin'," Toad grumbled. "He bought the
track a couple of years ago, when there wasn't nothing doing
on it. When stock racin' started in the other towns, he
opened the track. It's all his'n. You run his way, or you don't
run. You know how the boys are—they'd ruther race than
argue."

"What's his way?"

"About what you'd expect," Toad said. "He don't care
about racing. He wants thrills. Lots of spins and crashes,
even if he's got to buy 'em. Figures the crowd comes to see
smash-ups."

"Fixed races?"

"Naw," Toad said. "Not that way. Everybody tries to win.
But he'll give some guy five bucks to spin some other driver
off the track. Any time anybody gets spun out, the driver
figures it was on purpose. If it's bad, he'll tear into the other
guy right on the track. Makes for a lot of bad blood and mean
driving."

"But it brings in money," I said.

"Every time," Toad said.

"Doesn't anybody ever balk?"

"Yeah," Toad said. "The good boys want to run clean.
Bill tried to fight for some rules. He wanted to get away from
fender-bangin' and into hard racin'. Some of the guys were
with him—while he lasted."

I looked at Toad. He didn't have to put any more into
words. Bill had put up a fight. I knew the rest. Somehow,
somebody would always be spinning him out, forcing him
into the fence, hooking him and dragging him out of a race.
For five sure bucks. More than that "somebody" might make
all night just racing for the checkered flag. Hazards of racing.
You couldn't prove it was done on purpose. You had to take it

and fight back until you won. Until you proved you were too tough to take that kind of crap. If you didn't get the end of a fence rail through your guts first.

"Who did it?" I asked.

"A guy," Toad said.

"Paid for it?"

"I don't know," Toad said. "I didn't ask before I started in on his haid with a wrench, and he wasn't able to explain after."

Toad's lip curled back slightly in the furtive yellow-toothed badger grin. He snuffled out his cough-like chuckle and raised his head a little. I saw his eyes. There were tears in the corners.

As Toad and I neared the track we were passed several times by drivers bringing their racers to the tracks. Some were towed, some rode on trailers, a few were carried in trucks.

"Damn your long-legged soul," Toad gasped. "Slow down."

Seeing the racers go by had done it. Each one pulled me along a little faster. Just the sight of them going by—and knowing where they were going—made my throat dry, sent shivers through my middle, and pulled the canvas covers off my raw nerve endings. An old fire horse trying to gallop after the red trucks.

By the time we reached the track customer traffic was heavy, the PA system was playing a loud record, and above it all we could hear the rising and falling snarl of a gutty engine being revved. And I wanted to throw back my head and whinny.

A car came up from the rear. It sounded familiar. I turned to look, and it was my old car all right, with Joe at the wheel. He drove past slowly, trailing a steady wisp of blue smoke. As he went by our eyes met and I almost laughed at the forlorn expression that was still on his pale, chinless face.

But as I watched the stubby tail end of the Hudson disappear, and remembered what we had been through together, recalled the battles and the way the scars had been won, I wanted it again. Wanted it to be my own.

But it was gone, ridden by a pimply stranger who hated it. Gone, and with it, a big chunk of my life. All that it had been and I had been was over for us both. I was glad the end had come, glad I was out of the safety belt for good. We had nothing further to share, the old Hudson and I. Only memories to forget. But the parting, though planned for, was not easy. It was like being divorced, and seeing your ex-wife again suddenly, with a stranger, remembering all the good things she had given to you, and now offered to another.

Toad began to swear. "What's eatin' you?" I asked irritably.

"The ungrateful little punk," Toad grumbled. "It's six more blocks to the track. He knows we're goin' there. And after all we done for him, he wouldn't even stop and give us a ride."

The track was at the edge of town, near the shallow river I had crossed coming in. It didn't look like much. Not many small tracks do.

There was a high unpainted board fence that encompassed track and bleachers. There were a couple of little gates on the south, where the crowd was tunneled in, and a large gate to the west, for the racing cars to use.

It was at least an hour before sunset, and longer than that to race time, but the crowd was coming in. Their cars bumped along the parking field slowly, kicking up dust, directed by attendants wearing, sun helmets and carrying red-tipped flashlights.

I stopped to look the place over, listening to the sound of an engine that was being revved, detecting a high rpm miss. How many times, and at how many tracks, had I heard that sound? How many times had I made it, sun-broiled, sweating, and angry with an engine that wouldn't sweeten up, and time running out? How many tracks reached after a night-long drive? How many pits toiled in? How many last-minute adjustments to the music of warming engines on every side?

How much coffee gulped? How many hot dogs shoved down with a greasy hand? How much indigestion carried at top speed for twenty-five, fifty, two hundred laps through dust or mud, through fumes and heat-wave patterns, under the merciless sun, or the glare of lights at night?

How many circles turned? How much life spun away riding a roaring merry-go-round that let you off right where you got on, sick, dizzy, and minus youth ....

It never changed. The long lines of cars turning into the parking place, the noise, the talk, the laughter, the irritation, as people got out of their cars and walked toward the ticket office carrying blankets and cushions and light jackets.

The same people who were always there, everywhere.

The teen-agers in jeans, the boys slouching, the girls stepping like trotters in their tight pants, wearing men's white shirts that cascaded disturbingly over firm-tissued young breasts. The older folks, walking leisurely in groups. The women chatting as they picked their way around rough spots, the men in quiet thought, jingling their keys as they wondered how long it would take before the plank benches jarred aged prostates into back-aching protest.

Even the families were the same. Strolling, hurrying, with kids and without, holding hands or domestically chaste in public, they made their swarm at all the ticket offices everywhere. The same people. I knew them. They had been at every race, they would never miss one in the future. That girl with the dark hair and the white halter, the white-haired woman in slacks and a Mexican jacket, the new father who carried the baby while his wife carried the accessories, the group of fifteen-year-olds with their motorcycle caps and their hands in their pockets, trying to look bored, the young wife in a summer dress with two fussy children, trying to look interested.

I knew them all, almost by name. I had seen them at every race, in every part of the country. They had cheered my wins, booed them, screamed at my crashes, gasped with relief at my escapes, watched me a thousand times on a thousand tracks. Strange that now they could walk past me a pace away, look at my face and pass on, as though they had never seen me before.

It was the same, and I didn't want any part of it, I goddamned myself for stopping in Town, for getting snagged by the uptilt of a widow's breasts, for getting involved with the garage. Didn't I know it would lead me to the track? Didn't I know?

Toad made a funny grunting sound. I looked at him. He had his hands in his pants pockets and was huddled down into himself as though he were out in a blizzard in his summer underwear. His mouth was hanging open and he was listening. Listening to engines.

"Where can I find Herpgruve, Toad?"

Toad pointed toward a small wooden building near the ticket window. "In th' office."

"We'll get us some pit passes," I said.

We went inside. Herpgruve was a red-faced man, with egg-like eyes. He muttered, "Hello, Toad."

"This here's Ace Jones," Toad said, blinking in the light.

"He's takin' over Bill's garage. This here's Herpgruve, Ace."

Herpgruve looked at me, scowling. The hand he had started to stick out stayed put. "Seems to me I've seen you before," he said, narrowing his eyes.

"We've met," I said.

"I can't place you, offhand."

"On the highway," I said. "Just before noon."

His lips thickened around the cigar and his face went a shade darker. "You planning to run Bill's cars?"

"We don't know yet," I said. "Depends on what's in it for us."

"Same as anybody else," he said. "As much of the purse as you can win."

"We'll think about it," I said.

"Glad to have you out. Nothing like a full track to pull the crowd." He didn't sound very glad, and I didn't blame him.

"You don't mind if I look around a little," I said.

He pulled open a little drawer in the table. "I'll give you a couple of season passes. Good for the pits, of course."

"Thanks."

Toad and I waited silently while he filled out the passes. "We could use another good car or two," Herpgruve said, sliding the passes toward me. "Bill drew a lot of people. There's a place down here for a driver who ain't afraid to crowd on the turns." The eggs in his head popped out at me resentfully.

"Maybe you can help me find one," I said. "I'm just a mechanic. I never race, myself."

I went out with Toad right behind me. We walked over toward the pit gate and found a grassy spot where we could sit down and watch the cars coming in.

Looking through the gate, I could see the track. It was a rough quarter or three-eighths or whatever the hell it was. Almost more of a circle than an oval, the chutes weren't too long. By the time a driver came off the corner onto the chute, he was practically in the approach to the next corner.

I sat and chewed grass and watched the boys bring their cars in.

A convertible with three men in it bumped past towing an orchid-and-white coupe with a crumpled right side where it had been rammed or hit the fence. A stock truck covered with country dust ground past, carrying a stubby little '34 Chevy. In the truck cab was a husky, farmery-looking boy

who drove the truck and probably the racer. An older man
sat next to him, and on the right a young woman holding a
baby. A black rod like Ronnie's pulled a black-and-red jalopy
that had large patches of paint burned off, and the deep
gouges of a collision still puckering its body.

There were more. Red, yellow, black, multi-colored. All
with numbers, some with names like Bombshell, Speedy-
Eadie, Little Gem, Fencebuster. All but a few carried the
names of some sponsor. The garage-sponsored cars were
professionally lettered. The cars that were advertising grocery
stores or other merchants were crudely lettered.

It was like sitting at an aid station behind the lines
watching the corpsmen bring in the wounded. But these
wounded, these battered and crushed veterans, were streaming toward, and not away from the front. What happened to
their bodies mattered little. They suffered only when their
throaty, roaring guts were pierced, clogged, or blown apart,
and their toed-out wheels could no longer turn in combat.
The show here was not one of glitter and color. It was a nine-
act performance of noise and violence, of crush and collision,
of hurtling iron and smashed fences that pulled the crowd. It
was the spin, the rollover, the locked horns at sixty-five miles
an hour that attracted the slouching teen-ager, his high-
busted girl, the young parents with the baby, the old folks
with their pillows and piles.

"Here comes Barney Oldfield," I said to Toad.

Toad looked up and saw Loren Peak's car. "Haw!"

Peale was pulling his flashy charger behind a tattered
Buick that was twelve or thirteen years old. Its black paint
was checked and rusty, the windows were cracked and
discolored, the fenders undulated flabbily with each turn of
the old wheels. It growled in protest as its aged valves panted
and the dying pistons wheezed for compression.

As Peale drove by I saw Ossman sitting on the right
side, pipe in mouth. There was a. woman between two men,
but all I could see of her was a flash of very light fluffy blond
hair. The back seat was jammed with kids who peered out of
the windows like little gophers peeking out of their holes.

"Twenty-seven," I said to Toad. "Is that good?"

"We've had better'n forty and less than a dozen," Toad
said. "But twenty-seven ain't bad—if they'll all run."

More engines were starting. A dozen of them barked in a
wild, exciting chorus. I felt my hands shaking. Even here, at
this dinky track, stuck away under the crupper of civiliza-

tion, where machine cripples sputtered for five laps and exploded—even here, it was the same.

Toad felt it too, the same way. His mouth twitched, and there was a rigid, glazed look in his eyes, like a tomcat frightened by a dog bark in the middle of mating.

The engines roared, belched, fired shots of protest, settled into defiant, powerful snarls. A score of angry voices yowling in the pit. The exciting stink of gasoline fumes drifted through the gate and stung my nose. I wanted to jump to my feet and run into the pits. I wanted to be a part of it. I needed a car. Any car. I ached like the guy whose bride got locked in the hotel bathroom on his wedding night. To get what I needed I was ready to ram through a wall with my head, willing to fight with feet and fists, tear with my teeth, and smash with any weapon that came into my hand.

The crowd was where it belonged, the high compression beasts were caterwauling in the pits, the race would be on. And Ace Jones was sitting on his tail in the grass outside, looking on.

Half a dozen cars were on the track now, beginning their slow warm-up circling. They raised a swollen doughnut of dust, and the faint hot currents of moving air carried the dust into the stands.

"Where the hell's his water truck?" I growled.

"I tol' you," Toad said. "Herpgruve don't do nothing he don't have to. He lets the ram do the waterin', and the rollovers do the blade work."

"Isn't there anybody with guts enough to get a decent track to run on?"

"There was," Toad said.

"There'll be some changes made before we put rubber on that track," I said. "A guy like that oughtn't to be allowed to own a track."

"Why don't you buy it from him?" Toad snickered.

"Maybe I won't have to," I said. "Maybe he'll get generous and offer me a piece."

"What the hell do you want with a track?" Toad complained. "You're gonna have enough troubles keepin' the garage afloat without takin' on the track. I never saw anybody so greedy to git in trouble."

"I just hate to see a good track go to hell," I said. "That's all. Tracks have been where I made my living. I like 'em. I hate to see anybody mistreat 'em. If I could get my hands on this one, you'd see some changes made. Make something decent out of it."

I don't know what I was getting mad about. It wasn't any of my business. I was in Town for what I could carry away in a tote sack, and not to reform any evil conditions. Maybe it was professional pride. Maybe I saw a way to pick a few extra bolls while I was in the field.

I got to my feet and brushed the loose grass from my clothes. "Let's poke around the pits a little," I said.

Toad stood up. "I was wonderin' if we was gonna watch from out here."

We went through the pit gate to the track. When there was a break in the warm-up traffic, we walked across to the infield, where a couple of dozen jalopies were being readied to run. The pits....

Out of Control
a novel by Dan Gerber

"Dan, where the hell you been?"

That's Carroll Shelby on the line, creator of the legendary Cobra. Two decades after driving for the swashbuckling Texan, Dan Gerber has rung up his old boss wondering if a little memory jogging might be in order. That turns out to be not the case at all.

"You may not believe this," booms Shelby, "but I'm looking at your picture on the wall right now. Are you still writing that poetry?"

Ah, the poetry, yes. Not many racecar drivers write poetry, if any. Soft-spoken Dan Gerber is that rare exception. Did he take a lot of ribbing for it from other drivers?

"It wasn't much of an issue at the time," he says. "I think the only people who knew about it were people who were readers of poetry who also happened to follow racing to some extent."

On an overcast November day in 1966 at California's Riverside Raceway, driving a Mustang GT 350 for Carroll Shelby, the poet-racer's racing career ended abruptly against a cement retaining wall. With nearly every bone in his body broken, Gerber was fortunate to have survived. Several months later, he started a new career teaching high school English, beginning in a wheelchair. It proved a wonderful opportunity for the poet and writer in him to fully emerge.

He wrote poems and short stories and saw them published in various collections of his writings. He taught writing courses at a number of colleges. And he wrote about motor racing for Sports Illustrated and Playboy.

Out of Control is his second novel, written in 1972-73. He started it quite by accident. "I had just finished my first novel, and I was kind of recovering from that, and missing that," he says. "I just started writing and it was the experience of being in a racecar, which turned out to be the first chapter of the book. I think, probably half-way through that chapter I felt maybe I was on to another novel, and just pursued it."

The excerpt is from Chapter One. Roger Swain is about to win his first Can-Am race and realizes his life will never be the same.

Everything worked. He was driving to win and nothing could intrude. He had a feeling he was slightly out of control, never absolutely sure the car wouldn't fly off the road at each corner or soar at the crest of each hill. He'd had a nightmare in which the car became an airplane and he had no way to land it, exhilaration going up and terror knowing he must come down. The forces on his body were like movements in a dance danced in a space no larger than his body so it became more a dance of the mind, the road rushing into his car, the dips and bends and rises, the vibrations from the engine behind him, choreography for his toes in asbestos ballet slippers and the quick slight movements of his hands from the wheel to the shift lever and back.

The scream of the engine was behind him, pushing him as if he were trying to escape it. He imagined the twisting force, the flywheels and gears trying to drill through the firewall into the small of his back. He was more aware of vibration than sound. The fuel vapor rose from his injector stacks where the engine sucked in the air and shot it out the exhaust pipes as sound. But now it was all one, movement, vibration, sound and the smell of heat on brake pads, rubber and oil. The sign from his pit told him there was no one ahead and twelve seconds of vacuum behind. Three laps to go. In plain English this meant that if the car held together he'd won the race.

He didn't have a sense of it being a race anymore; he was simply trying to hold the car together, watching the oil pressure dial he'd ignored during most of the race and listening for the engine to falter. He silently apologized to the car for the abuse he'd given it and begged it not to die. He passed slower cars. He passed the pits again. Two laps to go. He braked for the left-hand bend and downshifted for the carousel right that followed. He feathered the car through the carousel and fed the accelerator on the way out. The long straight began to rush up on him. It was like driving into a green funnel. He spotted a red jacket and knew it was Frank. The red jacket was gone now and he set up for the bend in the straight.

It was the most perilous spot on the course, an almost imperceptible crick in the long straight when you passed over it slowly, but at 163 miles per hour it became a thrill. He had to place the car on the right-hand edge of the asphalt and let it drift to the left, hoping that he ran out of bend before he ran out of road. Each year the cars went a little faster and each year each driver had to find out for himself if the bend could still be taken without letting up on the gas. It could. But each time he took it, the bend was an adventure. Would there be oil on the road, would the tar be soft? The car weighed seven pounds when it got to the bend. Seven pounds distributed to four patches of rubber about a foot square each. He didn't like to think about that. He couldn't think about that when he drove. He watched the road slide from left to right under the silver of his car. He watched the green rush by and the specks of color that were the spectators. He picked his spot to shut off for the tight right-hander and anticipated the bumps in the asphalt that would make the car jump as he braked.

It seemed as if all the cars were driving themselves because the drivers were barely visible, a plastic or metallic-looking bubble of helmet protruding from the sleek wedge of the car, most of them a distinctive color or design contrasting with the body of the car; and then Roger's helmet passed, a deep metallic blue, looking really more black than blue above the silver body of the car; and nothing but the color and his name on the side of the car which he knew was there but couldn't read as the car hissed by in its pocket of air followed by the scream of exhaust as if the twin megaphone exhaust pipes were actual megaphones through which the engine was begging to be left alone. It seemed to be always on the edge of exploding, and when he had looked at it in the garage and listened to the mechanics warming it up and checking the timing he regarded it more as a bomb than a vehicle and wanted to stand clear in case it should explode and fill the air with shrapnel. The red blur on the side of the car that was Roger's name against the silver blur that was the car itself and the furtive helmet that was Roger were now gone, leaving only the scream from the black void of the mega-phones rising and falling, rising and falling like a baby alternately screaming in a tantrum and pausing to catch its breath, then the steady rising pitch as he picked his apex and accelerated through the unseen corner and into the unseen straight, then lost in the sound of the other engines and erased by the cars now passing the spot where he stood.

The cars were spread out so that it seemed there was really no race, simply an undetermined number of cars amusing themselves with speed and sound, as if hurtling their unseen drivers past the crowd in an attempt to disguise them, to smuggle them past without notice as a child might scream about pain or in justice to obscure the fact that he was stealing cookies. It somehow wasn't Roger in that car, at least not the same man he had seen that morning absorbed in his own thoughts, whatever thoughts he might have before becoming anonymous in silver plastic and traffic and the stew of sound punctuated by the mention of his name from a loudspeaker as if it were the only word he could recognize in a foreign tongue, the same Roger who had eaten a rare steak and salad and drunk over half a bottle of wine the night before and overtipped the waitress because she was pretty and certainly not the same Roger who read T. S. Eliot aloud to no one who wanted to hear it and drank straight tequila when he drank it at all, which wasn't very often, and had actually claimed he didn't want to screw his fiancee until after they were married. And suddenly it was quiet as if everything in the world had been switched off except the katydids or crickets or whatever kind of bugs that hum on a summer afternoon, now overcast and looking as if it might rain, the grass and trees a deeper green against the gray sky, dense and still and the crackle of the loudspeaker and the sound of engines sounding like toys passing the official's pagoda where the announcer stood. Maybe it was Roger's car he was hearing through the speaker like a sound effect on a radio drama he remembered as a child or a Memorial Day broadcast of the Indianapolis 500 he'd heard years ago while driving to a beach on Lake Michigan.

The man was standing on the apron of the track in front of the pit wall. He was a small man in a lavender suit. He seemed contemptuous of the cars passing a few feet from the crease in his trousers. He chewed an unlighted cigar and held a long stick in his hands. There was a piece of cheap muslin, dyed black and white, stapled to the stick and furled around it. He was looking down the track in the direction from which the cars were coming, watching for a silver car with the number 7 on the nose. Actually the car was so low that he wouldn't be able to see the number on the wedge-shaped nose from the level of the track, but the men in the tower would be able to see it and would announce it over the public address system. The man on the track would see a thin silver wedge with a dark blue helmet growing out of it. He unfurled the flag and held the loose end of it in his left hand. He began shaking the stick, still holding on to the loose end, a quick up and down motion, a motion of excite-

ment. He was about to perform. Now he could see the silver
car. It appeared out of a mirage, vague and shimmering at
first, then distinct, then it was past him and he felt the
vibrations in the ground beneath his feet. He continued to
wave the flag and to leap into the air again and again. To the
spectators he looked like a Milanese flag dancer. To Roger he
looked like a blur of black and white that meant he could
slow down, that meant he didn't have to listen to the engine
anymore, that it didn't matter if it faltered now, that meant
he'd won the biggest race of his life.

He'd won many races in the seven years he'd been
driving, but never a Can-Am. The win would open a lot of
doors for him. His picture would be in all the newspapers
and magazines that regularly covered racing and he'd appear
in advertisements endorsing tires, oil, brake pads, spark
plugs, gasoline and maybe even a certain brand of sport
shirt. Years ago racing drivers had endorsed hair tonic, but
not many drivers used hair tonic anymore. When his helmet
was off, Roger's dark hair hung almost to his shoulders. He
couldn't imagine himself endorsing shampoo.

Now the man with the black and white checkered flag
was behind him. Roger let off on the gas and coasted the
remainder of the straightaway. He lifted his right hand from
the steering wheel and waved to the spectators and corner
workers who cheered back. Roger couldn't hear the cheers,
he could only hear the engine popping and sputtering as it
loafed through the carousel and began to smooth out as he
picked up speed down the back straight.

He cut the engine and coasted to a stop at the start-
finish line. Sam Dandy, his mechanic (everybody kidded him
about his name), was waiting there, so was Walter Ellison,
the car owner, a flock of photographers and race officials and
the man in the purple suit who was the first to congratulate
him and handed him the checkered flag. Roger pulled off his
helmet and the flameproof balaclava he wore under it and
accepted a paper cup of tepid water from Sam Dandy.

"God damn, boss-man, you did it. You sure as hell did
it," Sam said. He said it again and again. Sam Dandy was
from South Carolina. Walter Ellison came over and shook his
hand, then turned and shook Sam Dandy's hand. Walter
Ellison was happy. His car had won an important race and
the Armstrong Tobacco Company would be happy because
they sponsored the car which carried advertising for Sylvan
Cigarettes, and photographs of the car with their advertising

would be in all those magazines and on the 11 p.m. sports roundup on all those television stations. Walter Ellison bent down and said something to Roger, but Roger couldn't hear what it was. He was looking for a face he couldn't find. He motioned to Sam and Sam bent down to him. "Carrie?" he shouted in Sam's ear.

"I haven't seen her, boss-man."

Carrie was Roger's wife. He'd left her at the motel that morning. She didn't come to the races anymore; at least she was never there for the start of the race, not since Roger's accident. She'd seen Roger's car stall on the grid at the start of a race several years before. There was always a lot of dust and smoke at the start, and always a lot of confusion. She'd seen one of the cars from the back of the grid crash into Roger's car and seen both cars explode into flames. Roger got out with a whiplash neck and a few minor burns, but the man in the car that had hit him died. The safety crew got to him quickly and put out the fire, but he'd inhaled the flames and there was nothing they could do for him. His body wouldn't hold water. They'd taken him to a hospital and kept him alive for three days, but they knew they couldn't save him. He was in the room next to Roger's when he died and his wife and his father were there. After that Carrie never came to the track until after the race had started. Usually she never came at all.

Grand Prix Monaco
a novel by Roderic Jeffries

*It seemed innocent enough. Take the American editor out
for a spin in your 1924 3-liter Bentley, show off a bit of English
countryside, and maybe drop a word or two about your passion—
restoring vintage cars. Says Jeffries: "My father wrote novels
that were published in the States, and his editor when in the U.K.
visited him. I drove the editor in my Bentley one afternoon and
he asked me if I would like to write a racing novel."*

*To write a convincing story Jeffries knew he had to get the
details right. "I went to each race I wrote about and either before
or after the race, walked the track, taking photos of the corners,
and so on. At the time, I met Graham Hill and seized the chance
to question him about cornering speeds, gears, etcetera."*

*Jeffries wrote four novels, each focused on a particular cir-
cuit: <u>Grand Prix Monaco</u> (1968), <u>Grand Prix Germany</u> (1970),
<u>Grand Prix United States</u> (1971) and <u>Grand Prix Great Britain</u>
(1973). Written for adult readers, publisher G.P. Putnam mar-
keted the series in the States as juvenile fiction, to boost sales.*

*Jeffries did not start out to be a writer, but an attorney. "I
decided to read for the Bar and when called upon as a barrister,
met with conspicuous lack of success." Thus, he turned to writing. "My father was a writer and so it did not seem to be an
extraordinary occupation."*

*Jeffries has written over 100 books, mostly serial myster-
ies, under his own name and various pseudonyms, including the
Blackshirt Series (as Roderic Graeme), the C.I.D. Room Series (as
Roderic Jeffries), and the Inspector Alvarez Mysteries (as Roderic
Jeffries). He wrote the Grand Prix Series as Jeffrey Ashford.*

*The chapter nine excerpt finds rookie GP driver Dick Knox
about to take on the world's best drivers on Monaco's unforgiv-
ing streets. His mount: a lumbering, year-old Cooper-Maserati.*

Dick lay in bed and stared up at the ceiling. It was Sunday morning, ten o'clock, and there were five hours to go before the flag was dropped for the start of the Grand Prix. He sat up and drank the half glass of milk that was his breakfast.

He recalled the sequence of corners, their characteristics, their danger points. He remembered Station Hairpin and the different lines he had tried, the line Langrigg had shown him, the rpms at which it was a reasonable corner, the rpms at which it was vicious. He remembered the awful second after he had hit the stone parapet, and he sent a silent prayer to the gods of chance that he wouldn't do that in the race.

Time moved on and it was 11:20. Harry had told him to stay in bed until midday, but he could not face another forty minutes. He wasn't exactly nervous, but he was excited and he wanted to be up and doing something.

He dressed in woolen underwear. That might seem crazy since the day was hot and would certainly get hotter, and in the car the near red-hot engine would be just behind his head, but wool mopped up perspiration and did not burn. He put on flameproof overalls. They were grubby and smeared with oil, but even if he had had a fresh pair to change into, he would not have worn them. These were the overalls he had worn in his first race and they had become a talisman.

There was a knock on the door at midday and Harry entered. "They're serving soup down in the office." The hotel did not provide meals other than breakfast, but the proprietor's wife had immediately agreed, on being asked, to provide some soup for Dick—*"le grand conducteur."*

"How are you feeling?" asked Harry.

"Fine, thanks."

"You're lucky, then. I feel lousy, like I was driving, not you."

Dick laughed, but quickly saw from Harry's expression that it had not been the best moment to laugh.

"When you drew into the pits at the end of practice last time yesterday, there was a noise from the back axle," said Harry.

"I didn't hear anything."

"Of course you didn't, not with your earplugs in. It wasn't a real whine, or a knock, and it wasn't very loud, but . . ." He became silent and stared unseeingly at the far wall. He mentally listed every malady to which a rear axle could possibly become prone.

Dick crossed to the window and looked up at the sky. "It's a bit cloudy."

"It's going to rain and we haven't any wet-weather tires."

"Harry, I'm the fellow who's supposed to need calming down, not you."

"What have you got to worry about? All you've to do is drive."

They left the bedroom and went down to the office. A space had been cleared among the mass of papers on the desk and the proprietor's wife served the soup with a care and a ceremony that would not have disgraced a dish of *tourte de truffes à la périgourdine.* The proprietor stood in the doorway and talked of some of the classic duels that had been fought out on the circuit: Nuvolari and Varzi, Fagioli and Caracciola, Fangio and Moss.

Harry had not finished a quarter of his soup when he pushed the bowl away. Immediately, in a flood of French, the proprietor's wife demanded to know what was wrong with her soup. Harry merely mournfully shook his head.

Afterwards, Harry and Dick left and went along to the garage, pushing their way through the small crowd of young boys who were staring at the Volkswagen pickup and the Cooper-Maserati loaded on it. Harry checked his watch and then muttered something when he saw that it was not time to leave. "I'll tell you one thing," he finally muttered. "It was never like this at Brooklands!"

The race for Formula V cars, over twenty laps, began at 12:30 and finished shortly after one o'clock.

By now, the clouds had rolled away and the sun was shining brightly from a brilliant blue sky. In the harbor, many of the yachts were full-dressed, and the central T jetty was being used as a landing place by two TV helicopters. All boats had been ordered away from their moorings at Quai des Etats-Unis, and were now moored out in the harbor. Two small motorboats stood by, one carrying a doctor and the other a diver in frogman's dress. Large TV trailers were parked in the roadway below Quai Albert Premier. At the back of stands A and B, national flags of those taking part in the Grand Prix had been hoisted and were flaring out to the stiffening breeze. The stands were filling up with people who wore brightly colored clothes, and many of whom bought gay paper hats and sun umbrellas. On the slopes of the Rock of Monaco, beyond Gasometer Hairpin, there was a dense throng of people who had paid nothing for their seats and would have a fairly good, if distant, view of the race; in the balconies of the tall buildings overlooking the course and on the roofs of the lower buildings, the more wealthy people gathered for their free view.

Police and course officials tried to keep the track free of unauthorized persons, but they were no more successful than was usually the case. Most of the pits were empty, but in two of them mechanics had begun to lay out tools. In stand F, the contingent of Ferrari supporters was larger than ever and now they had two large Ferrari flags to wave. Red Cross members, in their gray, blue and red uniforms, took up position in the pit area. Ambulances were parked at several points just off the course.

At 1:50, there was a small parade of vintage cars that had taken part in a rally and as they went around the course the less appreciative onlookers shouted out comments that were at times both witty and insulting. At 1:55, the first of the large transporters arrived and stopped on Quai Albert Premier to unload the cars. Mechanics drove the cars down to Gasworks Hairpin and around to the pits. The air became filled with the harsh scream of high-revving engines.

At two o'clock, as the vintage cars were going around the course for the second time, Harry brought the Volkswagen pickup on to the Quai Albert Premier and he and Dick unloaded the Cooper-Maserati down the ramps. Harry carried tools and spares over to the pit while Dick climbed into the car, started the engine, blipped it until his head rang to the noise—he was not yet wearing earplugs—then drove to the pits. He braked to a halt in front of the pit which was now numbered 22. He switched off the engine and stared for several seconds at the square sign hanging above the pit. "Cooper-Maserati. Harry Chambers. No. 22. Richard Knox." There it was, in black, red, and white! He climbed out of the car.

Penelope crossed the track, smiled at him, but said no more than "Hello" as she climbed into the pit. Many drivers became completely taciturn immediately before a race, as the tension built up, and she was leaving it to him to choose whether to speak to her or not. He stared down at the dashboard and the one-franc piece that was now fixed to the right of the tachometer. Might the good-luck charm work overtime!

Two Lotuses came up the road to the pits. Shortly

afterwards, an open Mercedes braked to a halt behind the Lotuses and Langrigg and Marcellin got out. Langrigg was in red overalls, Marcellin in blue. A third Lotus arrived and was followed almost immediately by a Cooper-Maserati and two Ferraris.

At 2:35, two Lamborghinis drove past the pits and then turned off the course and parked up a side road, the barrier of which had been opened by the police. The leading Lamborghini was a futuristic vehicle with highly swept-back windshield and two large sliding doors in which the glass was continued below the waistline and almost down to floor level.

A Ferrari started up and revved fiercely. The wha-wha-wha of its engine shattered the air and made those near to it cover up their ears. Three mechanics bent low over the engine.

Harry came running across the course, brushing aside a gendarme who demanded to see his armband, which he had forgotten to put on. He came to a puffing halt by the Cooper-Maserati and stared down at it, but did not speak.

More cars drove around to the pits and the track swarmed with people. Paradusa drove up in his Lamborghini, and as he stepped out of it the photographers closed around him in a solid bunch. The Italians in stand F began a chant of "Guido, Guido, Guido."

The Ferrari's engine was cut and, as always, for a few seconds the silence seemed strange. Mechanics wheeled the racing cars out on to the dummy grid; all other cars and transporters had left. Harry and Dick pushed the Cooper-Maserati to the right-hand mark on the second row from the back.

At 2:53, a black Cadillac with police escort, followed by a Rolls-Royce, drove up the course from Gasworks Hairpin and came to a halt by the royal box. H.S.H. Prince Rainier III and H.S.H. Princess Grace stepped out of the Cadillac. The cheerful national anthem was played. They then got into the glass-doored Lamborghini, which had been driven along from the side road, and Prince Rainier drove the car around the course, thereby officially opening it. Their car was followed by another, the clerk of the course's, from which was flown the red and white Monégasque flag. When the lap was completed, the royal couple left the car and went into the royal box. The car was driven away.

By now, all racing cars were in position on the dummy

grid and the photographers were waiting by the Lotus in pole position and the Ferrari alongside it.

Drivers were called to the head of the grid, there to be addressed by the clerk of the course. Most of them were wearing their helmets and earplugs so that the whole of the address went unheard. In any case, they knew what it would be. "You know the rules. . . . Drive like sportsmen. . . . Observe the flags. ... At the end of the race stop by pits. . . . Winning car only in front of the tribune. . . . Signals given at one minute, thirty seconds, twenty seconds, ten seconds, five seconds, then each second. . . . A false start will incur a minute's penalty."

The drivers returned to their cars, hardly any of them acknowledging the presence of friends and rivals. This was the moment when the tension built right up and the mouth went dry and it seemed as if an eternity would have to pass before the flag dropped. Only one driver in fifty had the extraordinary self-control that Moss had had —he'd been able to talk about anything to anyone right up to the last second.

Drivers climbed into their cars. The photographers took photographs by the score, almost defying the gendarmes and officials to clear the track. At last, only mechanics were left by the cars. A scuffle broke out near one of the pits as a gendarme tried to move a mechanic from where he was standing. The crowd whistled their disapproval and finally the gendarme released the man and angrily stamped away. Cars were started and the mechanics waited to see if any last-minute help was needed. A wet plug, caused by low rpms, might fail to fire—there was still time to change it.

Dick blipped the engine of the Cooper-Maserati. He checked that the temperatures and pressures were O.K. Harry nodded to show that from its sound all was well and stepped away. The track cleared and only the sixteen cars remained, vibrating to their revving engines, together with the starter, who would unleash their power and their fury.

The cars moved forward from the dummy grid to the starting grid. The starter, the clerk of the course, gave the one-minute signal. Dick revved up to 9,500, chided himself for taking it so high, held it down to 9,000 the next time he blipped.

The thirty-second signal was given.

He engaged first gear, pulled the gear lever back to neutral, engaged it again, suddenly found himself having to check that he had not by mistake engaged some other gear. The noise hammered inside his head, despite his earplugs. He eased the pair of goggles he was wearing a fraction higher up his face and checked that the spare pair were ready around his neck.

Twenty seconds. He found he was taking the engine up to 9,500 again, so forced himself to hold it down to 9,000. If it were held too long at very high rpms when the car was motionless and only a light weight on the engine, the plugs could get wet. What could be more ignominious than to be left on the starting line?

Ten seconds. The air shimmered to the heat of the exhausts. Time had never passed so slowly.

Five seconds. He checked once again that first was engaged. Starter's flag was up, starter's other hand fell to show one second gone; rpms 9,000; concentrate on the starter, but tachometer just visible out of the corners of the eyes; vibrations of car indicating the rpms fairly accurately; two seconds gone; feed the clutch in too slowly, burn it out before the race begins; let it out with a bang and stall the engine; three seconds gone; too few rpms and engine falls below power range, too many and wheels spin too much and melt the surface of the tires; four seconds gone; Bunsen in the car immediately ahead, always a wild starter and some-times too wild so be ready to swing out; clutch not biting enough; wheels spinning on Bunsen's car; cars creeping, flag down, clutch out.

He made a perfect start. The right amount of power was fed in to get the wheels spinning initially, then the clutch was out, the tires were gripping, and the car flung itself forward.

A Brabham and a Matra had made very poor starts and there was a traffic jam in the center. Dick swung over to the right and shot through the gap between the pavement and the Matra. He changed to second as he crossed the finishing line, and third soon afterwards. He was now one of four cars jockeying for position for Ste. Devote. In practice, a driver chose his line for a corner; in a race, as often as not, he was elbowed out of the best line and had to take whatever one was left. Dick was in the center and unable to close up on the right-hand side so that he had to be ready for the adverse camber to affect him. He braked and turned into the corner and immediately sensed the wheels were light. He put on opposite lock to regain control. The back twitched, but did not skitter; full tanks were making the car touchy.

Already, a Ferrari, two Lotuses, and a B.R.M., were a quarter of the way up Beau Rivage climb. Behind them was a gap, then a Ferrari, a Brabham, the Eagle-Westlake and the Honda; another gap, then a Lotus, a B.R.M., and his Cooper-Maserati.

He took the climb at 10,400, finding fourth at the beginning of the third curve, but the cars that had been with him were drawing away. They braked for Massenet and he gained fractionally on the B.R.M., which meant his brakes were set up better. He changed down to third and went into the left-handed Massenet and past the Hotel de Paris. The rpms were building up as he passed the crowd-filled terraces, windows, and glass conservatories of the hotel. He braked for the right-hander around the central gardens, breasted the blind bump and dived down the hill. In front of him were three cars; in his rearview mirror he could see a car which he judged to be between two and three lengths behind.

He braked, changed down to second and the railings came up on the left. He swung into Upper Mirabeau from the left, clipped the curb, and saw that a car had spun off and slammed into the stone parapet just beyond the point where the steel guardrail finished. The driver was climbing out of the cockpit.

Station Hairpin came in sight. He accelerated in second up to 10,200, braked harshly, took the corner as flat as he could by using all of the very slight right-hand curve just before the corner, as Doug had taught him, rounded the hairpin and found himself almost on the tail of Sven Nyström's Lotus. Nyström was obviously unhappy.

A quick squirt that took the rpms up to 10,300, then he was braking for Lower Mirabeau. Nyström had trouble at the corner and almost lost the car, forcing Dick to swing wide. He all but collected the Antar advertising banner on the stone parapet. A photographer leaped clear, but only after all danger was over because his reactions were not quick enough to keep up with events.

The Lotus drew away on acceleration, fell back on braking and in the corners. There was only a length between them as they took du Portier. Once around there, Dick fed in the rpms, changed up to third by the lamppost that was leaning out of the perpendicular, and to fourth just before the red-flowered creeper that spilled down over the high stone wall which buttressed the terracing of the ground above. He entered the tunnel. The violent change from harsh sunlight to artificial light unsettled him, even though experience had prepared him for it. Just for a moment, he instinctively eased back his right foot from the accelerator. Immediately, Nyström pulled ahead. Dick brought the rpms back to 10,300 as the exit came in sight. This was not a boy's race: there could be no easing up in the tunnel.

He roared back into the harsh sunlight on to the broad sweep down to the chicane. He grabbed fifth, saw the rpms reach 10,500, then braked, changed down to fourth, took the chicane in the line that came from the center of the road to the left to the center of the road, felt the car at the limit, then was on the brick-paved but smooth Quai des Etats-Unis. He had gained on Nyström at the chicane because the Lotus was clearly having trouble with its suspension.

They went down to Tobacco Corner and changed gear almost in unison, took the same line around that corner and up the slight ramp to Quai Albert Premier, clearing the stone steps by exactly the same distance.

Better acceleration took Nyström ahead. At the corner, Dick braked violently as he changed right down through the gearbox. He clipped the boarded-up apex and paid off to the left. In the corner he once again made up the distance he had lost on the straight. Now, however, on Boulevard Albert Premier, the pattern was again repeated and Nyström drew ahead, even though Dick got second well before stand E and third as he flashed past his own pit.

The first lap had been completed: 99 laps to go.

The Last Open Road
a novel by B.S. Levy

It was one those cosmic moments, the kind where planets align, mountains erupt, and rivers change course. Well, maybe not that cosmic, but close. Burt Levy was on the telephone trying to reach the one publishing house in New York City that had not rejected his manuscript—yet. After weeks of being "in voice-mail limbo," he finally got through. Here, let Burt tell it:

"One day I called and just by accident this woman picked up the phone, expecting a call from somebody else. I said, `Hi, I'm Burt Levy and you've got this manuscript which you've had for a very long time.' And she goes, `Oh, Jesus, you're not the guy I wanted to talk to. What's the title?' And I go, `It's* <u>The Last Open Road</u>.' *And she goes, `Oh, yes. That's a wonderful story, it really is, but we can't publish it. There's no market for it. Those people don't read.'"

Levy pauses a moment, to let the full meaning sink in. This is a guy who'd spent eight years writing the book and dreaming of the reception it would have among enthusiasts everywhere and among his racing pals which are legion—people he hung out with and knew intimately, his people. Levy continues: "She said it in such a snotty, arrogant, New York way, you know, that I thought, I'll show you. That became my whole business plan: I'll show you."

Burt Levy, ex-mechanic, ex-car salesman, journalist, vintage-car racer, and budding novelist, was about to become Burt Levy, publisher, promoter, and marketer of three successive hit racing novels: <u>The Last Open Road</u> *(1994),* <u>Montezuma's Ferrari</u> *(1999) and* <u>The Fabulous Trashwagon</u> *(2002). With a million dollars in gross sales to date, he has shown her indeed, and the world as well.*

The excerpt is from chapter seven. Young, impressionable Buddy Palumbo is having his first encounter with America's burgeoning, post-World War II sports car culture. It's an encounter that will begin his journey to a series of sports car races, from Elkhart Lake and Watkins Glen, to Mexico's Carrera Panamerica and the Le Mans 24 Hour in France.

Big Ed became a frequent visitor at the Old Man's Sinclair that spring and summer of 1952. Actually, it was Big Ed's Jag that became sort of a regular. I got to know that XK120 pretty well, on account of it always seemed to be needing a little attention here and there. The Jag was *fussy*, you know, like some rich, high-class woman who's used to nice clothes and servants and stuff. And I had to buy myself a special set of sockets and open-end combination wrenches because nothing in Butch's toolbox fit anything properly except the sparkplug wrench. That's on account of the English use something called British Standard nuts and bolts, and they're unlike anything else in the whole world. Probably on purpose. See, you measure a normal bolt – no matter if it's coarse thread, fine thread, or even that metric stuff they have over in Europe – by the diameter of the shaft part. And that makes sense. But the Brits decided (for some reason that absolutely eludes me) to measure their bolts by the length of one flat up on the head. So, while a seven-sixteenths American-style bolt would be considered pretty damn dinky, a seven-sixteenths British Standard bolt is a rather hefty item. Not to mention that they're sized in such a way that no standard-regulation American S.A.E. wrench will fit snugly on a British Standard nut or bolt. Oh, you can try, but you'll inevitably wind up with the wrench slipping off at an inopportune moment (like just when you're trying to torque that last little quarter-twist into a nut or bolt head that's hidden way down in the bottom of the engine compart-ment) and that's how you wind up leaving half the skin off your knuckles embedded in the radiator core like a smear of the suet my mom leaves out for her stupid damn birds in the Wintertime.

Those British Standard wrenches were expensive, too, and it took our regular tool guy more than a whole damn week to come up with them. And no way would Old Man Finzio lay out to money just so's I could work on Big Ed's Jag. But I didn't mind. Hell no. In fact, I was real glad to have Big Ed's XK120 dropping by for service and routine maintenance every few days, because working on it made me feel pretty damn special compared to the Chevys, Fords, Nash Ambassadors, Henry Js, and even Cadillacs, Packards, and Lincolns I was used to. Plus that Jag was nothing short of a Certified Goldmine for a decent automobile mechanic. And that's not even counting Big Ed's five-buck tips! Best of all, that XK120 intimidated the living shit out of Old Man

Finzio. Why, he couldn't even look in the engine bay without his eyelids starting to twitch and his jaw tightening up like a damn vise grip. Truth is, Old Man Finzio didn't understand or appreciate Jaguars one bit, and I did what I could to encourage the situation by sort of talking to the car whenever I had it in for service. Like my mom talks to her stupid damn birds, you know? I came up with this phony baloney Lord-Earl-of-the-Sinclair British accent, see, and every now and then I'd hold a dashpot dampener or voltage regulator or something up to my ear and pretend like it was answering me back. I guess it must've looked and sounded pretty loony, because soon I had Old Man Finzio creeping around the back of the shop on tiptoes every time I worked on Big Ed's XK120. In fact, sometimes he'd just give up and go hide in the can or hang around out by the gas pumps until he heard it fire up and roll back out of the service bay. That sure beat hell out of putting brake shoes on some rinky-dink tax accountant's Plymouth.

Of course there were a lot of little mechanical secrets to learn about Jaguars, and right there at the beginning, I didn't know *any* of 'em. Like I'll never forget the day Big Ed's Jag staggered into the station with the engine popping and banging something awful and these enormous sooty-black clouds blowing out the tailpipe. He'd only owned the Jag five or six weeks then, and boy oh boy, did he ever look *pissed*. In fact, I recall his face was about the color of a fresh radish, and you could tell by the droop of his cigar that Big Ed was someplace well west of merely disappointed. "This goddam Limey piece of shit," he snarled, reaching over and yanking the hood cable so hard it damn near came off in his hand, "take a look at it, willya?"

To tell the truth, I hadn't the foggiest notion what was wrong. But I pulled the sparkplugs (always a good place to start) and it didn't take a Nuclear Physicist to see they were all gas fouled pretty bad. So I sandblasted the plugs and screwed 'em back in, and then just kind of leaned into the engine bay and stared at those weird S.U. carburetors for twenty minutes or so, trying to figure out how the hell they worked. Can't say as I'd ever seen anything remotely like S.U.s before. They had these elegant-looking aluminum towers on top —standing up there at attention like the Queen's Royal Guard or something— and I had no idea on earth what they had to do with mixing air and gasoline into something an internal combustion engine might swallow.

Finally I gave up and punched the starter button —just to see what would happen you know?— and of course the Jag fired up instantly and settled down to an absolutely *perfect* 550 rpm idle. It was like a miracle!

Needless to say, my stock soared with Big Ed Baumstein, and this time he slipped me a tenner. Honest to God he did. But my newfound stardom as a British car mechanic fizzled out less than twenty minutes later, when Big Ed's Jag stumbled back into the station with its engine halting and bucking on maybe two live cylinders and even bigger, blacker-looking clouds belching out the back end. There was a purple cast to Big Ed's face this time, and his cigar was dangling straight down his chin on account of he'd bitten clear through it. *"Wh-what the hell's wrong with this G-Goddam thing!"* Big Ed sputtered, really on a boil.

So I checked it over again —same thing exactly— and to say I was mystified just about covers it. So I reached in my back pocket and fished around for Big Ed's sawbuck. "I'm sorry, Mr. Baumstein," I told him, sounding extraordinarily lame, "but your Jaguar is really, aah, *different* from all the other stuff I've worked on. It's gonna take me a little time to figure it out," and I handed him back his tenspot.

To my everlasting surprise, Big Ed's face came down three or four shades until it wasn't much more than a warm pink. Then he reached out and pushed the tenner back into my pocket. "You'll figger it out though, won'cha Buddy?" he said, staring me right in the eyes.

"S-sure, Mr. Baumstein," I nodded.

"Good fer you!" he nodded, and slapped me on the back hard enough so there was maybe a little hint of a warning in it. Like maybe I sure as hell better figure it out.

So I looked into the Jag's engine compartment again, and all those strange, shiny, foreign-looking pieces stared right back at me. "Y'know, Mr. Baumstein," I told him, "At the very least I'm gonna need me a shop manual. You got any idea where I might find one?"

"Well," he said, "The Jaguar dealership's way the hell over in Manhattan. Tellya what, Buddy, I'll borrow ya the black Caddy tomorrow so's ya can drive over an' buy us one." It was springtime, so Big Ed wasn't using his Sixty Special for much of anything. "And one more thing...." he continued, resting a hand the size of a calf s head on my shoulder.

"What's that, Mr. Baumstein?"

"Call me Big Ed, willya?"

And that's how I wound up driving into Manhattan in Big Ed's black Caddy sedan (which, by the way, had real thick glass in all the windows) for my first-ever look at a foreign sportscar dealership. Naturally I'd asked Julie if she wanted to come along, since it was always kind of exciting going into Manhattan. Especially in Big Ed's Cadillac Sixty Special with by far the biggest, widest, softest, most sumptuous front seat you ever saw (I don't even need to mention what the back seat was like). In fact, thinking about Julie and all that soft, cushy real estate was enough to get my hormones working overtime, but she couldn't make it on account of she had a date to go over to the beauty parlor with one of her girlfriends so they could get their damn hair done and nails painted. How that ever compared to visiting a Jaguar dealership in Manhattan was beyond me, but I guess that's just one of the many important differences between women and normal people.

Anyhow, the next day I found myself crossing the George Washington Bridge all by my lonesome (with that magnificent expanse of Cadillac front seat going totally and completely to waste) and followed the directions Big Ed had scribbled on the back of an envelope down towards the southern tip of Manhattan and Battery Park. The Jaguar agency was on a little sidestreet near the river, mixed in with a bunch of factory buildings and warehouses and stuff, and it was really just an ordinary cinder-block garage that somebody'd dressed up with a fresh coat of whitewash and some brown 2x4 trim to make it look like one of those two-door English houses. There was a small wooden sign hanging out over the door, and it was done up in the kind of fancy Olde English script that you commonly see on Scotch labels and eye doctor diplomas. It read:

Westbridge Motor Car Company, Ltd.
Thoroughbred motorcars for discriminating drivers
Colin St. John, proprietor

Two MGTDs and a bright red Jag 120 were parked out front, and gee whiz, did that Jag ever look sharp in red! The MGs were sorta nifty, too, come to think of it. I'd seen a few TCs and TDs around on the street, but I never paid too much attention on account of I always thought they looked kind of rickety and spindly —like old baby buggies or something— and I knew they weren't especially fast, either. I'd learned that fact when I got into a sort of drag race with one when I was out, uhh, *"test driving"* Mr. Altobelli's Plymouth sedan. It came out pretty much a dead heat as I recall, and that should tell you a little something about how screamingly fast T-series MGs are. But they looked snappy as hell parked by the curbside, no two ways about it.

Just as I pulled up in front of the Westbridge Motor Car Company (Ltd.), this tall, natty-looking guy with a tweed cap, leather elbow patches, and a gold-topped cane stepped out through the front door, took a long, down-the-nose gander at me, and limped briskly over to one of the MGs. He tossed his cane behind the seat, folded himself neatly inside, pulled the choke knob full out, yanked smartly on the starter, and listened with his head cocked to one side as the engine ground a few times and clattered to life. While it warmed up, he gave himself a thorough once-over in the little pocket-sized mirror you find perched on the dashboards of all T-series MGs. He straightened his tie, tweaked the ends of his mustache, realigned his cap, then wet the tip of his finger and ran it delicately over both eyebrows. "Right-0," he nodded at last, giving himself an appreciative wink in the mirror. Then he reached in the MG's door pocket and pulled out the most enormous curlycue smoking pipe you have ever seen in your life. I swear, that thing was big as a damn French Horn, and the guy spent the better part of five whole minutes getting it packed, tamped, leveled off, and fired up just exactly the way he wanted. Made a regular Church Ritual out of it, you know? Once the pipe was puffing away to his complete and utter satisfaction, the tweedy guy folded his tobacco pouch neatly away, pushed the choke knob all the way in, blipped the throttle once or twice, selected first, and tootled off down the street, looking jaunty as all getout and trailing an aromatic cloud of burnt Cavendish in his wake. He ripped off a crisp shift into second and yanked the wheel hard left at the next intersection —without even *touching* the brakes!— and I watched in awe as that MG skittered around the corner like a beagle puppy on a freshly-waxed linoleum floor. Right *then* I came to a new appreciation of what MGs were all about. So what if they weren't particularly fast in a straight line? Those things could scoot around tight corners like nothing you ever saw. Plus they had a certain style and spirit that was almost as good as sheer, pavement-scorching acceleration. Maybe even better, since a really fast car could land you in a heap of serious trouble if you didn't know what you were doing.

Or sometimes even if you did.

Inside Westbridge shop were more damn British automobiles than I'd ever seen in my life. There must've been five
or six XK120s and near a dozen MG TCs and TDs, and
almost every one of them had its hood wide open or was
perched up on a set of jackstands with the wheels off. Or
both. There were some other cars, too. Cars I'd never seen or
even heard of before. Up against the side wall was this
magnificent Jaguar Mk. VII sedan that looked like the damn
Lincoln Monument on wheels, and right next to it was a
pudgy little Morris Minor coupe that could have easily
belonged to Elmer Fudd. A few TDs and XK120s down from
the Morris was this *incredible* torpedo-shaped Frazer-Nash
racing car with cycle fenders and numbers painted on the
sides. It was done up in a deep stringbean green, and it sure
as hell didn't look like any Nash automobile *I'd* ever seen
before. Of course, I didn't know at the time that Frazer-Nash
was just one of several dozen pint-sized English sportscar
companies that nobody on this side of the planet ever heard
of, and it didn't have one single thing do with Nash automobiles here in the states. Over in England, it seems like
anybody with a gas welder, a pile of scrap steel, and a roof
over his head can set himself up in business as an automobile manufacturer. All you have to do is hang out a shingle.

Anyhow, I'd have to say that Frazer-Nash was the first
actual honest-to-gosh *racing* car I ever saw close up or stood
right next to, and gee whiz, did it ever give me goosebumps.
Oh, it was a little beat up and scruffy-looking, what with a
bunch of scrapes and dings here and there and all these
dried insect splatters and genuine, hundred-mile-an-hour
stone chips on the nose and fenders. But you couldn't miss
the little half-moon racing windscreen or the serious-looking
leather strap buckled across the hood to keep it from flying
open at high speed, or how the exhaust pipe ran right down
the side of the car, just below the driver's elbow. *Wow!* No
question about it, that Frazer-Nash was a War Machine.

I didn't see much of anybody hanging around inside the
Westbridge shop, and I started thinking about maybe un-
buckling that leather strap and taking a peek at whatever
might be lurking under the hood of that Frazer-Nash. That's
when an unknown finger extended itself out of nowhere and
tapped me on the shoulder. "Need any 'elp there, guv'nor?"
said a voice right out of Piccadilly Circus.

I wheeled around to find this short, hollow-faced guy in

a blue shop coat staring up at me through a pair of sad, watery-grey eyes. "Mister St. John?" I asked, real formal-like. A name like Colin St. John does that to you.

"Naw, Barry Spline's the naime," he wheezed through a nose that was pointy enough to open oil cans, "glad t'meetcher." Barry Spline had one of those rare British accents that never once made you think about royalty. "Yer missed 'is bleedin' 'ighness. That was 'im sportin' off in the TD just now. Bloody supercharged, that one is. Quick as a blink."

"I saw."

"But not near s'quick as *this* little beauty," he grinned, patting the Frazer-Nash on its nose emblem. "She's just got back from Sebring. Florida, y'know. Won the big bloody twelve hour there. Yer probably read about it in the bleedin' papers."

"Sure," I lied, wondering what in the hell he was talking about.

"Any'ow," he continued, extending a hand that obviously worked on cars for a living, "I'm the bloke gets most things done 'ere around the Westbridge shop. 'Ow can we be of service, eh?"

I explained as how I was looking for a Jaguar XK120 shop manual, and right away the smile melted off his face and Barry Spline's eyes narrowed down to suspicious little slits. "And just why would yer want a Jagyewahr shop manual for, eh?" So I told him about Old Man Finzio's Sinclair and Big Ed's Jag and the fouled plugs and clouds of black smoke, and as I did, Barry Spline's lips spread out in a small mean sliver of a smile. "Starting carburetor," he snickered.

"What?"

"Thermostatic actuator fr'the bloody starting carburetor. You'll find out."

"I will?"

Barry Spline nodded. "As a general practice, we don't h'encourage the h'untrained to h'attempt maintenance or repairs on Jag-ye-wahr automobiles. Company policy, you know. But seeing as 'ow you're way over in Jersey, and seeing as 'ow it's only one bloody car..." his eyes swept around the shop, "and seeing as 'ow I've got more flippin' work than I know what to do with, I suppose we might be able to make an h'exception. Just don't let 'is bloody 'ighness know about it, eh?"

I nodded. "Mum's the word."

"Right. Just step over t'the parts counter and ring the bell. Our Spares Consultant will be only too 'appy to 'elp yer out."

So I went over to the parts counter and rang the little bell and who pops up on the other side of the parts counter but Barry Spline. Only now he's wearing a *white* shop coat. "'Ow can I 'elp yer, sir?" he says with a perfectly straight face.

"I want a shop manual for an XK120," I tell him again, "You know that."

"Shop manual for an hex-kay-one-twenty," he says real slow, rubbing his chin like he's mulling it over, "I'm h'afraid we're fresh h'out of stock at the moment."

"All right," I said, measuring my words carefully, "When do you expect you might have one?"

Barry Spline the Spares Consultant rubbed bis chin some more. "Most normally, we don't sell Jag-ye-wahr shop manuals to the public at large. Matter of general company policy," then he leaned over the counter and added in a near whisper, "You h'understand, of course...."

"Oh, of course," I nodded, not exactly sure that I did. "But you said yourself it was just one car, and that it's way over in Jersey...." I was starting to get a little annoyed, you know?

"Ah, well," he said with an elaborate sigh, "I suppose we could put one on order for yer, seeing as 'ow its just one bloody car, and 'ow it's way over in Jersey...."

"Gee," I told him, trying not to grind my teeth, "that'd be real swell of you."

"Takes h'about six weeks...h'unless yer wanter pay Air Freight, that is."

"Air Freight is fine."

"Payment in h'advance, of course."

"Oh, naturally."

So I handed over a large wad of Big Ed's folding money and, after making a few quick mental calculations, Barry Spline returned to me a quarter, a nickel, and a few pennies in change. Judging from the price, they must write those Jaguar shop manuals on parchment from the Dead Sea Scrolls. Then I asked for a receipt so I could prove to Big Ed that I hadn't bought myself a gold watch or maybe booked a private railcar to Atlantic City. Barry Spline acted sort of offended that I'd ask for such a thing, but then he shrugged one of those home town New Yorker shrugs —*what can you do?*—and dashed one off longhand on an ordinary white paper notepad he had sitting on the counter. "There you are, guv'nor," he cooed through the self-satisfied grin of a man who has really put the screws to a fellow human being, "That oughter do yer up right and proper. And willyer be needin' anything else terday?"

"Yeah," I growled, doing a slow burn in front of him, "can anybody tell me how to keep one of these damn Jaguar shitcans *running?*"

Barry Spline stiffened up a couple notches. "If yer 'ave a *specific* sort of problem, yer might take it up with the Shop Foreman."

"And just where do I find the Shop Foreman?"

"One moment, eh," and Barry Spline the Spares Consultant (white coat) vanished, only to reappear a few seconds later as Barry Spline, Shop Foreman (blue coat). "What seems ter be the trouble, guv'nor?"

It took me awhile to get the gist of things, which was that Barry Spline/Spares Consultant and Barry Spline/Shop Foreman had to be *paid* separately. See, you could buy any Jaguar part you wanted from Barry-in-white (as long as you were willing to pay a left nut for it —in advance, of course— and wait until the Twelfth Of Never to get it) but then you still had to pay Barry-in-the-blue-coat for whatever information, advice, or encouragement it took to get the damn thing properly installed. And we're not talking about tips like the fivers Big Ed palmed off, either. Barry-in-blue charged "consultation" fees whenever he could get away with it, and he'd even write you up one of his plain white notepad "receipts" if you wanted one. At least if Colin St. John wasn't around to see him do it, anyway.

But once he'd relieved me of all the loose cash I had on my person, Barry Spline lightened up considerably and actually took me on a tour of the Westbridge shop – one mechanic to another, you know. "Yer've gotter h'understand about sportscars," he explained, waving his hand through the air. "The people who buy them could all drive bleedin' Cadillacs if they wanted. Cars like that great bloody black sedan yer rolled up in." His eyes glazed over just thinking about Big Ed's Sixty Special. "Oh, those are some marvelous smooth cars, Cadillacs are..." you could tell Barry Spline really admired Caddies, "but that's not what these flippin' sportycar people want. Oh, no! They claim t'*like* the 'ard ride and the 'eavy steering and enough bloody 'eat through the floorboards to roast bleedin' chestnuts. These people *h'enjoy* the engine racket and picking insects out of their 'air after every bleedin' run t'market. And believe me," he said, raising an important finger towards the rafters, "they absolutely *live* for the roadside breakdowns and h'expensive repairs..." Barry Spline looked me squarely in the eye, "...and do you know *why?*"

I shook my head.

"Because they're all bloody *masochists!*"

"They're what?"

"Masochists."

"What the hell are masochists?"

Barry Spline licked his lips and thought for a moment. "Before intercourse, 'ave yer ever been tied down to a bed with fine silk ropes and 'ad somebody go over yer private parts with an eggbeater?"

I couldn't say as I had.

"Neither 'ave I," he said wistfully, "But the point is that a masochist *h'enjoys* things like pain, suffering, and humiliation."

I looked it up in my aunt's dictionary when I got home, and Barry Spline was telling the truth.

Honest to God he was.

The Boondocks
a novel by Desmond Lowden

It's the dream of every writer. Write that first book and—omigoshyes!—overnight it's an international best seller. Faster than you can say "Hollywood", a movie deal is cut, with Richard Burton and Peter Ustinov as stars. Then, as often happens in the movie industry, production is delayed for a variety of reasons, interest wanes, and the movie gets shelved. That was the fate of Bandersnatch *(1969), a disappointment in one sense, but a hugely successful effort by first-time English novelist Desmond Lowden.*

Writing a follow-up seemed easy enough.

"My publishers wanted me to write another big book, with a big glossy international background," says Lowden. "I had always been interested in Grand Prix racing. So I said, How would it be if I went around the race tracks and then did a book after that? And they said fine."

Lowden hooked up with Team McLaren and hung out with Bruce and Denny for much of 1969 and 1970. It proved to be an exhilarating and deadly time in Formula One, with technology accelerating and the coming of commercialism, and the death of three of its star drivers, including Bruce McLaren. Lowden was put off by much of it but found the story he was seeking, of a private entrant waging a losing battle against the factory teams and the big money sponsors behind them.

The Boondocks *(1972), like so many racing novels, failed to connect with readers. Lowden went back to writing straight thrillers.*

The excerpt is from chapters 17-19. Veteran GP driver Frank Riley is at Spa-Francorchamps, sweating bullets as he faces two of racing's fastest and most dangerous curves—Burnenville, and the Masta Kink.

Frank Riley parked his Porsche at the side of the road and got out. He stood on the tarmac rim and kicked the soft core beyond. It was clay and sank beneath his heel. Farther on rain had cut a channel and there was a hole around the pebble bed where it drained. Just a hole the size of his foot at the roadside, but he stared at it. Then he walked on and found another hole on the inside of the next bend. It wasn't a section of the track that bothered him, he'd be slowing here for the hairpin at La Source. But he marked the holes in his mind and then stood still a moment, listening to the wind coming up the valley. It was wide to his right and the pines there were an old billiard green. While ahead up in the valley neck the pines were dark, a black arm reaching down from the horizon.

The wind was warm but he shivered as he went back to the car. Beyond it a line of white reflector posts marked the long straight up from the valley. Above the posts was a steep bank with telegraph poles leaning drunkenly downwind. And above the poles the trees began again, the pine forest where the evening was night. He thought about the bareness of the straight a moment, the trees and poles hovering over it. Then he told himself once more it wasn't a section of the track that bothered him. It just hadn't altered much in all the time he'd known it. But the cars had. The Lotus he'd be driving would come through these long curves at around 170 miles an hour.

He got back into the Porsche and drove on, the road getting darker as the pines closed in around the head of the valley. He came to a junction and took the sweeper turning to his right, La Source hairpin. The road swooped down past the grandstands that clung to the slope, and the squat concrete barracks of the pits opposite. He slowed, wondering if anyone else had arrived early. But the stands were empty of flags or people, sombre in the shadow of the hillside. Every time he came here Frank wondered what motorists must feel as they passed these strange empty theatres, staring hollow-eyed at the road before them. Because it was a public road, the track at Spa. The smoothest fourteen kilometres of road in Belgium. Which wasn't saying a lot.

The track was wide now, rushing down to the swerve at Eau Rouge, then narrowing and going steeply on uphill. Frank accelerated hard, enjoying himself. The road was smoother than he remembered and he drifted through the bends, climbing all the time until the pines were tipped with

flame. Then, the end of the world, a long left-hander called
Les Combes where the steel rail and the sky seemed to go on
forever. Through the bend Frank went down towards the
BASTOS bridge, then he braked suddenly. He reversed back
to the hilltop and got out.

He was high up in the evening and the whole character
of the track had changed. The chill of the pines was behind
him now and his shadow went on alone. A long way, the
plain below him was huge. He could see the track curling
away, cutting villages in two. That was the thing about Spa,
it was one of the last true road races. There was a straight
two and a half miles long, there were bends you took at 170
and you aimed the car at somebody's letterbox. To do well
here was a solid definite thing that you carried away inside
you. After it was all over.

For a long time Frank looked down at the plain. At the
single sunfired steeple that was Burnenville, and then across
to the village of Masta with its square white farmhouses and
cows kneedeep in the coarse grass of summer. Just for a
moment he wondered why he was so bothered about two
sections of tarmac three miles apart.

He knew why. Burnenville he knew as a long curve that
cut through the village, a curve that fell away and kept on
falling. It was wide there, you were out on your own in the
middle of the track with only your gut for a marker. And it
was very, very fast. Or could be. The big boys took it flat in
fifth gear, all six of them to Frank's knowledge.

Then there was the Masta kink. On the map it was just
an S-bend through a village called Masta. The road was
straight for two kilometres before, straight for two kilometres
after. It was the one sensation on this earth, coming down to
that unbroken line of Armco barrier from around 180, feeling
it with no damn gap in sight, and flooring your foot to get
through. The one sensation on this earth. Until the Group 5
Sports Car race at the end of last season, when Frank had
fuel feed problems and the motor suddenly cut out.

It was the strange army lorry shriek of the tires he
remembered most of all. Then the thunder of bounding metal
as he shaved the right-hand rail and watched the left-hand
rail line up. The car was sick, bulging at the Armco without
the power to push it round. And he couldn't go near his
brakes. The motor caught once, like a gunshot. He got
another foot and he knew it was going to be close. At that
speed he could only try to hold the car straight when it

touched and hope he didn't lose a wheel. It was only a brush. The noise from outside was huge, while his hands were tiny on the wheel. And he kept them tiny, feeling every crash, every explosion of gravel as he held the car to the left. Then he found the tarmac rim again. He was still straight, and for a moment he thought he'd got away with it,

*   *   *   *

"How long were you in the flames?" Jake asked. "Here, I mean, last year."

"Fifteen seconds. It doesn't sound that long." Frank leaned against the grey cushions in the Paco van. "But the side window went, that was the trouble. There isn't an extinguisher made that can take that blast. My eyelids were right up in my head."

Jake nodded. "Fifteen seconds. So what speed were you doing when you jumped out?"

"Between fifty and eighty," Frank said. "I took the tip off my big toe. Otherwise there wasn't a scratch."

"Did it hurt?"

"Did it ever? I knew I was okay as long as it hurt." He held out his hands. "These were like overcooked steaks, black, and sort of bent over. I was looking down at them and suddenly they seemed very small. So I crossed them in front of me and jumped. I rolled over and over, away from that prick of a car. I didn't want to know about it any more."

"But you were driving again? Not much more than a month after?"

Frank lowered his hands. "They reckon drivers are fools, getting out of hospital real quick, like it's a race. But you lie in that bed and you pick a certain day. And you know if you don't make it then you won't make it ever."

"Maybe you're right." Jake nodded. "But how're you doing now? I hear you're going a bit short."

"Short?" Frank tried to hold on to his anger. "It's all money now, isn't it? How you get connected? Suddenly Schlegermann buys himself into my sports car seat, and then the whole bloody season gets to be a disaster. My Formula 2 car's never looked like being ready, and now they tell me the sponsorship deal's fallen through for my Can-Am drive ..." He tailed away, feeling thin and pale in front of Jake. There was something about trans-Atlantic flights and a lot of people with your name on their lips that widened a man's shoulders. Since they'd last met Jake had got rich at Indianapolis and driven a race in Portugal. Frank looked at the calm face and thinning hair, tried to see the man he remembered under the tan. The man who years ago had sweated at his side over a battered Lotus Elite in a London garage, while the rich kids came and went with their factory-tuned cars.

Jake grinned at him. "Don't get so screwed up," he said. "You've got a drive at Le Mans, with me."

"Christ, I didn't even ask you."

"I know you didn't. But John Feeney rang. He thought it was a good idea too." Jake reached over and pressed his arm. "So come down to Le Mans when you want to get your hands on a Group 5 car. I'll be down there early next week, testing."

Frank turned and looked out of the window. He looked up past the Shell filling station to where the transporters were parked in a row behind the pits, March and Lotus red, Matra blue, BRM white, and the new Bison honeygold. This morning the circus had pitched camp at the head of this narrow valley. And suddenly he felt good about it.

But when he turned back Jake was no longer smiling. "The last time you drove here was when you had your shunt, wasn't it?" Jake asked.

"Exactly that."

"And it doesn't bother you driving here again?"

"Hell, no. I made the mistake. The motor was going sour, but I thought I could put in a couple more laps. You don't do that on a track like Spa."

There was a long pause. Jake was strangely serious. "I don't know if I like this place," he said at last.

Frank shrugged. "One or two people are saying that."

"And one or two people are saying there shouldn't be another Grand Prix here." Jake didn't look at him. "I reckon I agree with them. Tracks like this are getting kind of thin. And the cars are getting kind of thin as well."

Frank hid his surprise. He'd heard it from other people, never from Jake. Then he swung round, the mood broken.

The van door was open, and a girl was standing in the corridor talking to Max, the Paco attendant. From the back she was neat, a silk headscarf and blouse, and cord trousers that were very tight.

"Is that a bum or isn't it?" Jake brightened.

"It's a bum," Frank agreed.

But when Max moved away and she came towards them, it was difficult to tell. She could have been a woman or a girl, her face was carefully made up, bland and American, and she seemed unaware of the tight trousers. What they did was out of sight, she left her men behind her, and she made Frank want to come in from the corner of her eye. "Jill Samuelson, *New York Mirror*," she said. Her fingers were nervous on the small tape deck she carried.

"Maybe you want him," Frank said. "Jake Ballantyne, glamour boy."

"You're Frank Riley, aren't you? I'd like to do a piece on you."

"Moy loife." Jake grinned and picked up a newspaper. "She saw you drive at Riverside three years ago, boy."

The girl blushed. "D'you have a couple of minutes, Mr Riley?"

Frank nodded.

"Only I'm doing an article on the new professionalism in sport," she went on. "And you're the latest driver to get financial backing from a commercial combine."

Frank was disappointed. That soft mouth shouldn't be American, it shouldn't come out with those long gristly words. She was brisk as she sat down, setting up her microphone and opening her notebook. And the page she chose was full. Frank was the more disappointed. She was one of those reporters who had the answers written down, not the questions. "Ready when you are," he said.

She switched on the tape deck. "Mr Riley ..."

". .. Frank." He smiled at her. "Let's make a deal. You call me Frank and I'll call you Jill."

"Frank, I want to talk to you about the new professionalism in sport," she read the words from her book. "Like how big money's made the pressures greater. Like how on the golf course, the tennis court, on your British football fields even, there seems to be a war going on."

"I don't know about that," Frank said.

"You don't watch other sports?"

"There's only one sport. The others are relaxations."

"Pro tennis, for example," she looked up, "you don't enjoy that?"

"I'd rather watch two flies crawling up a wall."

She frowned, then read from the book again. "Okay, let's take motor racing, the second biggest spectator sport in the world, also the most expensive sport to put on. Big money had to come into it, and it came. D'you reckon it's made any difference?"

"Yes, the pay's better." Frank wished she'd throw the

book away and ask questions that went with a name like Jill.

"Right. But that's part of what I meant by pressures, commercial pressures. It's getting to be a vicious circle. Every race there's more money up front. Drivers are asking a lot more money, and the cars are costing more to get to the line. The only people who say they're losing out are the race organizers. It would seem they can't afford to do all the modernizing they maybe should on the tracks. And in some cases they're not holding the races at the right tracks even."

"What d'you mean?" Frank was wary.

"I heard talk that the Belgian Grand Prix should be held at Zolder and not here at Spa, because Spa's got too danger-ous. But I heard that the organizers want to stay here because they sell this race as the fastest track in Europe. And they're kind of stuck too, because the spectator facilities at Zolder aren't big enough to make it pay."

"I don't know where you heard that," Frank said.

"You don't agree that Spa's got too dangerous?"

"Any track's just as dangerous as a driver wants to make it."

"But there are . . ." She stopped suddenly and swung round to the tape deck. The spools had jammed. For a moment she was a girl called Jill as she swore softly under her breath, for a moment Frank really liked her mouth. But he was making her nervous standing there, so he walked over to where Jake was reading his newspaper.

"It's like walking into a pub," he said softly, "and telling the first person you meet how you make love to your wife."

*   *   *   *

Frank was in and out of love every second now. He was half out of his seat, tight against the right-hand side of the cockpit as he found the exit to Les Combes. Then the green of the downhill section flew at him, and the BASTOS bridge. He got fifth gear and he hesitated a second, thinking about the bend which was still blind, and about the wing they'd taken off to get more speed. But if you were going to try at Burnenville you started trying two counties away. He tickled the fat front wheels towards the inside of the road, felt the tiptoe then the godfearing slide. His foot almost flat, he came down the hill on a whisker of rubber and a great warmth in his chest. The long downhill curve was now open before him and he picked the spot marked X. Then he hit a bump, the car went, a vicious snake, and only his hand was calm. He backed off, sweating as he found the bend again. But slower.

Much, much slower.

Jake was close behind him as he came to the new chicane at Malmedy, grinning right through his Nomex mask. Frank put his foot down early, took a bit of grass, and watched a photographer jump clear. Then he was watching something else. The track just fell away through the green to the horizon. The Masta straight.

Suddenly the morning was bright again. Suddenly Frank knew he liked his motor, and Vic, and every bloody person who'd helped sit him in this car. He went through the gears, flooring his foot each time. The track became a narrow ribbon, widening where it held him. But only just. Because it smashed up at his wheels. The Masta straight was still a road, just as it always had been. Gently, very gently he found the smooth path, keeping left until the house with the tiled front, then nudging right and smoothing out the wind that hit him after the bushes. He was thundering through air that was like a wall. Still the straight was long, still Jake got no bigger in his mir...

But Jake was drawing up. Frank looked at the revs. Only nine-five, the engine wasn't getting on to the road. And it was bad road now. The ramp up to the smooth section, the telegraph poles swinging in from the left, the squat grey house straight ahead, the unbroken Armco rails. He knew they were herding him left like a cattle chute, but he couldn't see the gap, the Masta kink.

Frank backed off. He fought his hand, swore at it, but of its own accord it shifted down to fourth. And Jake sailed past. It was easy. He sat over on the right and tickled the throttle. Then he went through, hard on the pedal, laughing as he shifted just the cheeks of his backside.

Next time, Frank told himself. Next time.

The pits were a sloping line of shadows, dark after the track. Vic was waiting for him, his face clean of oil and problems this early in the day. Frank loaded them on to him.

"I need the bloody wing," he said. "It's a cow through the quick corners. It wasn't the wing pulling me back. I'm over-geared."

"They all are." Vic nodded up the line. "The fat tires they're using this year won't go through the air. They're all slower than they thought."

"Okay." Frank thought for a moment, staring at his gloves. "Set her up for the corners. We'll need to come up on the suspension if we're using the wing."

"Four clicks up on the shockers?" Vic asked.

"Try four." Then suddenly Frank got out of the car. "No, let's bloody get it right. Let's do the big things and put the icing sugar on later." He counted off on his fingers. 'Give us a decent fifth gear and bring fourth down. Do the wing and the shockers. Then maybe some camber on the front wheels so she still understeers, but only just."

Vic looked at his watch. "We'll have to hustle. Only 45 minutes left." He went away to get Lester and Sam.

Frank took off his helmet. Then he felt a hand on his shoulder. He didn't turn. He could smell the aftershave, the underarm, the spearmint gum, he didn't have to look at Grogan.

"Hey, fella, you going to drive around like that, without a wing?" Grogan asked. "Only on that wing is our message to the world. You know, Bison ... Press .. . Racing?"

"It's okay," Frank told him. "They're putting it back on the car."

"That's my boy."

Frank walked away. He held on to Vic's arm as he passed. "Somebody keep that creep away from me," he muttered.

But Grogan's handiwork was all around. Farther up the pitlane Roger stood with a shiny Bison Press girl on each arm. "What sort of time are you making?" Frank went towards him, "I mean on the track?"

"Oh that track?" Roger looked out at the pit straight. The girls split their damson lips and giggled. "I haven't been out there much," he shrugged, "I keep finding things wrong with the car."

Frank wasn't fooled. Roger's face was flushed, his hair was plastered round his head. "What time did you do?" he repeated.

Roger let go of the girls and backed to the pit counter. "3.32.5," he said softly.

"Not bad." Frank whistled. "How d'you reckon it then?"

"It's not my favourite stretch of road."

"Me neither. Where d'you make it up?"

"Round the back." Roger pointed over the pit roof to the long section that came up from the valley. "There are a couple of kids who can make up time round Burnenville and through the kink. Not me."

"Exactly that," Frank said.

Roger winked at him and took the girls off towards his

car. On the pitstool above was a slim dark-haired girl, soft in a mohair sweater. She was Sue, his fiancee. The way she smiled down at him made the two Bison Press girls look like cheap souvenirs. Frank turned away, remembering when his wife had come to race meetings. That was a long time ago.

Later he was leaning up against a pit counter waiting for Vic and the boys to finish. He didn't know it was Alan Prince's counter until Prince came freewheeling slowly down the line towards him. He parked clumsily, and he sat on in the car, his face a dirty white. Over by the barrier his two mechanics were finishing off a story and one of them happened to be looking at Prince when he laughed. Prince hauled himself out of the cockpit and ran for the pit counter. He climbed over it, the door at the rear banged shut, and he was gone.

A few minutes later he came back, nodding the mechanics to him. "Leave it like it is," he said. "It's okay." He got back into the car and drove off.

Practice was almost over and Frank was hurrying. He took the car hard down the hill and set her up for Burnenville back where it meant business. He felt better about the car, and he felt scared. Burnenville was a whole new feeling, grey and endless. He was a shot in a long hard sling, it curled around him tighter and tighter, waiting to hurl him off. The car hurt him, cutting into his left shoulder, sharp as a saw. His knee was hard against the metal, he was low in the car, and the car was low to the left. He watched the tires bulging against the slide, itching on the tarmac.

The Masta too was different. The wing took its toll. There were huge savage grunts beneath him as the chassis bottomed. It didn't bother him. He took a careful line between the bumps while the car set up a pattering motion of its own. But it took more than a mile to wind the engine up to ten. And he took it further, beginning to feel sorry for that motor now. He was doing over 180 and he'd never been so slow. There was a grey wire going from his head to that distant Armco rail at the kink, and coming back to his head and foot. Inch by inch it came in, there was this slow real understanding. He bounced up on to the smooth tarmac and the wire still held him steady, leading him through the gap he couldn't see. With a sudden shock he lifted his foot and a river ran down his spine. Then he was back on the power, heeling to the right and left. He was through with three yards to spare. Next time, he told himself. Next time.

He came back into the pits and sat staring at his hands.
"What's new?" Vic knelt down beside him.
"Nothing," Frank said. "Don't change a thing."
Vic got up. He motioned Lester and Sam away, and the
three of them left him alone. Frank stared on at his hands.
They were trembling. He didn't see them. He saw only the
Masta kink. And that three yards. There was more to come.
And there was more at Burnenville.
"Do us a teeny favour, fella."
Frank heard Grogan's voice. He didn't turn.
"I wonder if you could leave yourself clear of the other
cars down the Masta? Just once? Our photographer's out
there. He says he hasn't got a clear shot of you in front of the
Bison Press hoarding."
Frank looked up. He saw Vic running, grabbing Grogan
away. Then his thumb was on the starter. He snapped his
visor down and roared out along the pitlane, snaking on the
cement dust.

Stand On It
a novel by Stroker Ace
(alias Bill Neely and Bob Ottum)

"It was a lot more fun," says Bill Neely about racing in the 1960s, when he was Manager of Racing Public Relations for Goodyear and hanging out with the likes of Cale and Richard and A.J. "The drivers were a little wilder, and everybody had a much better time. There wasn't any money, or any sponsor demanding a squeaky-clean image from his driver. Funny things were happening: backwards races to the airport in Charlotte, putting a car into a swimming pool at Darlington.   So I got the idea, why don't I put these all together in some kind of anthology, as a novel, changing the names to protect me from being shot or sued or both (laugh)."

Enter Bob Ottum, senior editor at <u>Sports Illustrated</u>, *with a few ribald racing tales of his own. "We gave each other assignments," says Neely. "I would write a chapter and he would write a chapter, and we would exchange them. We would get together about once a month and just sit around and laugh for about two days. What* <u>Stand On It</u> *turns out to be is a thinly veiled biography. I mean, it's a novel, but most of it is true, with the exception of Stroker's childhood."*

Read Neely's biographies of A.J. Foyt and Cale Yarborough and you'll run across many of the same stories in <u>Stand On It</u>, *told almost verbatim.*

In 1966, Neely left Goodyear for Exxon. In 1970, he turned free-lance writer, with publication of <u>Spirit of America</u>, *a biography of land-speed record holder Craig Breedlove. It was the first of a series of biographies Neely would write, not only about racers but musicians such as Roy Acuff, Chet Atkins and Pete Fountain. In 1973,* <u>Stand On it</u> *was published. In 1975, Neely wrote a sequel in the form of a short story for* <u>Playboy</u> *magazine entitled, "Manhattan Pitstop."*

The backwards race excerpted here (from chapter four) is a retelling of a race between A.J. Foyt and Cale Yarborough. Neely: "Foyt was new to NASCAR. We were all sitting around drinking, and they were needling him, saying, You're just a fancy-pants Indy driver. You'd never make it down here. A.J. said, I can outrun all of you hoopies backwards."

The gauntlet thrown down, it's Turbo Ellison vs. Hack Downing, alias A.J. Foyt vs. Cale Yarborough.

This is the way it is: the sun was setting over the motel in Talladega and the air was full of race-driver romance. Which is to say that it was about eight o'clock or so and the sky had turned into a primer-color red over behind the Dairy Queen across the street and the air was a little bit cooler, with a hint of a faint breeze rippling the top of the swimming pool. The guys had all showered by now and had changed into their Going Out clothes. One by one they were coming out of the doors to their rooms, usually with a can of beer in one hand, and their hair all slicked down. The way a motel is set up, with a sort of courtyard in the middle and all the rooms opening off it around the pool, it makes for a very chummy setup, one of the best moments in racing. You have to experience it.

I was in my red and white checkered golf slacks and this pair of sixty dollar Gucci loafers, and no socks, which is a thing you pick up very quickly by racing at Monaco, where only the hayshakers wear socks at any time of day or night. And I had on this white knit polo shirt and my burnt-orange golf sweater with the very baggy sleeves right around the wrists. All put together it is an extremely sporty costume, just the sort of thing that race drivers are wearing more and more these days.

Also television people, for which, the hell with them.

Well, a guy has got to be comfortable to drink and do the town and the nice thing about an outfit like this is that, maybe at some point in the evening, a stranger is going to turn to you in some bar and say: "Boy, that is a very faggy costume you have got on, there." And you can carefully put your glass down on the bar and say to this stranger: "Ah, *hah.* I take it you think I am wearing a very faggy outfit, right?" And the guy, puzzled, will get a little more belligerent. And he will put down his glass and he will say: "That's what I said, all right. And what's more, I think you are a fucking queer."

And then you can take his head off. We do this a lot.

Towns like Charlotte and Altanta and Daytona are absolutely full of guys who have got up in the morning and looked into their mirrors at big goddam purple lumps over their eyes and cuts just alongside their noses and have made vows right there on the spot never again to criticize anyone's clothes in a bar.

Anyway, we are all coming out of our rooms now and, for a few moments, the air all around the pool is full of the smell of Aqua Velva and it is very pleasant.

"Where you gonna go for dinner?" someone will say.

"Well," the other guy will say, "what I thought I'd do first is to maybe go over to the bar here and suck up a few beers. Then you know Gordy Landen, right? Well, he says that, last time he was here, that there is this place over there in the colored section that serves maybe the greatest goddam ribs and chicken you ever ate in your life. So I thought I would eat me a whole mess of ribs and —— "

"And maybe change your luck?"

"Well, hell, it couldn't hardly get no worse than it is now, bright? You heard the way I was running out there today?"

"Running? Hell, you were in the pits all day."

By now, more and more guys are drifting out of their rooms, all of them slicked up for the evening and the motel courtyard is starting to look like a cocktail party. Occasionally someone will duck back into his room for another beer, or someone else — particularly those guys who have had a tough day—will come back with a glass of Seven and Seven.

"Hey, Stroker. Them are sure some fancy pants. What did you do with the stiff you stole them off of?"

"Hey, Stroke. You forgot your socks. Lissen: if you're all out of clean socks, you can borrow a pair of mine. I only wore them driving all day and I sure as hell wasn't going fast enough to even sweat them up any, I'll tell you that."

"Damn, I got to get me a clothing sponsor like old Ace here."

"Well, if you do, you also got to get you a guy who tells you what pants to wear with what sweaters and like that. Man, if that old sponsor ever sees old Stroker, he'll come right up and snatch all that stuff right off him. Then he can go out and get himself a really pretty guy to wear the stuff. Like me."

"They don't make these pants that big around the gut, Charlie."

"Lissen: you see this here gut?" Pat, pat "It took me maybe ten years and fifty thousand dollars' worth of beer to build a gut like this."

"How you running, Stroker?"

"Fast as that shitpot engine will allow. And I promise you right now it ain't near fast enough."

"Yeah, I saw you sort of loafing around out there today. Sounds like you need a lower gear, maybe."

"They're working on it tonight."

"You going to get some supper?"

"Yeah. I thought maybe I'd try that rib place. You doin anything?"

"Not special."

"Well, come along. Give the waitresses a real thrill for a change."

"Okay. But no panty-snapping tonight, all right? Chrissakes, the last time — remember, in Atlanta—you damn near got us all killed."

"Well, look: I didn't know her husband was the goddam bartender. How was I to know?"

"You see that double-barreled sawed-off he keeps behind the bar?"

"Well, no. I mean: I sort of got a glimpse of it going out the door. But I wasn't all that anxious to stop and admire the hand engraving on the barrels or anything like that."

"Funny thing was: I kind of thought his old lady really sort of *liked* it."

"Well, she *did* sort of back it right up there to me, sort of friendly-like, didn't she?"

"I'll tell you one thing: w'ell never know."

"Lissen: let's go over to the bar and get a beer, all right?"

Same night, four hours later.

"I think," says Turbo Ellison, "that what I will do is have one more beer and then we really got to get out and get something to eat."

Turbo Ellison drinks his beer right from the bottle and always waves off the barmaid when she tries to put down a clean glass. "Lady," he will say, "if God had meant us to drink beer out of *glasses*, then He wouldn't of put it in bottles."

"Another round," says Turbo, drawing a big circle in the air over our table with one forefinger. "Another round, which I am personally going to pay for. I mean, since I personally am going to take all the money out of this here race come Sunday. I feel it's only fair."

Everybody nods thoughtfully.

Except, of course, Hack Downing. Hack simply leans back in his chair and burps loudly. Then he gets the two front legs of the chair back down on the floor and he leans across the table.

"Turbo, my boy," he says, "you had better let me buy this here round and I'll tell you why: the reason why is that, come Sunday, your ass is going to be so broke that you won't be able to buy a sack of Bull Durham."

Everybody nods thoughtfully, passing around the new order of beer.

Now, you have no doubt read in fiction books about where some guy grins *wolfishly*, right? Well, never mind any of that. I promise you that you have never, ever in your whole life read about or heard about or seen a wolfish grin until you have seen Turbo Ellison grin. And he does this right now.

"What's that?" he says, his long eyeteeth showing wetly.

"I said," says Hack, "I said: come Sunday, your ass——"

"I heard you," says Turbo. He tilts the bottle back for a long swallow and then carefully puts it down on the table. "Yes, I heard you, and I got to tell you that it makes my old Mississippi heart sad to hear you say it. You are always, always, saying that before a race. And I am always beating your ass. Now you know that."

Hack burps again, this time getting in a two-tone effect. He is very good at that

"Most always," he says, nodding. "But not come this Sunday. I'm sorry, old buddy. But not this Sunday."

Old Turbo swings his head around and looks at us, each one in turn. "Does he know something I don't know?" he asks.

I shrugged. "He's running fastest in practice," I say, "and that's got to count for something."

Turbo nods again, digesting this new fact. "I swan," he says. "Fastest in practice. God Almighty. Why I didn't know that, Hack, old buddy. I mean, you finally got that shitpot all together, huh?"

Hack blinks modestly. "She's runnin' real good," he admits.

"Well, then," says Turbo, closing the trap. "It's just a by-God good thing that I'm so much better a driver than you, ain't it? Damn, you had me scared there for a minute, pal."

This is like the part in King Arthur where the guy tugs off his big iron glove and throws it down. We all sat there, nodding and grinning. Well, except Hack. He was puffing up a little bit.

"Driver?" he said.

Turbo grinned wolfishly. "Driver," he said.

Hack drew his own circle in the-air with his finger and got the bar girl's attention. "Another round," he said, "and this one's on me." Then he turned back to Turbo. "You know, old buddy," he said. "You know: for one little old second there I thought you said better driver. But, hell. That can't be right, and you got to forgive me for not hearing too well. I mean, after all, everybody knows that I'm not only a better driver than *you*, old pal, but I'm the best driver at this here *table*." He pauses a moment and half raises from his chair while he looks around the place. "Hell," he says, I'm the best driver in this whole fucking *bar*."

We all grinned wolfishly, as best we could. And everybody looked at Turbo.

He was shaking his head, with great sadness. "Shee-it," he said. "Lissen: I can drive a goddam car backwards better than you can drive it any way."

Hack carefully wiped the top of the new bottle of beer with the flat of his hand — the better to get the germs off it. Then he took a long pull at the bottle and made a declarative statement:

"No fucking way," he said.

Turbo swung out one long arm and pointed.

"Not in my eye," I said.

"Sorry," Turbo said. He corrected his aim just a bit and pointed at the door. "Lissen: I can take that bad-ass Hertz car right out there in the front of my motel room and drive it backward better than you can drive your goddam racecar in any direction."

"When?"

"Right now. Right this very minute."

Hack looks at me. "Whatta you think, Ace?"

I shrugged. "What the hell is so tough about driving backward? That's the way I spend half my time at Indy, for God's sake."

That seemed to decide Hack— and there I go, contributing to the delinquency of race drivers again.

"Okay," he said to Turbo. "What'll it be?"

Turbo thought about it, mapping out a route in his mind. "Airport and back," he said. "Backward."

"Both ways," said Hack.

"Shit, yes, both ways. You think this is a goddam sports-car race or something?"

"What kind of car you got?" Hack asked me.

"It's a Hertz-something. Ford LTD, I think. Who knows? The radio doesn't work very well."

"Yeah, well, never mind the radio. How's the reverse?"

"Oh, factory-fresh, I would say. I only drive the son of a

bitch frontwards, you know."

"Keys?"

I handed them over and we all trooped outside, leaving behind this round table absolutely jammed with beer bottles. Turbo stomped off to get his rental car and I instructed Hack.

"Brown metallic hardtop," I said. "It's in front of my room there. If you can't find it, try any one the key fits. Hell, steal one; you're not going to use it all night."

And in a couple of minutes they were both back in the driveway out beside the bar, parked side by side, both in neutral and both zapping their engines. Zap, vroom. Zap.

Sam Bartow stepped off the sidewalk and got out in front of the cars, then he held up both hands. He was weaving just a bit, but not bad. "Gentlemen," he said. "Gentlemen, start your engines."

"They are started, Sam. *Jesus.*" Charlie said.

"Oh. Well, in that case, let me have your attention."

They stopped zapping the engines for a minute and let the cars idle.

"Now, then," Sam said. "Here are the, rules. First —— "

Turbo stuck his head out the window of his car. "What fucking rules?" he said.

Sam shook his head like a teacher. "Shhh," he said. "I'm just making them up now. Now don't confuse me. Now when I drop the flag, you guys —— "

"Somebody get him a flag," somebody said.

And pretty soon one of the guys came back with this big goddam red and white checkered tablecloth he had jerked off somebody's table. Plus about twenty-seven diners who wanted to see the official start of the Great Backwards Race.

"Now, then," Sam said. "When I drop this here flag, you gentlemen are officially racing. Get that? It's backwards to the airport and back. Backwards back, too, I mean. And——"

"Get the fuck out of the way!" Hack yelled. Three of the diners jumped back inside.

Sam held up the flag and waved it in front of his face. "No, no!" he said. "I don't have to get out of the way, you asshole. Excuse me, there, ladies. Don't forget, you're going *backwards.* This here is the front of the cars, where I'm standing. God, you guys are dumb."

Zap, vroom! Zap. Crank. Both racers put their cars into reverse and sat there, riding the brakes and zapping the motors some more.

Then Turbo stuck his head out the window again. "Wait a goddam minute, dummy!" he yelled. The street is out *that* way. Out there."

Sam turned around and looked over his shoulder at the street. Then he turned back and nodded. "You know, you're right," he said. "But since I am making up these here race rules, that fact appears in your driver's manual under the chapter heading of Tough Shit. You are in the Great Backward Race and you got to get to the street any way you can. Are you ready?"

"Are they ready? They're damn near out of gas, Sam," I said. "Start the race, for chrissakes."

So Sam dropped the flag-tablecloth.

Both Turbo and Hack wheeled in their seats and looked over their right shoulders. And both of them jumped off the brakes and slammed down on the gas. There was a fine, swirling howl of smoke and dust and gravel and off they went— side by side around the motel driveway. Backwards.

Sam got back up on the sidewalk.

"I wouldn't anybody step out there just now," he said. They're headed for the motel parking lot, see, and soon's they get in there, they're gonna have to turn around somehow. And then . . . and then they're going to come back by here going to beat hell, headed for the street."

Exactly. We all stood up on the sidewalk and heard the roar of engines back in the parking lot and then — zambo! — here came Hack, holding a slight lead, looking over his shoulder, with Turbo coming on fast. Swoosh . . . and they were by us.

We all stepped out and watched them hit the street with terrible damn bounces and Hack got just a little bit sideways coming around an Allied Van Lines semi-rig that was barreling past The semi hit the brakes and his rig started to get a little sideways, but the driver wisely got it up on the curbing a little bit and saved it.

And then they were gone.

One of the lady diners shook her head at all of us.

"Race drivers," she said. "Honestly."

Sam stooped and picked up the tablecloth. There was a big, fat tire mark smudged down the middle of it.

"Here's your official souvenir race flag, lady," he said.

"How long do you think they'll take?" Duster Hoffman said.

"Well, let's see. Takes maybe forty-five minutes to make

it to the airport from here going frontwards. Oh, I don't know, maybe a couple of hours or so."

"If they don't get picked up."

"Well," said Sam. "Either way, we got time to have another beer, you guys. Come on."

Official Race Report:

Turbo Ellison won it easily, if you count driving time: 112 minutes flat until he walked back into the bar.

But Hack Downing, 162 minutes, more or less, filed a formal protest, which the Race Stewards accepted.

That's because Hack stopped at the airport circle and picked up a couple of girls. Even got out and put their bags in the trunk.

After the Race Committee meeting, there at the round table, Turbo was awarded the trophy (one case of beer) and the Special Grand Award (one of the girls). Personally, I think he got the worst-looking one.

(It also was decided, for the record, that neither of those bums was anywhere near to being the best race driver at the table.)

The Ragged Edge
a novel by Richard Nisley

How hard could it be? I'd just seen the motion picture Grand Prix *in 1967 and thought, I can write a better story than that. I knew enough about motor racing to get the details right. Dream up a plot. Create some characters. The story writes itself. I took typing in high school and majored in journalism in college all the while thinking about this great novel I was going to write. How hard could it be? Plenty hard, as it turned out.*

Nothing I wrote got past my internal censor that calls itself critical thinking, the very censor that served me so well writing straight news stories and feature articles. The creative muse, I was to learn, runs and hides at the first sign of criticism.

A developing career with a major tire company didn't help either; it fact, it became a convenient excuse not to write. But the idea of writing a racing novel wouldn't let go. A story developed in my head. Characters slowly emerged in various scenarios I dreamed up. One of them (John Wagner) often told me that I had great story to tell, if only I would write it down. Twenty-three years passed.

When my wife Cindy was carrying our first son, it dawned on me that I might never write the story. I had to get started and stay with it. I did. Much of what came I didn't like but I wrote on until it was finished. Reading it, I discovered it wasn't half as bad as I'd thought. Some ten rewrites later (and a trip to Europe to see many of the circuits) I sent it off to a literary agent who'd expressed interest—and who promptly sent it back requesting another rewrite. But that's another story.

The excerpt is from chapter seven. After winning the first two races of the season, American John Wagner is beginning to think his luck has changed and that this will be the year he fi-nally wins the Grand Prix world championship.

Wagner rolled off Viraje del Tunel and tried pushing his right foot through the floor. Inches behind his head, throttle slides drew open, exposing 12 shiny round ports, each one the size of a silver dollar, each one sucking air and fuel with hurricane velocity. He felt his body weight triple as speed exploded past 100 mph and within seconds touched 180 mph. On either side, the world blurred past. Ahead, at the opposite end of the front straight, Viraje Nuvolari leaped out at him, a speck one moment, huge and menacing the next. But his mind was fully absorbed and he was seeing the corner arrive in slow motion. He had plenty of time to brake and downshift. With the curve dead in his face, he even had time to come off the brakes gently, so the chassis wouldn't lurch up on him, but remain steady and balanced for a smooth, swift entry into the curve. Turning in, he fed in throttle and felt the tail slide, the car shift into oversteer. Coming out, Viraje Fangio winked into view. He stayed in second gear, accelerated, backed off, and eased on the brakes. Turning in, he felt his rear tires slide again, saw the guardrail spin past his eyes. Calmly, in complete control, he powered out, upshifted to third, and stayed left for Viraje Varzi. It was broader, faster, and taken in a heartbeat. He was on a chute now, speed climbing, wind pressing against his goggles. The magnesium-and-aluminum chassis enclosing him, containing a mere eight gallons of fuel, vibrated like some big empty can.

The car was better, but still far from perfect. Despite all the work of the previous day, it was still unpredictable around <u>Circuito Permanente del Jarama's</u> stop-and-go curves. If he got on the throttle too soon, the car wanted to understeer—go straight on—rather than turn. If he got on it too late, it wanted to oversteer—the tail slide out on him. He was having to finesse the car to get it through the curves reasonably quickly, and to guess, because in every one of Jarama's 14 curves the car responded differently. But with the morning session about to end, and desperate for a quick lap, he was hustling the car, pushing it faster than it wanted to go.

He braked very late for the first of a pair of sharp left-handers called the Le Mans Corners. He felt the tail become light, saw smoke flare from his front tires. Too fast. Too damn fast. With no time to steady his machine, he inhaled deeply and steered into the first left-hander. His inside tires ran up the curb. The car bounced, skidded, threatening to spin on him, but he caught it and angled out of the curve under increasing throttle. Now, for the second Le Mans Corner. Still in second gear, he braked and turned in. He clipped the inside curb again—harder this time. The car bounced up, airborne, hung there a moment, landed sideways and spun around backwards. All he could see was the white of tire smoke but he knew where he was headed. He switched off the ignition and fuel pumps, and braced himself.

The tail struck first, slamming his head back against the roll bar. The tail crumpled and the soft metal of the transmission casing split open and spewed out hot oil. The Garret-Hawk bounced off the rail and spun in the opposite direction, striking the rail again, nose first. The nose cone flattened, the radiator smashed and sprayed steam and scalding water. The car spun another half-turn and skidded to a stop, its path delineated by heavy skid marks, blotches of smoking oil, and steaming water.

In an instant, he was out of the cockpit, walking around the car. He didn't look at the damage. He knew it was bad. He removed his helmet and did something he hadn't done in 14 years of racing—slammed his helmet against the pavement.

It felt good.

*   *   *   *

"Yep," said Hacksaw, peering at the chassis; it was dangling by a hook on back of the wrecker, swaying back and forth. "You banged it good, Big Guy. The right-side a-arms are bent and it's going to need a new radiator and new trans and maybe a dozen other things I haven't seen yet, but I think the tub's straight. I hope so, anyway. I think we can have her ready in time for the four o'clock session." He looked at Walt Balchowsky, the fabricator. "What do you think, Walt?"

Balchowsky kneeled beneath the car and grunted. "Hard to say until we get it inside and look closer. But overall, it looks pretty decent. Wait. Aw, shit. Looky here, George." Balchowsky was probably the only person who called Hacksaw by his first name, other than Hacksaw's wife. The crew chief kneeled beside him and looked where he was pointing. "See that?" Balchowsky pointed to the front lower right a-arm mounting point. It was pushed in, forming a one-inch divot in the outer skin. "Sheee-it."

Hacksaw rose and hitched up his pants. "Tub's

damaged, Big Guy. Looks like you're stuck with the Mark Four."

Wagner shook his head. It was going to be that kind of weekend, where nothing went right. "It can't be any worse than this pig," he said, and walked off to the team's transporter. He needed aspirin for his headache. And time alone to regather himself. One practice session remained, one last chance to redeem himself. Somehow. He had to do well at Jarama. Monaco was in two weeks and it promised more of the same, trying to hustle a chassis that didn't like stop-and-go curves. He could see it: Parks or Evans or Bogavanti winning both races and getting a firm grip on the championship, his championship. He had to do better in the afternoon session, move up, get in the first or second row and be in position to pick up points in tomorrow's race.

Inside the transporter, he drank down some aspirin and lay back on the sofa. He couldn't relax. His mind was racing. He could hear engines revving over in the garage. He rose and went back to the garage, where his crew was prepping the Mark Four. The smashed Mark Five was shoved off to one side. The crew was working with purpose.

Hacksaw grinned. "Good news, Big Guy."

"Yeah? They're cancelling tomorrow's race?"

"Mikey's ninth quickest."

Wagner nodded. "So."

"It's a damn sight better than what he was yesterday—last. They got the front tires to stick. Unless you got any better ideas, we're setting up your car the same way."

"What have we got to lose? Do it."

Wagner was first out in the final session. Tires and brakes were new so he spent four laps bedding them in. Then he pitted. He stayed in the car while his crew made a quick check for leaks, retorqued the wheels, and added ten gallons of fuel. Then he was away again.

The corners named after the legendary race drivers—Nuvolari, Fangio, Varzi, Farina, Ascari—flew by with less effort than before. Then it was downhill through the Bugatti Esses, around the hairpin, up to Viraje de Monza, on to Viraje del Tunel, and onto the front straight again. The machine was cornering smoother and flatter, without a lot of fuss. Wagner allowed himself a small smile, then noticed his water temperature was rising quickly. Nuts. Nothing ever came easy in this business. He pitted, knowing he'd been quick, but how quick?

Hacksaw handed him his lap chart and nodded. "Not bad, Big John. A minute twenty-eight-eight. Sixth fastest."

"It's overheating," Wagner said, climbing out. He removed his helmet. "If it's something simple, I'm going back out. I can beat that time. Where's Michael?"

He found his teammate back in the garage, sipping on a cola while Rennie and Ray lay beneath his car repairing an oil leak. Wagner put out his hand. "Nice work, pal."

"Don't thank me. Thank Ray. He kept making changes and I kept telling him what it was doing to the car. Little by little, the car got better and better."

"Ain't it a bitch?" said Ray, from beneath the car. "Seems like every race we got to start all over again."

A food wrapper had found its way into Wagner's radiator inlet causing the engine to overheat. That removed, the Californian went out again. He knocked another four-tenths of a second off his time, then the engine lost power. There wasn't time to change it. But his latest time put him inside Row Two.

*   *   *   *

Edward W. Garret looked down imperiously from the VIP suite, atop the main grandstand. It was race day. Below, on the starting grid, a field of 16 cars was lined up in rows of three and two, revving, fuming, anxious for release. The starter signaled them to take a warm up lap. Garret watched them go around the 2.1-mile desert circuit, and return to the grid like birds returning to the roost. Engines switched off, crews returned, and several drivers climbed out and stretched. Garret's eyes were not on Wagner in Row Two, but further back, on Bravo, in Row Four. The Spanish Grand Prix marked Michael's Formula One debut, his grand entrance onto the world stage, and Garret was as nervous as an expectant father. Bravo was his discovery, the driver he had plucked from obscurity and intended to groom into a world champion. Wagner? He was the team veteran who would win some races, but not the championship. Guys like Wagner, who'd been around awhile, who'd never truly fulfilled their talent, their luck never changed.

Waiters in white jackets moved unobtrusively around the room, serving champagne and canapes to the guests: businessmen, promoters, and high-ranking functionaries, men of wealth and influence, with interests in the sport. Although they were Dutch, English, French, German, Italian, and Spanish, they all spoke the current language of Formula One—English.

Garret had arrived in Madrid the night before, establishing a pattern he would follow throughout the season: fly in for the weekend, see the race, and return to Southern California to run his business, Garret-Hawk Racing Enterprises, the largest U.S. supplier of performance and after-market auto parts. Garret's son Eddie managed team affairs in his absence, or did so on paper anyway. Everyone knew it was Hacksaw who really directed the team, and that Eddie was little more than a glorified secretary who answered the telephone and kept lap charts.

*   *   *   *

On the grid, crews topped off fuel tanks, retorqued wheels, checked tire pressure, and gave the bright finishes a last wipe down. Drivers climbed back into their cars, engines started, and crewmen hurried off to the side. The final seconds counted off, the flag waved, and the Spanish Grand Prix was underway.

Wagner watched Evans, Bogavanti, and Parks burn away, in front of him, and followed them over to the left setting up for Viraje Nuvolari. Loaded down with 43 gallons of gasoline, his car felt like some heavy bloated animal, wallowing this way and that through the slow, tight curves. He could feel his tires strain under the increased load every time he braked and turned, which was every second or two, the way the corners kept coming. On the short Pegaso straight, he had a brief moment to take stock. Parks' BRM was in front of him, running third, emitting puffs of blue smoke between gear shifts, and behind him was Edwards' Cooper-Maserati. Edwards seemed to be having a problem, because every time he braked smoke flared from his right-front wheel. In the split second Wagner looked back, he could detect nothing visibly wrong with the Cooper. Oh, well. It was Edwards' problem, not his.

The sharp Ascari right-hander rolled into view, demanding Wagner's full attention. Setting up, out of the corner of his eye, he saw the same telltale smoke flare off Edwards' right-front wheel. Exiting the turn, he hammered the throttle for the fast downhill run to the hairpin, felt the chassis lean side-to-side through the Bugatti Esses, and hunker down as he braked for the hairpin.

The next instant, he was slammed from behind, head flung back, stunned, uncomprehending, feeling his car lift, becoming very light, tilting lazily into a spin.

The thing's gonna flip, he thought, realizing what was happening, but no, the car was settling back on its springs just as it veered off circuit. He switched off the ignition and fuel pumps, released the steering wheel, and made his body as limp as possible. Dust and sand began swirling up around him, the car kicking and bouncing, rocks beating against the magnesium exterior. A tire ripped loose, banged against the side, and flew away. The car slid, dug into the sand and stopped. He heard steam hissing from somewhere and smelled something burning.

Fire! The mere idea of the car catching fire sounded an alarm in his nervous system.

He lurched forward trying to get out and to his horror discovered his legs were pinned. Something wet and stinging began running down his back. What the hell? He turned around to see a torn fuel line dumping raw gasoline into the seat. Frantically, he looked around for help. No one within 50 yards. Where were the bloody marshals? Damn it all. He had to get out of here. Now. This instant. He pulled and squirmed trying frantically to free his legs. Nothing doing. He pulled harder, felt movement, pulled harder still, one loosened. He wedged it free, which freed the other. He slid them both clear and raised himself up in the seat, and shit his back was on fire, and his arms too. He dove from the car into the sand and rolled over and over in it until the flames were out. Then he jumped to his feet and ran as hard as he could to get away from the car. When he was 30 feet away he turned and looked back. His car was fully engulfed in flames now, a thousand man hours of careful work, exotic metals, delicate castings, burning to the ground in seconds. He looked across the track at Edwards' Cooper, shooting flames 20 feet into the air.

A marshal ran up to him. "You all right?"

"Where's Jimmy? Did he get out?"

"Jimmy?"

Wagner pointed at the blazing Cooper. "The other driver. Did he get out?"

"He got out. I saw him."

That's what they always said. Wagner didn't believe him. He knew Edwards was still inside that car, past saving.

*   *   *   *

The accident was cleared and the race resumed. The two wrecked cars still lay on either side of the road, charred and smoldering throughout the afternoon. Bogavanti tried putting the whole sorry sight out of his mind, but each time down to the hairpin, the two blackened hulls rolled into view reminding him of what had taken place there. He hadn't seen either driver escape the carnage, but he had seen Edwards climb into an ambulance. The fate of his friend, Wagner, haunted him. He'd known the American for a decade, since their days as Ferrari teammates. Evans, in front, was drawing away, but Bogavanti didn't care. Parks passed him, then Phillips. The Italian did nothing. Ferrari team manager Zilli wrote a message on the pitboard: "Wagner OK." Bogo didn't believe it. Drivers were never told the truth until the race was over. The Italian soldiered on. Zilli held up a new message. "Evans Out." A few laps later, Phillips pitted, then rejoined the race. That put Bogavanti back in second place. Then smoke poured suddenly from Parks' BRM and he slowed down. Bogavanti repassed him and found himself leading the race, and not caring very much about it.

*   *   *   *

Wagner was relieved to see Edwards alive and unhurt in the trackside medical facility. The Canadian approached him.

"I'm sorry, John," he said, looking very sorry indeed. "My brakes bloody well gave out and there was nothing I could do, everything happened so quickly."

"Don't sweat it, Jim." Wagner grimaced. The pain on his arms and back made him want to scream. He hissed through his teeth, "I'm just glad as hell we're both around to talk about it, know what I mean?"

Edwards nodded. "I'm really, really am sorry, John."

"That's racing," he hissed. "Forget about it."

Wagner was given temporary treatment and put in a helicopter bound for a Madrid hospital. Garret appeared and climbed in beside him.

"I saw the entire accident," he said, as the helicopter lifted off. "Thank god you're all right. Jesus, what an unbelievable thing to happen."

Wagner nodded, turned and looked out the window. The circuit was shrinking beneath them. Whatever they'd given him was working, because the pain was subsiding. "If I never see this place again, it won't make me unhappy."

"I'm going to have you flown back to London tonight," Garret said in a grave voice. "A burn specialist I know will see you in the morning."

Wagner nodded. "That's very kind of you. But my car...."

"Eddie will drive it back. Listen, those burns might be worse than anyone thinks. My experience has been that it pays to get an expert's opinion."

Wagner looked back out the window. Rows of small houses rolled by as the Madrid skyline grew larger. The race, the accident, both seemed surreal. Only now did he have time to think about it, to grasp the reality of it, to feel truly frightened. And sitting beside him was Garret, acting strangely human.

The Ragged Edge
a short story by William F. Nolan

You've got to love a guy who owned not one but three Austin Healeys, one after the other, all four-bangers, the last a Le Mans 100M which he painted metallic candy-apple red with gold racing stripes, and raced in club events. To the surprise of fellow writers and racing buddies Chuck Beaumont and John Tomerlin— who had watched him spin and narrowly avoid disaster on more than one occasion—he actually won a race in his metallic candy-apple red Austin Healey, at Hour Glass Field in San Diego.

Bill "The Windmill" Nolan (as he was called in the heady days of the Group due to a habit of flailing his arms whenever excited about something) has written 75 books and some 700 magazine pieces as well as 40 television and film scripts. Eight of his books and 150 of his shorter works deal with motor racing. He wrote the first profile of Dan Gurney ever published. His racing books include The Barney Oldfield Story *(1961) and* Phil Hill: Yankee Champion *(1962). His most famous book is the sci-fi thriller* Logan's Run *(1975), a best-selling novel that resulted in a motion picture and a TV series.*

The Ragged Edge *was first published in* Sports Car Journal *in 1957 and subsequently reprinted in Beaumont's and Nolan's landmark* Omnibus of Speed. *About the story Nolan says:*

"I was a columnist for Badge-Bar Journal *in the fifties, so I used to write up every Southern California race. There was this 'special' driven by Dr. William Eshrich; I think it had a Porsche engine. He had two teenage sons that used to go to the races with him. Dr. Eshrich always did real well up to about the middle of the race—he'd be right up there with the leaders—and something would break every time. So I thought, what if I wrote a story about a fictional version of this guy actually winning a race. What would it do to his family? How would he react if all his competition dropped away and there he was in the lead? That's the basis of the story."*

As usual, Linda had remembered to have the thermos refilled at the last coffee stop just before dawn, and now Robert March held the steaming metal cup in his two hands, grateful for the steady warmth in the early morning. A clouded sun was just breaking over the tall trees fringing the track, and March inhaled the rich, moist scent of pine, carried to him by the chill ocean wind off the Pacific.

"At least we're good and early," he said to his wife.

Linda March smiled. She was a small-boned delicate woman with soft brown hair combed loosely back from a high forehead. "I knew we would be," she said.

March thought of his first race here at Pebble Beach last year, when they had arrived late at the track, and he had almost failed to run. This weekend would be different.

This weekend, he vowed, must be different.

Ahead of him, across the uneven ground, the long wooden inspection tables were already up, and girls in blue coveralls had arranged themselves in canvas chairs behind their charts and papers. Standing by the open door of the Chrysler, March sipped his coffee and watched the low-slung sports cars being pushed into line for technical inspection. His own machine, the March Special, was third behind a white Jaguar coupe.

"I'd better get on over there," March said, handing Linda his empty cup. "Keep the coffee hot."

"Tell Randy to put on his sweater," Linda instructed him, reaching into the Chrysler's rear seat for the garment. "It's windy this morning."

As March walked toward the inspection grid, he thought about the Special, about what the race tomorrow really meant to him. He thought of Bakersfield and the broken fuel pump in the fourth lap, of Santa Barbara and the wheel he'd lost on the hairpin, of Torrey Pines and the sudden, terrible dip of the pressure needle, telling him that his oil was gone; he thought of the long, uphill turn at Willow Springs, when the rear axle had broken and he'd spun out. And he thought, finally of the big one last year, right here at Pebble Beach, when he'd been doing fine, coming up steadily through the pack, and the transmission had blown. Always something. Something. .

You're a doctor, March told himself, a family man of forty with a fine wife and two nearly-grown sons. You don't belong in sports car racing and you know it. You're in it because you wanted to prove that you could take a car you'd built yourself and finish with the best of them. Well, you've tried; for a year now you've tried, and you've failed. You haven't finished one race, not one. So, why go on playing the fool?

"Hi, Dad!" The voices of his twin sons, Glenn and Randy, cut into his thoughts.

"Hi, boys," he grinned. "We're up next, aren't we?"

"Yeah. Give us a hand, Dad."

March tossed Randy's sweater into the cockpit and helped his two sixteen-year-old sons push the big blue Special into the slot vacated by the Jag.

March handed the check-off sheet to inspector Bill Greer.

"Think you'll blow off all the competition tomorrow, Doc?" asked the beefy little man, beginning his methodical safety check. He chuckled softly.

"Don't worry about Dad, Mr. Greer," Randy said stiffly. "Just let the other drivers do the worrying."

March could see that Randy was upset.

How do you feel, wondered Robert March, when you've got a father who never finishes? The boys had helped him put the Special together, worked with him on every detail, pitching in after school and on weekends to get the car ready. And then—eleven races and he'd never crossed the finish line. The constant ribbing from the other drivers had been hard to take, and he could see that Randy and Glenn were badly shaken by each new disaster. For them, the scorn and barbed humor cut deep.

Then why go on? Even Linda, who understood him completely, was beginning to worry. She knew the risks he took out there on the track, and accepted them calmly because that was her nature, but even Linda was concerned now over the boys. She had watched them become nervous and unhappy as the months went by, as the failures mounted, and she was worried.

All right, then, tomorrow would be the last one, the last time he'd race the Special. After tomorrow, if he couldn't finish with the car, he would quit for good. He'd give himself and the Special one more chance.

"Okay, Doc," said Bill Greer, checking off the last item on the sheet, "take 'er away."

Inside the cockpit, March jabbed the starter button and the big modified Mercury engine boomed fiercely into life under the long hood.

"She sounds sweet," Randy said, as they rolled toward the pits. "Real sweet."

Saturday practice was scheduled to begin immediately after the noon drivers' meeting, and already the crowds were pressing in, filling the grandstands along the main straight, posting themselves behind the sloping wooden snowfencing which lined the entire course, settling down with blankets and food and programs, waiting to see their favorite drivers and cars bullet over the treacherous 2.1 mile Pebble Beach circuit.

March was glad that the entire afternoon had been given over to practice. Here was the most beautiful and the most dangerous circuit on the West Coast, slightly over two miles of narrow blacktop, twisting through thick forest above exclusive Del Monte Lodge, with a deadly proportion of uphill and downhill turns. The massed trunks of pine and cypress waited along every straight and curve, ready to crush car and driver. A serious mistake here could well prove fatal. Practice, at Pebble Beach, was very necessary.

"Clock my last three laps," March told his wife, as he climbed into the cockpit. "Up to then I'll just be feeling out the circuit."

"Take it easy, hon," she warned him. "I've only got one of you."

He was pulling on the white crash helmet when Lou Coppard walked over to the Special. Tall and relaxed with the lean face of a wolfhound, Coppard had been openly contemptuous of March from the beginning. He never missed an opportunity to needle him about the Special.

"How's the patient, Doc?" he asked, grinning crookedly.

"She'll live," March said, his voice edged and cold.

"I should have remembered to bring flowers."

"Save 'em, Lou. Maybe you'll need 'em yourself."

"How long do you figure she'll stay pasted together out there, Doc?" Coppard asked, the grin still fixed on his lean face.

"Long enough," March replied, and decided against adding more. Don't let him get at you today, he told himself. Tomorrow, out on the track, maybe you can take him and settle the score.

The starter gave the signal to move and Coppard returned to his car. March eased the big Special through the pit gate and onto the starting grid.

As he was flagged away he forced himself to think only

of the track, of how soon he needed to downshift for the-
uphill hairpin, of his best line through the fast corners, of
when he needed to use the brakes and when he didn't.

He had a lot to learn before tomorrow.

In the late evening dusk Robert March walked back to
the hotel, smoking, moving leisurely over the darkening
streets, allowing himself to be caught up in that rare atmosphere characterizing such a weekend. Tonight, the small
towns along the length of California's Monterey Peninsula
were transformed, magically charged with a festive pre-race
electricity. In dozens of shop windows tall posters boldly
announced: PEBBLE BEACH SPORTS CAR ROAD RACES.
Neoned NO VACANCY signs glowed above every roadside
motel and the streets were filled with the ragged thunder of
sports cars, a veritable sea of out-of-towners gunning their
swift machines through traffic, shattering the cool night air
with their loud exhausts.

Practice had gone well at least. The Special had per-
formed perfectly throughout the entire session; she seemed
ready for her biggest try. March had lapped within a second
or two of some of the hottest pilots, proving the Special had
the juice if she'd only hold.

She'll hold, March told himself, because this is her last
chance; tomorrow she's got to hold.

Sunday morning dawned hot and clear at the track,
with no hint of the rain that had been threatening all week.
The sun rode down a cloudless blue sky, filtering through the
trees in checkered patches of light and shade.

Robert March had spent the early part of the day on the
winding cliff roads above the Pacific, relaxing with Linda in
the cool breeze from the ocean.

He told her of the decision he'd made.

"If I don't finish today, I'm quitting, Linda. Things can't
go on this way."

"Are you sure, Bob? Is it what you really want?"

"Yes, I'm sure. You can't go on beating your head against
a stone wall and expect the wall to give. This is my last try."

She had looked at him silently for a long moment, then
taken his hand firmly in hers. "Whatever you *really* want is
what I want too. I won't worry, no matter what you decide, I
promise. Just remember that, darling."

They arrived at the track after the Cypress Point Race
had been run.

March left Linda with Randy and Glenn in the pit and

walked over to have a look at Jeffry Moore's Monza Ferrari. Moore was a nice guy, and a hell of a driver. Whenever he was out there with the Ferrari the competition had something to worry about.

The car was undergoing wheelwork. The low, scooped snout of the fierce Italian car almost touched the ground, the sweeping lines of the compact body proclaiming sheer speed. Of course the Monza had been geared down for Pebble, but it would be reaching 130 on the back straight, and that was moving. However, Moore would have to reckon with Fischer's powerful D-type Jaguar and Wyndham's Maserati. A furious three-way battle to the checkered flag was in prospect.

"Going to ride her all the way home today, Doc?" asked a familiar voice, and March turned to face Jeffry Moore, resplendent in immaculate white coveralls. Like most of the aces, Moore wore his fame with a casual indifference, but behind the easy smile, behind the friendly squint of the narrow gray eyes, March was aware of the nervous pulse of electricity which only the track could completely remove. Only on the track, screaming down a long straight or fighting a tight curve, could a man like Moore wholly become himself.

"I'm going to try to keep you boys in sight," March replied. "I figure the Special is as ready as she'll ever be."

"That's just it, Doc," said Moore, his tone serious. "We all give you the business about the Special, but I, for one, hate to see a guy knock himself out for nothing. The car hasn't got it. She's full of bugs and bad luck, and you know it. We all know it. If you want to race then get into a car that will give you an even break. Right now Ray Boucher has one of his Ferraris up for sale. You could handle her, Doc."

"Thanks, Jeff, but I've got other plans."

"Okay. Hope she holds for you today."

"Yeah," said March. "I hope so too."

The furnace-heat of the sun seemed focused on the starting grid as the glittering line of cars rolled slowly into position for the last race of the day. This was the main event, the one the crowds had been waiting for. In just a few breathless moments the green flag would drop on thirty-two of the world's fastest sports cars, on one and a half hours of all-out driving for the coveted Del Monte trophy.

From his assigned position in the fourth row, next to a modified Healey 100S, Robert March could feel the tension, a thing alive, growing around him.

"You stick with 'er, Dad," Randy was saying. He patted,

the lean aluminum shell of the Merc-powered Special. "She'll go all the way for you this time, I know she will."

"You'd better get on back with Linda and Glenn," March said, as the clear-grid order crackled over the high black cluster of loudspeakers. They shook hands and Randy stepped away.

So, here we are, thought Robert March, flexing and unflexing his gloved hands on the spidery racing wheel. This is the last one, the one that really counts. He adjusted his goggles against the raw glare of sun on polished metal and waited.

A gradual silence fell upon the crowds in the grandstand and along the length of wooden snowfence fronting start-finish.

Tensely they waited for starter Al Tucker to begin his final check-run down the line of cars.

The sun lay on March's neck and shoulders, a hot, blazing weight, pressing him deeper into the bucket seat. Already the sweat had soaked through the back of his coveralls, and the safety belt felt like a band of steel across his hips. Damn it, Tucker, let's get the show on the road! Every second he sat there in the broiling heat, a taut spring was winding itself tighter within his body.

He thought of the men and machines around him, of Al Fischer in the incredibly fast D-Jag, of Jeff Moore's Monza Ferrari, of Wyndham in the Maserati. What a battle these three would wage! He thought, too, of Tim Mulford's huge 4.9 Ferrari. Tim might take an early lead with the brutish car, but he would be unable to hold it on a tight course like Pebble. Chuck Quavale in the Buick-Kurtis was always a solid threat. Finally, March thought of Lou Coppard. He could see Lou's face, framed in the rear-view mirror. His black Cadillac-powered Special was two rows back, on the inside. The rest of the leadfoots could battle it out for the cup; March only wanted two things in this race. He wanted to finish—and he wanted Coppard's scalp.

He pulled his helmet strap tight and forced his full attention to Al Tucker as the little man signaled start-engines.

The sudden thunder of thirty-two finely-tuned racing engines washed over the grid, the sharp roar of the Buick-Kurtis blending with the knifing shriek of the Ferraris. Every eye was on Al Tucker as the harlequin-shirted little man fell into his jogging Indian-run down the line of poised machin-

ery. March raised a gloved hand to let Tucker know he was
ready and firing.

At the end of the line Tucker pivoted gracefully and
loped back to the front row, the green flag furled and ready
in his hand. He paused dramatically, back to the drivers. The
engines screamed. Only seconds now.

I've been here for a century, thought Robert March,
belted to a tiger, waiting. Dear God, man, will you jump?

Tucker leaped high into the air and the green flag
swirled free.

The taut spring in Robert March's body uncoiled. He
mashed down on the gas pedal and felt the dizzying surge of
acceleration as the massive Special rocketed forward.

He saw Tim Mulford's big Ferrari rip into the first
sweeping turn just ahead of Fischer's D-Jag. Moore and
Wyndham went in snapping at the leaders' heels. Just ahead
of March, Chuck Quavale powered his Buick-Kurtis in wide,
passing two slower machines in the apex of the turn.

March was seventh coming out of turn 3 into the
winding, uphill hairpin, and he was hanging on to Quavale.
As they roared through the dog-leg bend Lou Coppard's black
Cad-Special whipped into sight in his rear view mirror.

So, he wants his dice early, eh? thought March. All
right, Lou, make your bid. I'm ready.

He'd planned on conserving his brakes through the
beginning laps, but now he saw this was not possible if he
wished to take Coppard.

They swung into the long back straight, down through
turn 6, and swept full-throttle past the pits and grandstand.
A rough circuit, March thought, a really mean one.

They boomed past Donaldson's stalled V8-60 Special on
the main straight with Coppard pressing hard, a scant two
car-lengths to March's rear. On the short, twisty stretch into
the hairpin, the cut-off markers jumped at them, and March
braked, dumping into a lower gear for the tight corner.
Coppard moved up another two feet.

The tachometer needle climbed crazily as March floored
the pedal on the long back straight. The straining Merc
engine shrilled under full-throttle, and the haybales, solid as
stones at this speed, flashed by in a yellow-bright pattern
under the sun. Behind the bales the threatening bulk of
trees blurred with speed into a single dark line.

A modified Triumph had spun into the bales on turn 6,
and March was forced to cramp the wheel hard-right to avoid

an accident. He saw Coppard slew by, barely missing the derelict car. The pace quickened.

Coppard, driving at the peak of his form, closed to within a half car-length on the front straight, and March wondered if he could hold him through the dog-leg at this speed.

At that precise instant Coppard's right rear tire blew, with a flat crack, sharp as a rifle shot, and the black Special skidded across the width of the track, spun twice, and came to rest with the other three tires smoking.

As he entered the first sweeping bend March could see Lou Coppard, obviously unhurt, gesturing wildly to his pit crew. By the time he could get a new tire on the car March would be half a lap ahead. The dice was over.

All right, let's start saving those brakes, March told himself. You've got better than an hour left to run.

On the next lap, as he swept past the pits, he caught the chalked numeral on the blackboard that Randy held out for him. P-6. Which meant he had emerged from the dice in sixth position!

He recognized Mulford's 4.9 Ferrari in the pits; Tim, of course, had pushed too hard. That meant Fischer in the D-Jag was leading somewhere up ahead, probably followed by Moore's Ferrari and Wyndham's Maserati. He could see Quavale's Kurtis and Gene Waring in the C-Jag ahead of him as he entered the back straight. He was running sixth, behind Waring.

March felt the heat from the straining engine fire up along his legs; he inhaled the bitter-sharp scent of burned rubber and hot oil—and he thought, by God, she's holding, she's doing fine.

Forty-two minutes to go.

According to Randy's pit board he was now picking up on Gene Waring at the rate of three seconds a lap.

He was still closing when Waring's car hit a patch of spilled oil, fishtailed wildly, and slid into the bales.

March roared by into fifth place.

He began to push harder, moving up on Quavale, lapping slower machines, using the car as a fencer uses a foil, darting and slashing around the 2.1 mile circuit.

Quavale fell back with every curve. Out of 3 March drew abreast and passed the big Kurtis in a short, savage burst of speed, using every inch of the narrow blacktop to get by.

He was fourth.

By God, you've taken one of the really hot boys. Let's keep moving'. He could see Jerry Wyndham in the blue Maserati breaking early for turn 6, and Randy's pit board told him the story.

Wyndham was running out of brakes!

Okay, then, let's get him!

Brake, downshift, accelerate, upshift, accelerate, brake. Over and over until his wrists ached, until his mouth was cotton-dry and his eyes burned through the dusty goggles. Closing.

Closing.

And behind March, another threat. Sifting masterfully through the pack, Lou Coppard had driven his black Cad Special to within a quarter-lap of March. Since the tire change, Coppard had passed all of the slower cars and was trying for another bid.

I can hold Lou, March told himself; he hasn't enough time to catch me unless something goes on the Merc. So, let's get that Maserati!

Wyndham was forced to slide through the curves, skimming the haybales with his rear wheels, fighting for control. March picked up another foot out of the third turn.

The two cars swept into the back straight, a pair of twin projectiles shot from giant cannon. March's foot was hard to the floor, a part of the machine itself, draining every ounce of power from the laboring engine. Through the separate leather flesh of the driving gloves he felt the wheel's rock-firmness in his hands.

I can take him at the end of the straight, March decided. He'll have to back off early to save what little brake he has left, and I'll pass him into the turn.

As the 5-4-3-2-1 cut-off markers leaped at them, Wyndham's brake lights went on and March blistered past, stabbed the brake pedal, snapped a quick downshift and drifted the turn, all four tires screaming. Wyndham fell in behind him.

With fifteen minutes remaining in the race, Robert March was third.

Randy's pit board told him he was almost three-quarters of a lap behind the second-place Monza of Jeffry Moore, and was about to be lapped by the leading D-Jag.

At least he'd been able to make Glenn and Randy proud of him, and of the Special. Now all he had to do was hold.

March saw the D coming up fast in the rear-view mirror.

Fischer would lap him into turn 3, so March cut wide for the turn, braked early, and waved him in.

Engine howling, Fischer scalded by. March saw the Jag's brake lights wink on as Fischer began his slide. Suddenly, at the apex of the turn, the black car seemed to explode. Orange flame gouted from the engine compartment, and Fischer, blinded by smoke, lost control, mashing into the stacked bales, bursting through in fiery petals of burning hay.

March slowed, saw Fischer leap from the twisted machine, saw the flagmen rush forward with extinguishers—and then he was around the next turn and moving away.

Robert March was second.

Look at your hands, March told himself, look at them! You're trembling like a novice in his first race. He felt the sweat, sour on his lips and under his goggles, felt it flushing over his body like a coating of warm oil. Fischer's okay. He's all right, so come out of it and drive. Drive!

He glanced in the rear-view mirror. Coppard! The flying Special was only a car-length behind him. Lou had taken neat advantage of Fischer's spin to move up fast.

As they flashed by the pits Randy held the board high and a single, hastily chalked word stood out in bold relief against the black: GO!

March, furious at his own weakness, began to drive deeper into the turns, braking at the last possible instant, drifting to the edge of the bales. Coppard, unable to maintain the pace, dropped back.

Ten minutes remaining; ten minutes to hold his position.

Then March saw the red Ferrari of Jeffry Moore off the track and deserted! The car had thrown a front wheel and Moore had retired. With a cold shock of surprise Robert March realized he was now in first place!

So, he thought, you've driven the Special, the car they all laughed at, the car that never finished, into the lead—and they're all behind you, Waring and Quavale and Coppard, all of them. An hour ago all you wanted to do was finish and look at you now. Winning.

Winning!

As he roared over the sun-splashed macadam, under the dark wash of trees, past the flickering faces of the cheering crowd, Robert March felt suddenly cold; a chill sense of loss began to build within him.

If he won this race, March knew, things would never be the same. If he won today, his victory could never be erased in the minds of the crowd. He would no longer be "ole Doc," the poor, unlucky guy to cheer for, he would be the man to beat. A winner had to keep on winning. If I take this race they'll say, "He did it once, why can't he do it again?" How many times would Wyndham's brakes fail, or Fischer's Jag catch fire, or Moore's Ferrari throw a wheel—all in the same race? Sure, today had been a freak affair from the beginning, but that wouldn't matter to the crowd. And it wouldn't matter to Randy or Glenn. They'd want to see me do it again, and when I lost I'd just be a fool in a slow car. I just can't let myself win today.

Starter Al Tucker gave him the blue flag as he passed the main grandstand. One more lap to go.

Robert March made up his mind. If you've got no business at the head of the table, move aside for the man who has.

It would be simple, really. All he needed to do was keep his foot on the gas for a second too long. Every curve has a ragged edge. If you push your car beyond the ragged edge, beyond the point of minimum tire adhesion, you lose control. Beyond the ragged edge you spin out, and there is nothing you can do about it.

Let Coppard have the race. If his luck held, he could re-enter and finish behind the leaders.

Coming down the back straight at full-throttle, Robert March watched the cut-off markers growing in the distance. 110 miles per hour. Tiny dots, growing larger with speed. 112. Becoming sharp and legible. 115. Easily readable now. His speedometer needle bumped 120 miles per hour.

When he was certain that he could never make the turn, when he was sure he had held the pedal down long enough, Robert March tramped the brake, downshifted, snapping the stubby gear-lever into place, and began his drift.

He caught a single, quick glimpse of Lou Coppard entering the far end of the straight. Okay, Lou, take her away. She's yours.

He felt the car breaking away into the long slide which would carry it into the bales. Now he was no longer master, no longer in control; he was simply a weight the machine carried with it toward the packed bales, a soft, helpless weight which could be crushed instantly to death or burned to sudden ash.

And then, in that long, dream-like slide, March realized why he was allowing this to happen.

Because he was afraid.

He was afraid of the truth about racing and what it actually meant in his life. He'd kept it carefully hidden from Linda and the boys, even from himself, but now he faced it.

You race for only one reason, March told himself. Not just to prove you can finish with a car you built yourself, not to have the crowds cheer because they feel sorry for you—you race to win. You really didn't know, until today, if you had the guts to get out and drive the way a winner must drive. Now you know. You proved you can match the best of them, so it's time to stop fooling yourself. You're in racing because you've got to be in it, because it's a thing you love—and if you throw away your big chance now you'll keep on being afraid to do what you really want to do. You were worried about Linda, about what she would say, but remember her words before the race: *"Whatever you really want is what I want too."* You stuck with the Special because you knew it wouldn't win, because you could put the truth aside in such a car. How could you win if you never finished? Jeffry Moore had been right when he told you to get the Ferrari.

So, all right. Why throw this race when you have it in the palm of your hand? Win today and then buy that Ferrari Boucher has for sale. Drive this damn car out of the turn and take the checkered flag because that's what you've wanted all along. Let's GO!

In that timeless, suspended instant between the beginning and the end of the slide, all these thoughts flickered through his mind like quick images on a screen.

Then the Special's rear deck struck the first bale. March felt the car tipping, poised for a roll, and he instinctively lowered his head. But the Special maintained balance. It crashed back on its wheels, spun around twice and slid to a smoking halt, facing the straight, the engine stalled and silent.

Down the straight at full-bore came Lou Coppard, leaning over the wheel, a crooked victory grin on his grease-blackened face.

The flagmen were frantically waving March back on the circuit; another second and it would be too late.

If only she fires, breathed March, punching the starter button, if only the bales didn't finish her! With a dry cough, the Mercury came to life and Robert March bulleted onto the track just as Coppard began his drift.

The scream of the crowd was lost in the savage thunder of racing engines as the two cars roared out of the turn wheel to wheel.

Lou Coppard had the edge. With a stabbing burst of acceleration, he passed March out of the bend into the front straight.

Far ahead, the late afternoon sun glinting on the gaudy silk of his shirt, Al Tucker crouched with the checkered flag ready at his side, squinting down the long strip of blacktop at the two leaders.

Coppard, his mouth now hard and unsmiling, his foot mashing the pedal, led March by half a car-length at the pits, but it was not enough. In the final one hundred feet, with the crowd wild and shouting his name, Robert March edged past the streaking black Cad Special to take the checkered flag.

The Pebble Beach Del Monte Cup was his.

He saw them coming, Linda and the boys, running across the track to meet him as he rolled the Special slowly into the winner's circle.

He wasn't sure exactly what he would say to Linda. How do you tell a woman that you've suddenly discovered another force in your life as strong as she is—that you need both, deeply, genuinely, each in a different way?

Robert March watched his wife push through the crowd, waving, smiling, tears in her eyes, and he thought: perhaps I won't have to tell Linda anything.

Perhaps she already knows.

Le Mans 24
a novel by Denne Bart Petitclerc

Le Mans, France, 1967. Screenwriter Denne Petitclerc is there with producer Bob Relyea, advance men for the movie Le Mans. They're stationed in the pit between Ferrari and Ford, between old world craftsmanship and machine age efficiency, waiting to see which will prevail. "We couldn't have been in a better place," says Petitclerc. "The Americans were like a military organization, clean and sharp, everything by command. The Ferrari guys had sandwiches in their back pockets. It was the first time I had a chance to see big-time racing, and I must tell you it was absolutely fascinating."

Petitclerc wrote a narrative, first as a novel—mostly to orient people who were going to work on the film—then as a screenplay. "It was a very different kind of screenplay because we were going to do it originally in a multi-screen process which was brand new at the time. It was fun and exciting, but it never got made."

Indeed. Having total creative control, Steve McQueen rejected Petitclerc's treatment (and the efforts of subsequent writers) and ultimately made a movie with very little story. Petitclerc's novel was dusted off and published in 1971.

Petitclerc covered the Korean War for the Santa Rosa Press Democrat and Castro's revolution in Cuba for the Miami Herald and the San Francisco Chronicle. He moved into television as a story editor of the "Bonanza" television series, and went on to create and produce two other series, "The High Chaparral" and "Then Came Bronson." His screen writing credits include Red Sun and Islands in the Scream. One of his more recent books is The Hallow-Point Birthday, a memoir of a near-tragic weekend in the 1950s at Hemingway's villa in Cuba.

The excerpt (pages 79-92) follows aging driver Chris Breslin as he readies himself for the race. For Vali Beaufort, his new girlfriend, it is particularly trying, knowing the risks drivers take every time they strap themselves into a cockpit.

Chris Breslin stood at the open window and watched the morning light come over the rooftops of the town. The slate of the roofs looked shiny and wet, and he saw the lights go on in the windows as people got up. He saw smoke drifting up from the chimneys and heard the cars going past below on the street. It had stopped raining before first light, and the clouds were broken, so that he could see the pale sky, with the light gradually increasing in it, until the sun appeared, blindingly bright. It was going to be a hot day.

After a while he went back to the bed and looked at Vali sleeping. Her mouth was open slightly, and her lips lifted from her teeth, as though she were going to smile. He watched her eyelashes tremble and her expression change as she stirred and turned against the pillow. She was the most beautiful girl he had ever seen, and he knew that he loved her now and wanted her more than anything he had ever wanted in his life.

There had been a moment yesterday, he was thinking, when he had closed his eyes and, in the dark, lost himself and felt as though nothing else in the world existed. They had been one being, together. It had never happened before, and as he looked at her now, at that familiar face, which was still a stranger's face, at her white neck and the curve of her shoulder, he was grateful, as he was grateful for many things that had happened in his life; but for this he was also humble and somewhat bewildered. He had never expected it to happen to him.

"Is it still raining?"

He realized that she had been looking up at him for some time.

"No. It's stopped," he said.

"Is it time to go?"

"No, sleep if you want. We've got a lot of time."

He sat down on the bed and looked at her. She looked sleepy. She smiled at him and yawned and stretched. She sat up and shook her head. "You're here. And I'm in love with you. It isn't a dream?"

"Probably."

"You don't know what you're getting yourself into," she said. "You truly don't know. . ."

"Neither do you."

"Oh, yes, I do, Chris. I know so very well."

He shook his head. "After this race—then make up your

mind. After you see it, then you decide."

She started to speak in protest, but he touched her lips with his fingertips and shook his head. "I want you to go through it once. So you'll know. I'm not going to quit racing. I'm going to go as long as I'm alive. It's where I'm at. It's what I'm all about. I'm not going to be an old man. Understand?"

"Yes, I understand—I do."

"I want you to see it. Go through it. Whatever happens out there this weekend will happen so many times you'll wish you never saw a car. But it'll go on as long as I'm alive. And one time I'm going to pull out of a pit and not come back. You have to know that. You have to expect it. Nobody really beats this rap."

"But some have. You said so."

"Yeah, a few. Maybe I'll have that kind of luck. Maybe I won't. That's just one of those things you never know about. But I've got to tell you this, because I love you. I'm going to ask you to marry me, Miss Beaufort. The moment the race is over."

"You don't want me to say yes now?"

"I don't want you to say yes at all." He looked at her straight. "I want you to say no. I want you to pull out and forget you ever met me. And then maybe I can forget, too."

"I'll never do that."

"Don't make any bets on it."

She moved close to him and curled herself against him. She could feel his heart beating.

They were in the hotel dining room, eating eggs at the long table and, occasionally joking with each other. Collins sat beside Vali. He looked rested and relaxed and talked more than usual. Reg Stuart had grown even more quiet. He ate listlessly and seemed preoccupied by his own thoughts. Blinn came in late and sat down beside Chris.

"Did you hear the rain last night?" he said. "I thought it was going to melt the town. What a rain!"

"Just hope you don't get it tonight, old boy," Collins said. "Le Mans is famous for its mucking weather. Have you ever driven in a bad rain?"

"Never," Blinn said. "Here in practice was the first."
Chris looked at him.

"Yes," Collins said. "Yes. You have to watch the little cars here in a real rain. They have a habit of bunching up on your line at the corners, eh? Goddamn sticky situation. Most of the drivers don't know their chins from their rumps about driving to begin with. Damn sticky. I wish I didn't; have to drive this bloody twenty-four hours, anyway."

"Hear, hear," Stuart said. He had been so quiet they all looked up at him. "All I said was hear, hear."

They laughed.

Vali looked at Collins and said, "How is Hadley?" Collins stopped his fork and looked over at Vali. He smiled faintly. "She's in good form. Put her on the plane last night. Talked to her this morning by telephone. Can't get into any trouble trussed up in plaster the way she is." He looked at Chris and then down at his fork and spiked a piece of egg. "She sends all apologies to you chaps for her—accident. And wishes us luck. She's in good form." He put the egg in his mouth and chewed. "Damn relief to get rid of her, though."

Stuart laughed. "I say, Derek, do you remember my saying that very same thing once?"

"Yes, as a matter of fact, I do. It was at the Targa Florio, two years ago, right?"

Stuart turned to look at Vali. "I have rotten taste in women," he said. "Three wives—all corkers."

Vali glanced at Chris and then down at her plate.

Blinn was saying, "I will never marry. Better to be alone."

While driving to the circuit they had all grown quiet and detached. They had to leave the hotel early to get in before the heavy traffic crushed into the roads. The route was already thick with cars. Vali watched the crowd of vehicles and the people who were walking to the race, streaming along the side of the road in long columns, carrying baskets and coats, sweating in the sun, and getting dusty from the cars passing on the road.

Chris braked as the line of cars ahead slowed. "We should've left earlier," he said. "This is a helluva lot of traffic."

"It will get worse," Collins said.

"I know it," Chris said. "We should've come out earlier."

"Well, we didn't."

Chris glanced at Collins sharply. There was a nervous, taut, detached manner about him.

"Look, Derek, you want to drive?"

"Hell, no, old man. You're doing beautifully."

"Then shut up."

Collins did not look at him but sat back in the seat and

turned his head away.

"It wasn't me that started the thing," he said.

"What?"

"Nothing, Chris. Just being nasty. Sorry."

"Yeah."

They drove in silence and turned off into the road that ran along the camping places. Vali saw rows and rows of cars in the parking lots. Mobs of people sat on campstools or in the grass beside their cars, eating lunch. Beyond, she could see a newly built bridge, the wood showing fresh and yellow against the green pine trees, and over the bridge moved a massed mob that seemed to have no end or beginning. When the car turned again and came to the gate, the two guards at the entrance waved them through. Vali saw the grandstands and the people flowing in steady lines along both sides of the road and going through the gate. The car moved slowly, and Chris honked to get the crowds out of the way, but the mob moved on and did not seem to notice or care. Finally they got inside, and, as far as she could see, heads and bodies were moving and dust rising from that great herd. Once inside, Vali saw the huge red Ferrari car van. They were just then unloading the blood-red brute that carried number 21.

"Well," Collins said. "There's our friend Ernst's little buggy. I suppose we'll be seeing a lot of it from now on."

"Gentlemen, we want you to note that you do not leave the pits thus—"

The slender, gray-haired man, with the sun-browned face and loud sport coat, shifted one of the model cars on the huge map of the Le Mans circuit. All the drivers were sitting around in the big hall in their white driving suits, listening to him. Beside the huge map of the oval track stood a long table, at which the officials of the Automobile Club del'Ouest sat in profound and silent dignity, their backs erect, their eyes on the speaker. The drivers lounged in their chairs and occasionally yawned.

"You see? This can lead to grave consequences, gentlemen. You must leave the pits properly." He shifted the angle of the cars again. He smiled. "Like this." He repeated the whole performance again in French.

"Now, gentlemen, we want to have a fine race. We want you all to have a fine race." He smiled and slapped a small plaque on the board: 24. "Twenty-four hours, gentlemen. That is the time of our race. Starting at four o'clock this afternoon. Twenty-four hours." He slapped down another plaque: 1440. "Fourteen hundred forty minutes, gentlemen. That is the time of our race. Fourteen hundred and forty minutes." He repeated himself in French, then slapped down another plaque beyond the other two: 86,400. He looked sternly at the drivers. "Eighty-six thousand four hundred seconds, gentlemen. That is the time of our race. The important thing you must remember is this—twenty-four hours. You must drive your cars twenty-four hours, fourteen hundred forty minutes, eighty-six thousand four hundred seconds, to win. But if you try to make up one of these seconds, pressing beyond the limits of your machines, you will not finish these twenty-four hours. Thank you, gentlemen."

There was a scraping of chairs and a mumble of conversation as they all stood and started to file out. Vali walked beside Chris. When they came to the door, there was Ernst.

"Breslin," he said. "There are no hard feelings. We both race to win, eh?"

"Yeah, champ." Chris smiled.

"But no hard feelings, eh?"

"You figure it out," Chris said, and they went outside into the sun. From the track they could hear the martial blaring of the music on the loud-speakers. The crowd beyond the fence was unbelievably huge.

They came into the tunnel under the stands out of the intense sunlight and went through the cool shade to the pit door. Chris stopped and looked at Vali. He smiled.

"Don't worry, huh?"

"Not even a little bit?"

"Not at all." He opened the door for her. "Not even if you want to."

A mechanic came into the concrete pit, nodded at Chris, and went past them. Instinctively Vali pressed close to Chris. Down the line a car started up, with a racking pop-burst, like an explosion. The music on the loud-speaker was deafening. And all around was the sound of the mob. When they stepped out of the concrete bunker and into the sun again she looked up and saw it.

The crowd seemed to have a life and surging movement of its own, a vitality that electrified the air. Currents moved through it the way wind works through wheat standing in a field and changes its color. So many people packed together, so many colors and sounds, so many papers fluttering and faces turning that it seemed as if a wave, invisible but powerful, had passed over and changed and rechanged the facade of that massed mob in the stands. It stretched out of sight, from it came one long, continuous, rolling roar of voices, and through it echoed the loud-speakered music and then the fierce sputtering crack of the cars being started. The air smelled of burned gasoline and castor oil, dust and wet cement and wet wood. People on the track walked past the cars, observing, filming, talking to mechanics and to drivers, and there were officials wearing tags on their coats and arm bands, and policemen in their dark-blue, white-gloved uniforms. Ranks of cars were lined up in front of the pits, with mechanics and spectators milling around them, the way bees mill and dart around flowers in a field. Towering above it all was that slanted, living, half-mile-long mosaic of eyes and mouths, set in faces that moved and shifted and changed color, and changed it again. And above this was the clear blue dome of the sky.

Vali caught her breath and held Chris' arm tightly. It was crowded around the pit, and she saw people turning their heads to look at them. Several took pictures, with their cameras slung around their necks by leather straps. She turned her head and saw the line of private booths just above the pits; each cubicle packed solidly with people who were laughing and smiling, and peering down at them through glasses. A woman pointed at Chris, and they all looked at him then. Vali felt herself growing smaller and more timid. Chris had become completely detached. Someone was leaning close to him and shouting to be heard above the din. Chris nodded, but Vali saw that his eyes were far away and that he was not listening.

Richard Hedges pushed his way through the crowd. Chris left the man who was still shouting at him and walked over to Hedges.

Vali tried to follow him, but the press of the moving line of spectators blocked her path. The man who had been speaking to Chris looked down at her and then away, as though he were ashamed. Vali turned away and tried to get through to Chris. The crowd had suddenly swelled at his appearance. It spilled over onto the track. News cameramen ran forward and clicked the shutters of their cameras. She caught glimpses of Chris and Richard Hedges talking together beside the Lola, which glistened green and shiny in the sun. She could not move in the crush of bodies.

"Here, let us through there!" a voice said sharply behind her. She turned and saw Derek Collins, followed by Blinn and Stuart, all in their white driving suits and carrying their helmets and gloves, trying to get through the mob from the pits. "Damn it, let us through!"

Bodies shifted, and Vali felt the hard press of shoulders and elbows. She was being crushed backward. Collins and Stuart went past her without looking at her, and Blinn glanced at her when she called his name. There was no recognition in his eyes, and the smile on his round, boyish face was fixed. The mob closed in behind them, then pulled back again as Henry Tripp, the mechanic, came back. He saw Vali and stopped.

"Bit crowded. No place for you. Come on, now." He reached out a greasy hand and led her to the ramp. It, too, was jammed with spectators. "Here now, clear out of there," Tripp shouted. "We've got work to do. Clear out, now, or I'll get the gendarmes after you."

The spectators grudgingly gave up their vantage point. Tripp lifted Vali onto the stand.

"Take your chair and hold it," he said, and smiled, showing his crooked teeth. "I'll bring you your clipboard and watches, miss. Don't let them crowd you out, now."

Then he was gone.

From her seat Vali looked out on the broad, paved track and down on the cars parked in the pits. To the right she saw the rank of red Ferraris. The mechanics, in their scarlet coveralls, pushed and shoved and shouted their way through a clutter of spectators, journalists, cameramen, tools, rags, spare parts, and tires. There seemed to be a great deal of confusion and animated excitement around the red cars. The drivers had not yet appeared. Hands waved frantically in the air as mechanics shouted to each other. Shoulders shrugged. Red-clad figures moved in and out, and the effect, she thought, was charming. The cars looked brutal, squat as toads, with their humped front fenders and thick, blunt, cut-off-looking rear-engine compartments. There was a stirring inside the pit, and she saw Ernst's blond head appear in the crowd and Campari's porcupine hair; beside him was Mietta Campari, looking dark, cool and aloof, and as detached as her husband. Behind them came the other Ferrari drivers, whom she did not know. She looked at Chris below her and saw that he was watching Ernst, too. She looked over at Ernst and saw that he had something in his hands. He stared over at Chris, smiled, and lifted his hands for Chris to see two magnum bottles of champagne. Campari looked over at Chris and grinned. He gave Chris the thumbs-up sign and laughed. Ernst placed the two champagne bottles on the timekeepers' table in clear view, so that Chris could see them every time he got out of the car. Then he turned his back. The mechanics in scarlet thought it a great joke. They were all looking over at Chris and grinning. There was a smattering of applause from the booths above the pits.

Chris smiled to himself and lowered his head to listen to what Blinn was saying to him, and then they both laughed and looked over at Ernst.

Someone in the stands above hooted and whistled, and a ripple of laughter and shouts came from the crowd.

Vali looked to the left and saw the two white Chaparrals, with their strange, strutted wings perched stiffly above the rear ends, looking like a pair of short, low-slung, box-shaped mechanical birds. A big crowd had gathered around them, and she saw two of the drivers, both with young faces and gray hair. They stood talking to each other as the crowd surged around them.

Beyond were the Fords. She craned her neck to see them. The pit area had been roped off, and a squad of policemen kept the spectators back, so that the cars stood free of the mob. The area looked clean, uncluttered, efficient, and, in contrast to the Ferrari pits, sterile. The cars were beautiful to see: painted rust-red, bright yellow, flame-red, and pale blue, with a broad white stripe on the hoods, in which was a white circle bearing the number of the car in black numerals. Vali saw Yarborough, in his white coveralls and broad-brimmed Stetson, standing beside his rust-red number 2 car talking with two mechanics. His face looked still and grave. She had never seen him unsmiling before. Other drivers walked about the uncluttered area, but she did not know their names. They all seemed extremely calm, confident, and aloof. The whole atmosphere around the Fords impressed her as one of Spartan, military, no-nonsense efficiency, which seemed American and threatening, and made her somehow resentful, as though they had no right to be so powerful, so rich, so uncluttered, so very, very efficient.

She turned back to see Chris. He was seated behind the wheel, signaling the mechanic with his hands. The mechanic adjusted the rearview mirror until Chris waved that it was

right. Another man was wiping the already shiny surface of
the car with a rag. Another was washing the windshield on
the number 18 car, while Collins, arms folded, looked on.
Vali saw another mechanic placing a plastic cover over each
headlight and applying masking tape to hold it. She looked
at the big clock, which jutted out from the upper grandstand
to her right, hanging at the end of a metal frame, with the
yellow warning lights above it, and saw that it was five
minutes until three o'clock. She felt the mounting tension in
the crowd and heard the helicopter chop-chopping overhead,
and the first car start up down at the Ford pits, racking her
ears with an echoing, smashing roar. When she turned her
head back to see Chris again a half-dozen cars had started.
The noise was deafening now. The smell of exhaust fumes
became intense. More and more cars were being started. The
music stopped, and a blurred, magnified voice made some
announcement, which she could not make out above the
roaring. She saw Chris get out of the car and lean forward to
shout into Richard Hedges' ear, and saw him nod.

There was an increase in the noise from the crowd, as
though someone had turned it up with a switch. Looking
down the track, she saw the line of policemen at the upper
end of the slight grade, standing loosely at attention. They
had formed a long line across the track. The crowd hooted
and whistled at them. The mob's voice roared louder as the
line of blue-coated, blue-hatted, white-gloved policemen
moved toward her down the slope, sweeping ahead of them
all of the spectators and photographers, some protesting
violently. One man started running, so as to circle around
the end of the line of policemen, and as the huge crowd in
the stands roared a policeman caught the man and they
argued angrily. The crowd hooted as he was led off the track.
The line of officers was closer now, and the crowd milling in
front of it was bigger. Vali saw the people moving into the pit
areas and being ushered out, leaving behind the line of
policemen only the cars and mechanics and drivers in their
white coveralls. Several of the drivers were putting on their
helmets. She saw Chris lift his helmet and slip it on, the gold
on the white helmet glittering in the sun. As the line of
policemen went past, two went by below her and looked up
coldly. One stopped and shouted something to someone
above. She looked up. A man with a cigar in his hand smiled
and put the cigar out of sight. The policemen went on.

Chris came over to her, and she got down from the chair

and leaned toward him. The roaring, ear-cracking sound of
the cars smashed away the sound of his voice.

"I'll see you soon!" he shouted.

She noticed the way his lips moved when he smiled. His
eyes looked at her, but she saw how detached and far off
they had become, and, suddenly, there was a rush of panic
inside her. She grabbed at his arm, feeling the soft, fireproof
material of his sleeve, and kissed him. She could smell the
acid scent he had and feel the clammy, hot touch of his
sweating skin. He smiled at her again and turned aside. She
watched him moving away.

The mechanics were shoving the cars into place up the
line. She glanced up at the clock; it was three twenty-five.
The drivers were starting to drift across the track. Below,
Chris had stopped to say something to Mario Campari.
Campari took his hand, suddenly, and leaned forward to say
something to Chris above the noise. Chris smiled—he looked
faintly embarrassed—and replied. Campari grinned, but the
grin faded, and he suddenly embraced Chris and patted his
shoulders with his gloved hands. Then they started across
the track. Collins, Blinn, Hedges, and the mechanics
watched them go. Stuart was already standing in his position.

Vali turned and saw Mietta Campari looking over at her,
with her bright, dark eyes. She smiled, lifted her chin, and
turned away.

Vali sat in the chair, beside the empty chair that Hadley
had occupied. She had never felt so alone in her life.

After he left Vali and started across the track, feeling the
pavement through the soft soles of his driving shoes, Chris
felt increasingly better. When Campari had stopped him and
embraced him, saying, "God be with you and me and all of
us," Chris had felt a surge of embarrassment, although he
knew how truly sincere and religious Campari was. Even
then he had been only vaguely aware of what was going on
around him. He caught glimpses of the mechanics pushing
the cars up. He heard the noise of the crowd and felt it when
it changed. He saw the other drivers moving with him and
alongside him and heard them saying something to him but
paid no attention.

He reached the embankment wall and turned, leaning
back against it, and saw the big limousines moving onto the
track, all black and shiny, with the men and women seated
in the back. He looked to where Ernst was standing, leaning

on one foot, the other drawn up against the embankment. Yarborough was beside him, his face sullen and drawn. Chris looked over and saw his car across from him, third in line, parked at an angle pointing up the hill, the sun glinting on the green surface, the number 17 showing big and clear. He looked up at the sky and saw the clouds moving. The light changed, darkened, and then it became bright again, and, as he watched, another cloud appeared, and the light darkened again. A big slow-moving airplane circled slowly. The engines, rumbling deeply, shook the earth under his feet. In the plane a side door had been removed, and he saw a photographer leaning out as the plane banked into its turn.

The loud-speaker announced, "One minute!" and the crowd gave a pulsating roar. It has begun! he thought. This is it! He felt the tightness grip his chest and the blood rush to his heart. This is it!

He took a deep breath of air, swelling his chest, and let it out. The next came automatically as a yawn, and his confidence rose as the tide rises, coming in a rush now. It was his greatest gift, the thing that fitted him for race driving: the ability to ignore what might happen; to anticipate with a growing excitement, with an enormous, surging confidence, ignoring all the rest of it, knowing it is there, completely, but giving it absolutely no thought; thinking instead of the car, which he could see there, the light blinding on the windshield—the car, yes, absolutely the car, just the car, and getting from here to the car.

It started in the upper tiers of the 400 yards of grandstands and rippled across the masses of faces in a rushing, rolling, building, hissing sound: "Shhhhh!. . ." Then: silence.

Overhead the steady droning of the camera plane as it circled into position.

Silence.

Acres of people jammed together in utter silence. The wind blowing across the stand stirred the flags and unfurled them in the silence. A little dust blew across the pavement to where the drivers stood in a long line, like skirmishers in white uniforms, tensing, bent forward like sprinters.

Across from them, separated by a road width, stood the cars, lined up in perfect echelon, waiting, in silence. Behind the cars squatted the mechanics and the team managers, each ready, watching the man with the checkered flag in his hand standing above them, each waiting, in silence, ready to signal their drivers to sprint.

The wind picked up and made a rushing sound, and through it the steady mechanical chatter of the airplane engines.

Chris could hear his own breathing. Sweat glistened on his forehead. He had deadened everything inside him. He could hear the wind hitting the helmet he wore. Inside him, nothing. His eyes flicked quickly down the line of fifty-four cars, then back to his own. Again, nothing. Richard Hedges lifted his hand, and Chris bent, tensing his muscles to spring. His eye caught the flash of Hedges' hand, and he ran.

The green car grew larger and bounced in his vision as he sprinted. He could hear, behind him, the padded scuffle of running feet. Then the door. The handle. Grasping it, he pulled the door open and swung smoothly into the seat. Grabbing the wheel with his right hand, he touched the starter.

For an instant his heart stopped.

All around him cars burst into life, roaring, cracking, smashing out the sound of exhausts and engines. He caught a glimpse of the rust-red Ford beside him pulling away, and a glimpse of the red, vented tail of Ernst's Ferrari just ahead, moving away in billowing clouds of blue smoke. Then another and another patch of color flashed past his windshield.

The starter ground and ground and ground.

When the black-and-white-checkered flag fell, fifty-four men broke and ran. Simultaneously, you could hear the massed, whispered clicking of 200,000 camera shutters going off; and, an instant later the pulsating roar of the crowd. As the doors of fifty-four cars were flung open the drivers ducked quickly inside, slammed the doors, and started their engines. Chaos ensued. Car after car after car pulled off the line, roaring viciously, lunging forward up the hill toward the curve. The noise was shattering. Smoke and fumes swirled in the air. Another car and another and another. Then four and five and six all together. The crowd broke into a sound like a great-throated animal howling. It thundered behind the more specific cracking of the exhausts.

They pulled away en masse, and, somehow, out of the chaotic scramble of moving machinery, an order evolved, and the growling, jammed-up mass of cars followed the leaders over the hill and vanished.

The smoke hung in the air for a moment, caught the wind, and blew away. The second hand on the big clock jerked, jerked, jerked around its circle. And every pair of

400,000 eyes looked down at the green car, with its white stripes, still motionless and alone at the edge of the track, the starter grinding, grinding, grinding.

Chris felt the sweat break through his pores. His face was extremely hot. He tried to subdue the mounting sense of panic.

The starter ground and ground and grou-ounnnd.

Vali stood in the pits, holding her breath. It seemed that time had stopped. The other cars were gone. There was no time. In her vision was frozen the image of the green car still standing beside the road, while the lingering smoke from the other exhausts drifted across into the stands.

Abruptly, a roaring, cracking, mechanical growl emitted from the little car. Smoke blasted from the multiple exhausts. The crowd boomed and shrieked.

As she watched, it moved, slowly at first, then picked up speed and climbed the hill, growing smaller and smaller. The noise tingled and ripped in her ears, and through it she heard the exhaust bellow of the green brute as it zipped up the hill, banked, and went out of sight.

Then she looked at the trail of bluish smoke it had left hanging in the sunlight.

Change of Plan
a short story by Ken W. Purdy

Put simply, Ken W. Purdy (1913-1972) was the most impor-
tant and influential automotive writer of his time. Gearheads,
not known as the most voracious of readers, read him. People
who didn't give a hoot about cars or motor racing read him.
Purdy's Kings of the Road *(1949) stayed in print a remarkable*
17 years. All But My Life *(1963), written with Stirling Moss, was*
the first motorsports book ever to make the British best-seller list.
Purdy was that rare writer who could switch effortlessly from
straight reporting to fiction, and win awards in both categories.
Perhaps the finest sampling of his art is contained in the anthol-
ogy Ken Purdy's Book of Automobiles *(1972).*

Purdy started out writing for a newspaper at 19, and went
on to become associate editor at Look, *editor-in-chief of* Victory,
Parade, True, *and* Argosy *magazines, before turning freelance*
writer in 1954. His articles and short stories appeared in some
50 magazines, from Atlantic Monthly *to* Vogue. *He contributed*
73 articles and short stories to Playboy *alone.*

Purdy also had the fortune—"misfortune" might be a better
word for it—to work on the Le Mans *screenplay. He was one of*
three writers at Le Mans working overtime to produce a script
that met with Steve McQueen's approval. The other writers were
John Kelly and Harry Kleiner. In the end, Harry Kleiner was
credited as screenwriter.

It would be nice to say that Change of Plan *is one of Purdy's*
unknown writing gems, but that would not be true. First pub-
lished in the Atlantic Monthly, *it has appeared in a dozen an-*
thologies here and abroad, beginning with The Best American
Short Stories of 1953.

The setting is a postwar World War II Grand Prix, probably
1949 or 1950. Veteran Pietro Lonetti (easily mistaken for Mantua's
favorite-son racing driver, Tazio Nuvolari) plans on retiring in a
most unusual way.

Pietro Lonetti sat in his car, a little man, very erect, well back from the wheel. He looked confident and happy, and so he was. In about one hour and a half he intended to kill himself. The decision had calmed him; it had put an end to the torments of the five years that lay leaden behind him; it had restored the lilting serenity, the certainty that all was for the happy, happy best, that he had, as a younger man, worn like a feather in his hair. Pietro Lonetti felt very well indeed.

He looked around. Most of these people were new to him. Lots of them had still been driving sports cars when the war started. He knew Pierre Marten, in the Ferrari, an old competitor. He knew Lyon, of course, with his bull neck and wrestler's arms, and Ignace Manelli. Manelli had one of the new Alfa Romeos. But so many of the others were young and new. The boy next to Lonetti, for instance, in the blue Talbot. Maurice Lascelle, called "Popo." He had been a great hero in the French Resistance. He drove very hard, but with no style. The Englishman, Danton, in an old E.R.A. That pink skin, Lonetti thought, that bland blue eye. A thin old man of about twenty-nine summers. He looks a bit like Dick Seaman, but Seaman is a dozen years dead, burned in a Mercedes-Benz at Spa. Varzi, too, dead in a skid in the rain. Rosemeyer long dead, Christian Kautz dead, Ted Horn dead, Hepburn dead, Lonetti dead ... the dour little man grinned to himself. Not yet, he said, not quite yet. Lonetti will die when he wants to. And not in bed, no matter what the damned doctors say. And after he has won this one. And in no accident.

The sixty-second gun boomed out and one engine fired, coughed, and settled down to an undulating roar as the driver gunned it up and down; another started, then two, three, another, two more, until the hot July air was pulsing with the sound of thirty open exhausts.

Lonetti hunched his shoulders a bit and stared at the fat man who was the starter. The fat man held the bright flag over his head as he counted off the seconds on his stop watch. He will be late, Lonetti thought. He loves himself and what he is doing and he will do it for as long as he can. In thirty years of watching starters, Lonetti had learned to read their little minds, he was sure of that. This one would hold the flag for a bit too long, and before he dropped it, he would lift it a bit, to get a wider, more spectacular swing. Lonetti would go on the lift and make a fifth of a second for himself.

He ran the engine up. The fat starter's shoulders bulged,

the flag imperceptibly lifted and started down. Lonetti let in
the clutch, bore down on the gas, and got away in a rush. He
was a clear half a length ahead of the blue Talbot. It was
enough. He grabbed the Maserati's crooked gearshift; banged
it into second and wound the engine up tight, snatched third
and ran it up to 7000, slid through the first corner with the
ease of a boy pulling a toy around the floor on a string and
settled down into the first straight, three miles long. He stood
on the throttle and locked his knee. There was 175 m.p.h. in
the car under him and Lonetti wanted all of it.

It was a good French road, string-straight and lined with
poplars that had watched two wars. The trees slid past in a
smooth and solid wall and the road rushed hysterically
under the bellowing Maserati like something in a nightmare.
Lonetti knew every pebble in the road. He had carted plenty
of silverware, plenty of francs, away from this circuit before
the war. They had called the race something else, in those
days. Now it was the "Grand Prix Robert Benoist." Benoist,
another hero of the Resistance, like Lascelle. He had driven
in Bugattis before the war. The Germans killed him. Lonetti
remembered him well, a big, pleasant man. He would win
Benoist's race now, and a few of them would mutter about it:
"Why did it have to be Lonetti?" Lonetti shrugged. He would
not be around to hear them. He shot a quick look into the
left-hand mirror. The Talbot was fifty yards behind him, the
Alfa hard on its tail. Lonetti grinned. "Driving Lessons Given
Here," he said to himself. A right-angle turn, one of the nasty
ones, loomed ahead. Lonetti braked at the last possible tenth
of a second, yards past the normal point. The engine
screamed as he kicked it into third. He put the right wheel
six inches from the grass and kept it there, to a hair, as the
car cornered in an insanely fast four-wheel slide. He flicked
it straight and roared at the hill ahead. He had doubled his
lead on Lascelle and he screamed with laughter and pounded
on the side of the car. They'll write about that one all right,
he thought.

". . . at the second corner, Lonetti clearly demonstrated
that his fifty-first winter had taken nothing from his legendary skill. He laid the elderly Maserati into the bend at an
incredible rate of knots, causing grief to the novice Lascelle,
who foolishly imitated him and lost vast yardage in the
subsequent skid. Il Maestro slid the corner in his patented
position and was obviously looking at 8000 r.p.m. as he
urged his ancient mount up the hill, steering with one hand

and beating happily on red tin with the other . . ."

The red car left the ground at the top of the hill and sailed like a bird for fifty feet. It came down square and straight and Lonetti grabbed fourth gear and rocketed away. He felt wild exhilaration and he screamed again.

". . . at the 20th lap, Lonetti had increased his lead to 22 seconds, but the little man was obviously in distress. He was seen to be coughing continuously, and blood began to show on his sleeve as he drew it across his mouth. He held the comparatively slow Maserati in front by dint of black wizardry and a refusal to entertain any regard whatsoever for the welfare of the machinery. Manelli and Lascelle, in faster vehicles, were able to stay in sight and pray earnestly that the Maserati would disintegrate under the punishment ..."

The brass-bright July sun was hot enough, but the shadeless grass beside the road looked cool to Pietro Lonetti, because the car was a moving furnace. There never was a cool one, Lonetti thought, they all roast you to death. Or gas you. The noxious smell of burning gasoline and half-burnt oil was sweet to him; it opened the door of his memory on all the good and happy things that had ever come his way; it meant more than the remembrance of violets in the hair of one's first girl, or the longed-for smoke of boyhood's chimney, or the crystal scent of rain in autumn. The smell was the warp and woof of his life, but the stuff itself was killing him. He coughed, and felt the bleeding, and he leaned out to gulp clean air, but it was no use and he knew it. Still, he had lasted the first hour and he would last the rest of it.

The faster cars had lapped the others now, and there were only signals from the pits to tell position. Lonetti didn't need signals. Until somebody passed him, he was first. He waved as he went by for the thirtieth time, and came up fast on the car ahead. He thought of passing him in the corner, but it was Danton, the Englishman, and Lonetti backed off and let him go through the corner alone. He could take him at will on the long straight, and he would humiliate him there if he could, but he would not take a chance on crowding him in the corner. Lonetti was not notorious for his sportsmanship, and in the old days he would crowd any man in a corner if he felt like it, but he did not feel like it now. They said he hated Englishmen, and so he did, maybe, but he was not going to kill one on the road. He blasted past Danton in the straight, staring at him.

He flew on. He knew he would win. He was happy. He

sat up straight, so proud of what he knew was being said of him that he could almost hear them talking. For twenty years Lonetti had been the standard by which other drivers were judged. There were many serious men who said that he had been born great, that he was the only authentic genius motor-racing had ever produced, that his skill could not be explained in rational terms. Lonetti believed them. He knew that he could tell, for example, exactly how many pounds of a car's total weight rested on any single wheel at any time, cornering or straight, braking or accelerating. He believed that he could drive at 150 miles an hour through a slot an inch wider than the car. He had done it, so he believed it. Other men had to practice in cars, get used to them, feel out their peculiarities. Not Lonetti, Il Maestro. They were all one to him, so long as they had four wheels, something to steer with, and a loud pedal that could be held flat on the floor.

He put it down hard now, to try to pass the two cars looming up ahead. One was Marten, a notorious road hog, the other was old Lyon. They were having a private race for the corner, and when Marten saw Lonetti coming up behind he moved over imperceptibly, blocked him off and let Lyon get around first. The three cars went around nose to tail in a hellish howling racket and slid into the straight like triplets. The others drew away there. Lonetti put the whole weight of his body on the throttle and shook the wheel in rage, but the revolution-counter needle would not go up where he wanted it: past the red danger line. He moved to the right-hand side of the road. The pits were only a couple of miles ahead.

He stopped the car where they waited for him and old Giorgio threw up the bonnet, the question in his eyes. "Plug," Lonetti croaked.

Giorgio savagely swiveled out the plugs. Nobody could do it faster, but he couldn't do it in twenty seconds, and Lascelle and Manelli roared past him. They were out of sight when the bonnet banged down and he was pushed off.

Lonetti had never been beloved by other drivers; he gave them good cause now to hate him. He drove as if he were alone on the road. He passed them in bunches as they braked for the corners, slamming through them flat out to stand viciously on the brake for a second and then drift through the corner in his own weird slide. He went into every corner with the nose of the car pointed dead wrong for the entrance but right for the exit, stealing yards and seconds from the lesser men who had to do it by the book.

He went into one corner behind Marten, caught him in it and slid around him, staring arrogantly out at the six inches that lay between the two cars and instant death. He was coughing constantly now; the blood ran unheeded down his chin and he grinned wickedly at Marten as he left him. He had terrified the man, he knew it, and he ran away from him roaring with mirth and pounding the side of his car like a maniac blacksmith. Manelli he passed at pits, his Alfette blowing out a fog of blue smoke, and he could see the Talbot ahead. He had two laps in which to take it, and as he passed the stands he pointed ferociously ahead, his big white teeth stripped. Let no one miss this, he thought. We will see how much resistance is in this hero, he thought. We will separate the men from the boys here. We will motor a little bit now.

Lascelle saw him coming and he tried everything he knew. On the straights he took every ounce of power the car had, and held his own, but it was either slow up for the corners or crash, and the insane Italian behind him crept closer with every bend in the road. Lascelle wanted to win. It was the first big race in which he had had any luck; it would make his reputation. Too, he had served under Robert Benoist, and the very idea of an Italian taking the cup away made him want to kill again. But every time he looked into the mirror Lonetti was a little closer to doing it.

At the beginning of the last lap, on the long straight in front of the stands, it finally happened. Foot by foot, the red Maserati pulled up beside him. Lonetti held the red car dead alongside, and when Lascelle looked over the little man grinned wolfishly at him. There was blood all over his shirt. As they went by the stands, locked together, Lonetti bowed graciously to the people, and suddenly then, in horror, Lascelle knew why he had not pulled on past: he intended to amuse them with the spectacle of two cars running suicidally together into a corner that was, at that speed, but one car wide. He was going to make the kid quit, brake, and pull over. Lascelle knew, and everyone knew, that Lonetti had done this a hundred times in the past, and that in the end, and always, it had been the other man who had felt terror slam his foot down on the brake. Lascelle decided, suddenly, that he would be the one who did not quit. Live mouse, dead lion, he thought. He kept his foot down. After all, he just might live through it.

Pietro Lonetti was surprised, fifty yards from the corner, to find the Frenchman still with him, but he drove the bend the way he had intended to, coming out of it slightly faster to clear the road, since he knew that otherwise nothing in the world could keep Lascelle from sliding into him. As it was, he felt the cars tick, nose to tail, when the blue Talbot moved behind him. It seemed to him that he heard the scream of the rubber, in two great howls, as the Talbot spun; and when he topped the hill he heard the crash and saw in his mirror the first orange burst of flame as the car exploded against the great trees beside the road.

He had it won, now. It was all over, they would give him the flag as he swept past, the crowds would scream his name, the journalists would pound their typewriters, he would take his victor's lap and at the end of it, as he had so long planned, he would fold his arms, proudly lift his head, and smash himself to death against the wall in the exit road, where everyone could see that it was no accident, and no one could come to harm by it. That had been his plan. That was why he was in the race. But suddenly now it didn't seem so much of a plan. It was empty. It was nothing.

Pietro Lonetti lifted his foot and let the red Maserati run along the side of the road at a bare 50 miles an hour. He felt as if he could get out and walk. He could see the separate blades of grass, each petal of the flowers along the ditch. He coughed and was surprised to taste the blood. His arms trembled and for the first time he felt the blisters on his palms. Everyone went past him. They roared by like a long freight train. He coasted into the pits. None of the din was for him. The photographers were elsewhere.

"Jesus and Mary!" Giorgio screamed at him. "What happened? What broke? What let go?"

"Nothing let go," Lonetti said. "The car is fine. This is good iron. I took my foot off, that's all."

"Man, man, you threw it all away!" Giorgio said. "For what? For that kid, that dumb Frog? For what, for Christ's sake!"

Lonetti looked up at him. "Take off the steering wheel, Giorgio," he said. "Take it off, and lift me out of here. I want to go home."

The Racer
a novel by Hans Ruesch

Hans Ruesch wants to set the record straight. It was he who set fastest lap that half-drizzly afternoon at Donington Park in 1936 and not Richard Seaman, as some reported. "I had a two-minute advantage when I turned over the car to him," says Ruesch. "Seaman needed to win the race in order to win the British championship. The track was very slippery by then, very dangerous to drive, so there was absolutely no reason to force it."

Ruesch has had an amazing life. At age 23, he won the Donington Grand Prix (with Richard Seaman as co-driver). By age 40, two of his novels had been made into motion pictures. By age 70, when most men are retired, he was the world's leading spokesman against vivisection. Today, he is most proud of being among the 90 thinkers and writers whose works are published in Past to Present: Ideas That Have Changed Our World *(2002).*

Ruesch competed in over 100 races between 1932 and 1937, winning 26, including three Grand Prix. Like Seaman and ex-patriot American Whitney Straight, he had the means and the talent to compete and win as an independent, and likely would have been called up by Mercedes Benz or Auto Union had an accident not interrupted his racing career.

The Racer *was first published in Switzerland, in 1937. Having recovered from his accident, Ruesch moved to the United States in 1938 where he free-lanced for several magazines and wrote a second novel. Before returning to Europe in 1946, he met publisher Eric Ballantine, who purchased the rights to* The Racer. *The two became lifelong friends, sharing a love of motor racing and united by their efforts to stop vivisection.*

The Racer's *main character, Erich Lester, is based loosely on three-time European champion Rudolf Caracciola. The novel opens with Lester competing in the Mille Miglia, which is excerpted here. Ruesch finished fourth in the 1935 Mille Miglia despite being delayed by electrical problems.*

Mille Miglia, Italy's thousand-mile road race, in the early Thirties.

A lean, long-nosed two-seater was streaking southward along the Via Emilia in the first light of day, scattering the patches of low-hanging mist like tatters of a veil. The tires hissed angrily on the wet asphalt which mirrored the slender trees along the road, and the bright song of the high-revving engine pierced the morning stillness like a stone dropping into a pond.

Erich Lester's face showed no tension whatever. He sat almost motionless at the wheel, chin on chest as if he were weary. Only his gray eyes, protected by giant goggles which lent him an owl-like appearance, were constantly on the move. They swept from the rev counter to the road and from the road to the telegraph poles, railings, milestones, trees, or any landmark ahead which might help him anticipate the course unraveling before him; for slippery turns, holes and bumps, gravel patches, narrow bridges, and stretches of fog kept alternating with each other, demanding constant attention.

And Lester felt none too comfortable as yet, driving all out in a car with which he was not entirely familiar. He was accustomed to racers, stripped to essentials: chassis, motor, wheels, a scant body, and that was all. This car instead, in order to qualify as a sports car and be permitted to compete in this event, had to carry a spare, a self-starter, a horn, lights, fenders, battery, a second seat of prescribed width, and—ultimate folly—a passenger.

Lester had taken along his Italian mechanic, Piero, who was seated at his left, a little sideways, to allow him more elbow room. From time to time Piero took his hand from one of the grips to which he was holding fast and pointed out some danger, to be sure it would not be overlooked: a railway barrier that was just being lowered, an oxcart crossing the road, some competitor ahead who was beginning to swerve and skid, or the needle on the rev counter passing the safety limit.

The air was still cool and Lester could go full throttle along the straights, regardless of the length of the course. The tops of the telegraph poles enabled him to keep speed up even where the pavement was blotted out by the mist. One by one he was overtaking the long line of cars that had started before him. They were either smaller jobs or otherwise negligible as competitors, but nevertheless they represented a constant hazard: they might crash just in front of him, or suddenly change lane, or purposely hinder his passing. Although in populated areas the crowds were fenced off or kept back by police and efforts were made to reduce highway traffic as much as possible, this was still an open-road race, not a closed-circuit event; yet the competitors ignored the traffic rules, passing one another on the right or left and on the turns—wherever it might save them a second or two.

Lester was hurrying hard. He was racing to win. He and his car were well prepared. He knew almost the entire course by heart—how wide the shoulders, how sharp the bends, where the loose patches lay and which pavements were more slippery than others when it rained. He felt fit and was spoiling for mileage. And there wasn't a bolt, a screw, a gasket, a line or cable that he and Piero hadn't checked, installed, tightened, and secured with their own hands.

The race had started in Brescia, at the foot, of the Bergamasker Alps, when long before daybreak the smallest car among the 185 entries had taken off, the others following in one-minute intervals according to engine displacement. The starting order of the same type machines was decided by lot, and it was Lester's bad luck that he had started one minute ahead of Santamaria, the star of the official Milano team: if the Italian overtook him, Lester had as good as lost the race, for Santamaria would never allow him to pass. So there was only one course open for Lester if he was to win: to outdistance Santamaria with everything he had, racing for his life from the first minute to the last.

The route led across the plain of the Po down to Bologna, Florence, Rome; from there back north over a different course to Ancona, along the Adriatic Sea up to Venice, and over the foothills of the Dolomites back to the point of departure, covering more than half the length of the Italian boot and crossing the Apennine range three times.

The field included almost forty Milanos like Lester's. The Mille Miglia seemed made to order for these sturdy, lively, quick-handling sports cars, and they in turn were made for it: all alike down to their color, like a big family of brothers, all fighting one another. Lester, however, was concerned only about Santamaria, who was one of Italy's ablest drivers and whose factory car was bound to have a more powerful motor—though how much faster it was Lester had no way of knowing as yet. For this was a race against the clock, control points were hours apart from one another, and no one could know his immediate standing in the contest.

The 150 miles to Bologna over which Lester was now rushing were one of the fastest stretches of the race, thus offering Santamaria a good chance to catch up with him, and half an hour after the start Piero began glancing over his shoulder; but the only cars he saw were those they had just overtaken. The wily Santamaria was obviously husbanding his strength and sparing his engine; for this grueling race, riddled with road and mechanical hazards, could not be treated like a three-minute hill-climb to be won by a split second—as Lester was doing.

He was taking all the chances that Santamaria avoided. He didn't lift his foot from the throttle even when, hood to hood with a twin Milano he was trying to pass on the straight, he neared at full speed one of those tightly packed villages of northern Italy that the highways slice in half. The passageway was narrow, for the sidewalks were brimming with crowds of onlookers held back precariously by a few carabinieri who showed more interest in the race than in their assignment

The two cars tunneled into this corridor with no more than a couple of inches between them. As the angry snarl of the two motors, reverberating from the first house-walls, shook the air, Lester saw that he was uncomfortably close to the throng, and the path was narrowing. His whole body tingled in anticipation of disaster; but his foot remained on the throttle. Then the other driver lifted his, and the rival hood dropped out of Lester's field of vision.

Lucky he's more reasonable than I am, he thought, smiling to himself, and a second later had forgotten the incident. He lacked the time and desire to be reasonable. He had been reasonable too long. Now, in a few unreasonable hours, he might change the course of his entire life.

At Bologna was the first control post, marked by high banners spanning the road. Grandstands had been erected. All around, roped off and kept in check by *carabinieri*, stood screaming throngs of *tifosi*—Italy's race fans, raging with the typhus-like fever of sporting enthusiasm. Officials with arm bands waved at the car. Piero had the control book attached to a string around his neck. He held it out open, and an official, trotting beside the coasting car, stamped it.

The fast, level stretch had come to an end, and the road

began to wind in gentle bends into the uplands. By now the
sun was out and the southern spring heat made itself felt,
even in the open, speeding car. Though Lester wore nothing
but his white overalls and a light cotton cap, sweat poured
down his face and along his thighs and legs. He felt the oven-
hot draft coming from the engine and the heat of the ten-
gallon oil tank which lay under the seats was rapidly working
up to its normal operating temperature of 180° Fahrenheit.

When the car snarled into the climbing twists and turns
of the Apennines and Piero tapped on the gauge to show that
the water temperature was nearing the boiling point, Lester
began sparing his engine a little, but tried to make up for it
on the corners. Then the entire weight of the car pulled on
the steering wheel, his arms shook, and the tires screeched
loudly, leaving black marks on the hot asphalt which
gleamed in the sun.

All along the thousand-mile course, uncounted millions
of spectators were watching the event; the rest of Italy
followed it on the radio. Even the sparsely populated mountain passes had groups of peasants on the vantage points. At
every checkpoint and refueling post, some excited *tifosi* broke
through the police cordons in order to toss soda and beer
bottles, fruit and cheese, sandwiches and chicken legs into
the cars. Lester ate nothing but a couple of oranges that
Piero fed him, and sucked sugared milk through a pipeline
leading to a Thermos under his seat. To keep up their
strength, some drivers swore by milk and some by coffee,
some by sugar and some by kola, some by Ovaltine or by
maltose or dextrose. Lester didn't care what he took as long
as he didn't take much of it.

In less than six hours he had reached Rome, the south-
ernmost control point, and started on his northbound trip.
By then he had his car well in hand. Those few hours of
racing had done what weeks of practice had failed to do:
welded car and driver into a single body, with one single
brain and will.

On the rugged mountains after Terni the weather broke,
and for three hours the drivers were drenched in heavy
squalls which turned the winding stretches of loose surface
into mud and rock tracks. There they saw two competitors
smashed against the concrete retaining wall. Lester hoped
the rain would keep up, helping him to offset the advantage
of Santamaria's faster car on the speedy Adriatic highways
ahead. But when they came in sight of the sea, and the

fastest stretch of the race began, the sun was out again, drying the last dampness from the ground.

It was night when they reached Venice. They had been under way over twelve hours. All day Lester had perspired, even in the rain, more than Piero who had only the heat of the motor and not the exertion to cope with; now cold air blew through the overalls which the sweat had molded to their bodies. Piero unbuttoned Lester and, taking care not to interfere with his movements, slipped over his chest a folded newspaper that he had kept under the seat—the most effective protection against the wind of the ride, and easy to put on. But under the Dolomites, deep in the night, the riders' hands and faces became numb with frost.

Lester's back hurt from prolonged sitting in a car that was built for stability at the cost of comfort and in which every stone and ripple and seam of the road was transmitted to the driver's seat; and the pain grew steadily. At every refueling point, a crew of mechanics took over the car for a minute or two, changing wheels and filling it up with oil and gas and water. These were the only occasions for Lester to unlimber a little. But at the last stop he had found it impossible to leave his seat: the stiffness in his back riveted him fast. Now he drove bent forward over the wheel, his fingers numb with cold and fatigue, kept awake mainly by the pain in his back and a splitting headache from eyestrain and the glare of the sun.

But the knowledge that success might be within reach renewed his strength. He cut the corners sharply and drove hard along the houses in the towns and villages and lost no time in overtaking other cars. At the last fuel stop, before Venice, he had learned that in Rome he had been in the lead—with four minutes' advantage on Santamaria and a good half hour on the rest of the field. But Rome was a long way back, and he could not afford to ease off for a single minute, for Santamaria must have taken up the chase.

Meanwhile they were passing more and more of the smaller cars that had started several hours ahead of them, and Lester doubled his efforts to keep up his speed without endangering his ride. He was taut and alert, striving not only to avoid mistakes but also to be on his guard against someone else's mistakes. But no one could guard against everything.

They had passed Verona, the last control point. Then, on the flat, gently winding stretch that made up the final portion of the course, less than an hour before the finish, it happened: Lester's headlights went out. All at once. As if someone had thrown a switch. One moment he was rushing into the silvery cone of his lights, and the next he was plunged in total darkness, with his car still speeding. It was all he could do to bring it to a stop unharmed, Piero vaulted out, flash in hand, lifted his seat, and a few seconds later announced: "The battery plates are busted."

"Always the damned electricity!" Lester cried, dismayed. "And a brand-new battery, too!"

He never trusted the electrical system. Something was always going wrong with it. That was why this year the more experienced Italian stables had appeared at the start equipped with a third powerful headlight fed directly by a generator, thus ruling out the hazard of battery failure.

In a contest where for long hours cars fully equipped to pass regular inspection rush at full tilt over long straights or up and down mountain roads, heedless of bumps and holes, and rough stretches, even the best-prepared may break down. With constant battering the strongest exhaust pipe may crack, the spare wheel may drop off with part of the aluminum body, the seats may break loose, the battery go dead, the radiator or tank burst, the ignition go on strike, the oil line break, or the fuel line clog. The most careful preparation is to no avail if one forgets to pack a dose of luck.

Lester was almost breathless with helpless rage. His eyes had grown adjusted to the dark, but moon and stars lit the road so dimly that he could see the reflection of his red-hot exhaust on the dark pavement while he cruised, waiting for one of the small cars he had just overtaken. When it came he let it go by and tailed it closely, driving in its light.

He drove thus for several frustrating miles. Then he felt Piero tapping his arm and, turning around, he noticed three powerful headlights emerging furiously from the dark: Santamaria. The Italian also recognized Lester's car as he overtook it, and immediately eased off. He had won the game. As long as he was ahead of Lester, nothing could rob him of victory; he could even let Lester pass, and if he came in only 59 seconds after him, he would still win the race. The decisive factor was a competitor's time— not who crossed the line first.

As soon as he was overtaken, Lester swerved away from the slower pacemaker and went after Santamaria's lights. But Santamaria was no longer in a hurry. What pleasure he must be getting from playing cat-and-mouse with his rival who had remained so long out of reach! When he accelerated, Lester also had to accelerate; when he slowed down, Lester also had to slow down. Sometimes Santamaria amused himself by driving into the shoulder of the road, then gunning his engine and blinding Lester with dust and rocks which drummed against his windshield and goggles, making it difficult for him to stick to his leader close enough to profit by his lights. But if Lester lost him now, all was lost—though he didn't know what good could come from this pursuit; and he dogged him recklessly through the dust screen, feeling like a wild animal struggling in a trap.

All at once, Lester's eyes lit up: unexpectedly, incredibly, an opening was presenting itself. He had no precise idea of how far the finish was—maybe five minutes, maybe half an hour—when he spotted the electric lights over the trolley tracks that started somewhere on the road from Verona and ran all the way to Brescia. The lights were tired and yellow, insufficient to illuminate the whole width of the pavement, but at least they allowed him to drive on his own.

This had not yet occurred to Santamaria, who was lolling along at not more than a hundred miles an hour over the softly curving highway, feeling safe. And already Lester had whizzed past him: He covered the last hundred yards in the dark, aiming at the street lights ahead, then leaned over to the left of the road, skimming the bed of the trolley tracks to raise a hail of stones with which to repay Santamaria's courtesies.

Now he forced his engine beyond the safe rev limit, preferring to drop out of the race rather than come in second. Fatigue was gone as if by magic as his whole body and mind cried out for more and more miles on which to whittle down Santamaria's one-minute lead. Much as he had yearned for the lighted archway that would mark the end of the ordeal, he now wished it far off. For there was no doubt that Santamaria would take fewer chances, had to take fewer, with victory practically in his pocket.

And all the Italian's skill and experience could be no match for the desperation of a young hopeful who had too long gone unfulfilled and who saw at last within his grasp the big chance that might never return. For Santamaria it meant merely one victory more or less on his crowded record; for Lester it could mean the entrance to the golden gate he had already been seeking for too long.

He drove like a man possessed. His car lay mostly sideways, broadsliding in the fast, sweeping bends, but never snapping into time-losing counterslides. He perceived the sudden tenseness of Piero who pushed his head back and stiffened his legs when they neared a turn. He couldn't talk to him, for the roar of the engine drowned what voice the rushing wind didn't carry away; otherwise he would have told him to relax, that he had nothing to fear, for in spite of the gloom Lester had never felt more the master of the road nor safer at the wheel. Everything was there: the rhythm of the ride, the feel of the four wheels in the seat of his pants, the deadly coldness in the brain besides the burn of anger in the chest.

He had no idea how many miles he had been driving in the lights of the trolley tracks when he saw, blazing in the distance, the lighted arch that stood across the finish line, at the end of the last straight. Several banners over the road spelled out: SLOW DOWN—FINISH AHEAD. Lester elbowed Piero in warning. Let others coast into the crowded finishing area; he was not going to ease his foot on the throttle—no matter what happened.

Beyond the naming arch, he could see the dark outlines of curious heads stretching from the mass of *tifosi* at the risk of their necks. He felt briefly the heat of the light bulbs on his face as his car rocketed through the narrow archway; then it screeched with locked wheels across a brightly lit expanse, paved with racing placards that were ripped by tire marks and soaked with oil.

The wings of onlookers on either side, seeing the car burst in at much higher speed than its predecessors, opened up. The Milano covered another two hundred yards before it reached the rapidly parting throng, and Lester had to bank it into a skid, bringing it to a stop with its side against the stockade of the paddock.

Piero jumped out at once, but Lester remained doubled up, his forehead against the wheel. Grabbing his arms and shoulders and almost tearing him limb from limb, eager *tifosi* lifted him out of his cockpit. He thought his back would crack as he straightened up. Then he pulled his goggles down on his chest, swept the cap from his head, took the control book from Piero, and tramped towards the judges, hunched forward, while the loudspeakers announced his time. Dell'Oro's old record was smashed.

But already the high song of a powerful engine was

rapidly filling the air, the silver beam of three strong head-lights came dancing out of the gloom, and Santamaria flashed through the archway, stopping some hundred yards beyond. It seemed to Lester that his rival had come in just behind him. He wondered how long he had been walking back towards the judges. It seemed a very short time—certainly less than a minute. If so, the race was lost

Weary reporters with note pads and excited *tifosi* with coffee cups crowded around him. Somebody said:

"In Venice you led Santamaria by five minutes. Did anything happen to you after that?"

"The damned electricity," Lester said, turning his back on him.

He was furious. He didn't want to talk or listen. He dropped his control book on the judges' bench, which was set up alongside the arch, and shuffled to the nearby timing stand, while a great sickness rose in his body. These were the last, bitterest dregs.

"I clocked you!" cried one of the *tifosi* who had followed him, waving his wrist-chronometer. "Santamaria got in one minute and thirteen seconds after you. So you won!"

"No!" shouted another. "He came in only fifty seconds later! You lost!"

"One minute and one second!" screeched another, waving his timepiece.

"Both same time," cried a few others. "Let's call it a draw."

Santamaria came up with his book, surrounded by a circle of fans who stretched to touch his mud-spattered overalls. His face was encrusted with dusty mud except for the goggle area, which was white. One of his goggle panes was cracked, and Lester hoped it was from one of the stones his tires had kicked up.

The three official timekeepers raised their heads from their score cards, compared notes and chronometers, ex-changed a few words. Silence fell on the crowd. Lester had to lean against the stand, feeling faint. Then the center man took up the mike and the loudspeaker crackled:

"Lester leads by four seconds."

Wordlessly Santamaria pressed Lester's hand, then walked off.

"It's your race, Lester," one of the sports writers said. "You can go home now: you two had the rest of the field outdistanced by almost an hour."

Lester refused to believe it until he had made sure. He remained propped up against the stand, waiting for the other cars to come in. The babbling bystanders looked like red devils jumping up and down in the hazy glare which hurt his eyes after the gloominess of the road. He was almost deaf from the incessant roar of the engine and didn't understand a word that was being said.

Meanwhile the other cars were arriving in quick succession—all mud-spattered and rock-battered—and lined up inside the stockade for future inspection. Though they appeared to him in a dreamlike haze, Lester noticed every detail about them. One had lost both front fenders. Another had smashed its side. Another's headlight was hanging loose on its wire. One had broken the support of the spare, and the co-driver was showing his bleeding hands with which he had held it up, for a car without a spare would be disqualified; the same went for the mufflers which some cars were dragging, after their occupants had fastened them with wire, burning their hands on the glowing metal. Everyone's eyes were glassy and all the faces wore the same mask of mud and dirt. Several competitors, hurt by stones, bled from cuts, and many had smashed goggles and windshields.

A repeated tapping on his shoulder finally awakened Lester to reality. Vaguely he saw Piero's face, felt Piero grab his arm and heard him shout into his ear:

"It's all over! We've been waiting fifteen minutes. This time you've won!"

Challenge the Wind
a novel by John Tomerlin

It's a wonder John Tomerlin ever found time to become a writer, considering his varied interests and many talents. He started out in radio, running a disc-jockey show, including writing copy, handling newscasts, and doing play-by-play sportscasting. While trying to succeed as a writer, he was media director of a Los Angeles advertising agency.

His first novel, Run From the Hunter (1957), was written in collaboration with Charles Beaumont under the pen name of "Keith Grantland." He went on to write nine more novels, some three-dozen teleplays, and countless short stories and articles for several publications, including Road & Track, where he served as technical editor for 15 years. He also played bridge, golf, tennis and learned to fly. And got Charles Beaumont and William F. Nolan interested in motor racing.

"I think I had something to do with it," says Tomerlin, "but it was Chuck who volunteered his 1954 Volkswagen for our first race, at Torrey Pines. We drove it again at Santa Barbara, and after that Bill and Chuck pitted for me for a year or so while I campaigned a 1955 Porsche Speedster at several tracks around Southern California."

About writing Challenge the Wind, Tomerlin says: "It was kind of a breakout thing. I'd been sort of trapped in television up to that time (1964). I was very, very sick of writing for television, and looking for something else to do. I paid my way to Europe. I received an advance from Dutton (the publisher) and spent it all and more in the first few months I was there. I established a base in the south of France, in Nice, actually. From there I travelled to the Nurburgring, for that race, and to Monza, and also to Monaco. The experience was worth every penny."

The excerpt (chapter 7) finds California club racer turned-F1 pilot Pete Langely at Monza, driving for Volanti, France's answer to Ferrari.

Milan. Milano. He'd always heard it called Milan, but the maps added the extra "o," and the maps were right: That final syllable, its softness, the hint it contained of music and grace, these were right for the place.

He'd felt the change the moment he crossed the border from France, a lightening and lifting of his spirits, a reaching out from himself toward the luminous, blue-white bubble of sky, the gentle, powdery Italian landscape. For him, France had been too definite a place; not all its admitted charm and beauty could quite remove it from this category: a terminal point for the business on which he'd come, one end of the link that yet tied him to his past. Italy, then, was a breaking of the link, an escape.

The drive from Monteville, begun on Saturday, had taken him down through the mountains and valleys of the southeast, skirting west of the Alps as far as Lyon, from Lyon east to the border. After a late start, taking his time, he'd stopped for the night in the village of Modane, at a tiny auberge, then driven across to Turino in the morning. Along the way, the scenery had undergone a gradual change, less an actual transformation than a slow process of miniaturization: Mile by mile the trees became smaller, more scattered, dwindling down from the larger, darker pines of the north to dwarf cypresses and low ledges of a paler, sparer verdure. The vineyards that, along the Rhine and the Moselle, had been planted in beds of coarse gray gravel — steeply ter-raced, like giant stepping-stones up the ragged hillsides — here spread across undulant fields of iron-red, sun-kilned sand. The air itself, charged with late August heat, became softer, more embracing, less a pressure than a presence.

It was noon when he arrived in the city, a place of broad black streets and wide white sidewalks, arches and monuments and statuary. Of main routes, lined by trees or divided by little parks, converging like the spokes of a wheel toward the civic center. Of smaller routes, spreading in concentric circles toward the rim of what once had been battlements; walls that had seen the Lombards, the Prussians, Napoleon himself. It was an industrial city now, and parts of it, farther in, were less pleasant to see: the over-crowded sections of black-stone tenements and close-packed little shops with their faded awnings, soot-obscured windows. Even here there was a sense of space, though; a contact with the sky above, established by a quality of light.

He drove slowly, held by the magic of Milano's ancient

newness, went along the Corso Sempione and around the edge of the great park where stood the Palazzo dell' Arte, continued through the jackstraw maze of streets beyond until he found Piazza Duomo. It was Sunday and traffic wasn't heavy, but what there was of it — tiny Fiats and Lambrettas, an occasional larger car, countless three-wheelers and motorbikes — coursed past him on every side, swerving and lunging in a desperate and rather comic haste. The high, narrow trolleys trundled obliviously down the wrong side of streets that had once been "left-handed." Spice to the game.

He found Corso Vittorio Emannuele and the address of the hotel that Gehrmann had given him before his departure. He parked Kettering's car and got his luggage out and carried it inside.

He went to bed at the end of that first day in Italy with a sensation not unlike that of having fallen in love.

He began work the day after his arrival in Italy. He drove from Milano, north to the suburb of Monza, eight miles in a little over ten minutes. Another ten and he'd located the entrance to the park and grounds surrounding the Monza Autodrome. It was laid out like a huge country estate, with picnic areas and playgrounds, and, at the heart of it all, the great black-roofed grandstands. At one end of the buildings was a road leading to a tunnel that passed under the start-finish straightaway and came out in the garage area of the infield. Chain-link gates stood open to the front straight, and since there was no one about, he drove through and set out to have a look at the course. After having gone only a short distance he could see the truth of all he'd heard and read about the need, here, for power and good brakes.

As he came onto the back straight, he had an urge to let out a little and see what Kettering's car would do. He was up to an indicated 120, and still had some revs left, when he began to run out of room and decided to back off. He turned into the giant banking at the south end and flew around it high on the wall, the little English compact skittering like a rollerskate on bricks, then coasted back toward the pits grinning to himself and wondering if he could have Gordon order him one like it. As he came into the pit area, he saw two uniformed men on motorcycles waiting in the center of the track.

Both of the cyclists had their engines running, ready to give chase if necessary. As Peter slowed to a stop, one pulled his machine in front of the car. The other approached on foot, a hand poised threateningly near his hip. Peter thought: Swell, I'm under arrest.

He was in fact.

The hope that either man might speak English was wasted; he was given to understand that he should get out of the car—and, no, leave the keys in it. He was marched back past the administration buildings toward where an olive-painted patrol car waited; was about to begin a trip that could lead only one place, when it suddenly occurred to him to try a phrase in French:

"*Je suis un conducteur de course,*" he said. "*Pour l'equipe Volanti.*" He had to repeat himself a couple of times before the officer in charge would accept that anyone with such an accent could be taken seriously.

"*Vos papiers, m'sieur,*" the man said at last, suspiciously. Considerable conversation accompanied the examination of his passport, driver's license, and other I.D., all of it in Italian so that he could gather only that the majority opinion favored jailing him first, and checking his story later. At last, one of the men went over to the administration building—and reappeared a few minutes later beside a tall, cadaverous man in a business suit. Peter felt a ray of hope.

"Mr. Langley?" the man inquired.

"Yes, that's right. . . . I'm with the Volanti team."

"I know. Mr. Langley, one applies for the special-practice pass before entering the course. It is fortunate for you I hadn't left for lunch when this happened, or there's a very good chance you would have missed the race."

The whole statement seemed so incredible to him that he could not even get angry. At the same time, he could see that the pompous little ass was quite serious. "I'm sorry, I didn't know it was against regulations."

"It was your business to know, Mr. Langley. However—" He turned and said something to the officers. One of them returned the keys to Peter's car, reluctantly. "You can go now. Please obtain your pass from the Auto Club in Milano before doing any more practicing."

Peter walked back to his car, and returned to town.

If nothing else, the experience provided him with an anecdote for dinner that night. Darrol had phoned to say he was in town, and they'd agreed to eat together, along with Mike Callenbera of the British Vanguard team.

They sat over plates of fruit and cheeses, and the

glasses of coffee-colored dessert wine their waiter brought them. Callenbera said, "That was a nice job you did at the Ring, Peter."

"Thanks, but it was a fluke. Carlotti had it."

"Oh, well, don't shed any tears for Ferrari. They'll have things their own way this week."

"I'm not so sure. I think Gordon could win."

"Not likely. Oh, he could, of course; Gordon can always win because he's that good . . . but Ferrari and Maserati are up on power, and that's what it takes here. They always are, of course—it's why Monza's the kind of ruddy track it is, and why the Italians usually win on it."

Darrol said:' "It's a national disaster when they don't. But you'll see for yourself, Pete; everybody goes nuts when anything painted red shows up."

Callenbera said, "What have they got you in, Peter—not the guinea pig?"

"Yeah, looks like it."

The Englishman shook his head, looking even sadder than was normal for him. "It's damn funny, you know, this business. You'd think when a new boy came along and showed promise they'd start him on something nice and tame, give him a chance to get the hang. Instead, he ends up with some ruddy beast no one else wants. When I think of the goats I drew when I was coming up ... it was frightful! Man's not only got to be good, he's got to be lucky to get through the first year or two."

Darrol said, "Let's not build up his hopes too much."

The sarcasm was lost on Callenbera. "I don't know, though, Peter, seems to me you've got some sort of chance—which is more than the rest of us have. I mean, supposing your new car picks this Sunday to sort itself out and go? Who knows? I assume you've had a try in it."

"Not much of one," he said, not wishing to discuss any of its problems with another competitor. "It's got good power."

"Well, there, you see? You've got to rate yourself a chance."

He laughed and said, "I'll be satisfied just to finish, and not get in anyone's way too much."

"Well, yes, there's always that," Callenbera sighed. "And Monza's a ruddy awful place to find out something's going to break. . . . Ruddy awful," he repeated glumly.

On Tuesday, having picked up credentials at the Auto Club, he and Darrol drove out to the track. Peter was beginning to appreciate his friend's ability to describe a course, to pick out the subtleties in it and communicate, not a mere technical description, but a sense of the difficulties posed. Darrol would point toward a section of pavement and say, "You can just jitterbug on through here, and it don't mean a thing, 'cause the asphalt up ahead smooths right out again." Or: "Got to watch that little seam over there; if you go in shallow, it's like trying to get a drunk up the front steps." And, put this way, there was a feeling of what would be required that could not have been expressed with all the talk in the world about "spring rates," or "rear-axle tracking."

From the beginning it was clear that the problem at Monza, though different from the one at Nurburg, was as worrisome in its own way. Where the German course had seemed a nightmare amplification of the California tracks he'd driven, Monza bore no resemblance to them whatsoever. He'd heard it was a fast race, but only now did he begin to achieve an emotional understanding of what that meant: Three hours at speeds generally higher than any he'd ever driven, interspersed with violent braking at the end of the chutes. He told Darrol:

"This place reminds me of Indianapolis, with wiggles in it."

"Boy, you aren't telling me anything!" Darrol looked thoughtful. "But if you got to drive there—or here for that matter—thing to do is go along the way you think's right for you, and never mind anybody else. Just no future in pushing at a place like this."

In a way, it sounded like more of Darrol's defeatism; in another, he wasn't so sure. For his first Formula I performance, in a relatively undeveloped car, on this kind of a track—it might be pretty good advice.

By Wednesday, most of the teams had come in, and this was excuse enough for the first party, a grand, if rather mixed affair, thrown by Senor Louis Valenzuela at his estate on the outskirts of Milano. (This was, in fact, the headquarters of the Spaniard's racing organization, and the grounds included the facilities where the cars were maintained.) The attire of the guests ranged from formal gowns and dress suits down to the working garb of some who'd been at the track all day and hadn't had time to change. This marked no distinction in rank, but all the same Peter thought it odd to see Valenzuela, in ruffled shirt and black cutaway, standing in conversation with Max Catalon—in overalls.

Peter had been able to return to his hotel and put on a suit and tie before driving back with Gordon and Lepic, both of whom were staying at the same hotel as he. Since arriving, he'd been introduced to a number of the guests—other drivers and members of the Milano Auto Club, and some of Valenzuela's staff. Few spoke English, and after a while he'd settled on a stool near one end of the bar where he could sip sherry, and watch. He felt rather comfortably isolated—by language and by the fact few people recognized him—at leisure to observe, to see here and there a figure of importance: one or two of the owners of famed racing marques, their team managers, and some of the leading drivers. He saw Rossi of Ferrari, now ahead for the World Championship (after Kettering's "DNF" at Nurburg); Aguirre, the Mexican, who drove for Maserati; Corbin and Turtle and Ford-Ogden, all with E.M.I., the English racing syndicate. And in one corner of the terrace he saw Darrol Anderson, talking energetically to a young woman in red chiffon; leaning intently toward her, his face alight with pleasure, his eyes riveted to her rather amazing décolletage, Darrol was "havin' a lot of fun."

Delmondo and his wife had arrived, and Harry McBride, escorting his young daughter, Gillian—a not-unattractive girl Peter had met that afternoon, at the track. He thought he might go over and talk to them. Suddenly he caught sight of a new group coming in; saw Marcienne, a figure in silver and white, stunning as always, and turned in her direction. He was stopped, however, by a British journalist, and by the time he was able to disengage himself Marcienne had taken a place at a table with Gordon, Telford-Grey, Celeste, and two or three others he didn't know. They seemed to be having a heated conversation about something, and he hesitated, uncertain whether he should break in on them or not. The matter was decided when Gordon glanced up, saw him, and waved.

"Peter, have you got a minute?"

He crossed to the table. Gordon made an encompassing gesture and said, "You all know Peter Langley," cutting through any need for formal introductions, in spite of the fact that it wasn't true. "Peter's from the States; he's got a different point of view on things like this. I'd like his opinion."

There was a vacant chair next to Marcienne, and he took it. He hadn't seen her since the morning of his race, and as he sat down she smiled at him and said, "You see? I was right. . . . About Nurburg."

"Yes. Thanks."

Gordon said, "All right, now, ask Peter—and no coaching, any one."

One of the women at the table—thirtyish, blonde, and quite handsome, English by her accent—who was sitting on the same side as he leaned forward to see him. "Yes, Mr. Langley, tell us what you think: are there sexual overtones to racing? Yes or no."

Everyone laughed at his reaction. He wasn't sure whether they were pulling his leg or not, but Gordon seemed serious:

"No, really, now. Peggy started this—the automobile as a sex symbol, racing as a substitute—and I say it's pure jealousy. A woman has to find something to blame when a man is interested in anything but her."

"You said no coaching," the blonde objected.

"Very well, then. Is it nonsense or isn't it?"

He still wasn't sure what level the argument was on. "I wouldn't say it was nonsense, exactly," he said cautiously.

"There, you see?" Peggy crowed.

"On the other hand, I don't entirely agree with the idea, either."

Gordon slapped the table with his palm. "Damned right."

The girl across the table from Peggy, next to Gordon (whom Peter suddenly recognized as the one Darrol had been talking to earlier), said, "But Mr. Langley, why is it that men refer to a car as 'she,' and give the good ones pet names, and call the bad ones 'bitches'?"

"Mere terminology," Gordon said. "It's arbitrary."

"That's the point," Peggy said. "If it's arbitrary, then the fact that it's 'she' and not 'he' or 'it,' proves something."

Gordon started to raise his voice again, but Celeste broke in with, "We still haven't heard from Peter."

The others looked at him, and he shrugged. "I really don't know. I've heard this discussed before, and it seems to me there's something to be said on both sides."

The man beside Peggy, an older man, gray at the temples, said, "Here we go. ... Why is it that all Americans these days think of themselves as mediators?"

This annoyed him. "All right then, if you want to know, I think there's a kind of comparison. A racing car can be a beautiful thing, and in fact it ought to be. It's a challenge; there's a desire to master it, or maybe I should say to measure yourself against it. There's the lure of the unknown, because no matter how much experience you have, every car is different! You expose yourself to it of course, and—maybe I'm wrong, but I've always felt that love was a little like that. A matter of exposure. The closer you come to the best that's in it, the greater the danger, physical as well as mental.

"The trouble with all this is that it's so damned egotistical. The challenge, the conquest, the possession of something, as it were, just because it's beautiful or difficult or unattainable. This is a side of love most men respond to, in one degree or another, but it certainly isn't the best side. So, if racing is a 'sexual substitute,' as you suggest, then I'd have to say it's a substitute for the kind of sex I don't admire much."

The older man said, "It almost sounds as though you didn't admire racing itself much."

"Admire it? If you mean in the sense of it's being a particularly worthwhile human endeavor, then I'm not sure I do."

"Which brings us to the hoariest question of all. . . . Which I assure you, I'm not naïve enough to ask."

"Why not? If there'd ever been a good-enough answer, it wouldn't still be asked so much. You mean, 'Why do you race?' I don't have the answer, but if it exists, I don't think it has anything to do with admiration. Do you admire what you do for a living, Mr.—"

"Carlson. Yes, I would say I admire, at least, the end result. My work has been with mineral exploration for the British Government, and I would think this has its place; a rather important one."

Peter nodded. "I agree, Mr. Carlson, the end result is important. The same could be said for racing: Most of the technical advances in automobile construction of the past forty years—safety features in particular—have been a direct result of racing. This is admirable, but I don't think it's why anyone does it. It's simply the end product, or one of them; it doesn't explain the act itself. With the obvious exceptions such as medical research, or social work, or something like that, it doesn't really explain why a man spends his life doing one thing instead of another."

"You're saying, then, that you think the motive must be more immediate. . . . More 'interested' as the French put it."

"Yes, I think so. That, and a matter of opportunity, individual capability. . . . Expediency, if you want."

Carlson nodded agreement. "Then it's the old answer, after all: You do it because it's there, because it's something you can do, and because it answers a need."

"Like sex," Peggy said.

Laughter ended the conversation, and talk turned to plans for the weeks ahead. Several members of the party were intending to spend a few days on the French Riviera, prior to returning to Italy for the Targa Florio.

While the others were talking, Marcienne turned to Peter. "What will you be doing?" she asked. "There are no other races till then."

"I don't know. I hadn't thought that far ahead."

"Have you ever been to the Riviera?"

He shook his head. "I figured on seeing it next year, when we go to Monte Carlo."

"It's really very lovely," she told him. "This time of the year in particular."

"Where will you be staying?" he asked.

She took a slip of paper and a pen from her purse and wrote down the number. "It's in Villefranche," she said. "We'll be there through the end of the month."

"I might make it by," he said.

Darrol Anderson looked in at the entrance to the salon. So, there she was, cuddling up: to Kettering. Damned little tramps were all alike, bunch of butterflies, turn your back for a minute and they flutter off someplace else. He wished now he hadn't left her, wasted his time talking to Hauser. Because it had been a waste all right; he knew that much. He'd been watching the man out of the corner of his eye for about a half hour, waiting for a chance to catch him while he wasn't talking to anyone. He'd seen his chance at last, had told Sandra, "Back in a minute, honey," and hurried down the terrace steps to the lawn, where Hauser was standing.

"Hey, boy, how you keeping?"

"Darrol! Why it's nice to see you again, Darrol. I'm just fine, and you?"

The man certainly seemed friendly enough, now. He'd have sworn, earlier on, when he'd tried to catch his eye, that Hauser had looked right past him.

"Oh, keeping real busy . . . can't complain."

"Good, I'm glad to hear it."

"You know, it's good I run into you tonight, Ian. ... I been wanting to ask you about your plans for next year. For the new cars?" Wellsley hadn't been in Formula I for a couple of years, but they were preparing a team for next season, and he knew they were scouting drivers.

"Well, we're not too definite on them ourselves as yet. I assume you mean for drivers? Actually, we've been too busy trying to get started on the cars."

"Understand the prototype went pretty good up at Silverstone the other day." He knew they'd broken the track record with it, unofficially, and that they would field a strong competitor; but, of course, you could never get these characters to admit a thing like that.

"Yes, we were fairly pleased."

"Well, you know, I did pretty good for you in sportscars, here 'while back. . . . Kind of like you to keep me in mind."

Hauser frowned. "I thought you were tied up with Louis for next year."

"Not exactly." He didn't want to admit that he was on a race-to-race basis with Valenzuela. "I'd like to get with a bigger outfit, and Louie'd let me go if I asked him. Not that I would, unless the deal looked right to me, you understand." But he wasn't fooling Hauser, he could see that. The man probably knew down to the small print what his setup was; in fact, he'd seen Hauser and Valenzuela with their heads together earlier on. It wouldn't surprise him if they'd been talking about him then.

The bastards were all the same; they stuck together; get a label with one, you had it with 'em all. He knew what his label was. Crasher. Ever since the time—a year and a half ago—he'd wiped out the two Alfas on the same weekend. Since then, any little thing went wrong, it was his fault: the Porsche at Avus, the Jag at Sebring. . . . And once you got the label, once you started down, why then you got stuck with the pigs; the ones that came unglued if you just looked at 'em the wrong way. Like a vicious circle. He could see from the look on Hauser's face that the man was trying to figure some way to let him down easy.

"Darrol, if you're really interested in doing something with us, we might be able to get you a sportscar, around the first of the year. Sebring or the Tourist Trophy. I don't know if that interests you, but as you say, you've done well for us in sportscars. It might be best to think about that first. So far as Formula I is concerned, we aren't making any commitments at the moment . . . though, naturally, if things went well . . ."

It was just the way he'd thought it'd be, the old run-around. "I don't know as I'd want to risk the deal I got, just for a couple of sportscar rides."

"Of course, I understand that would have to be between you and Louis. I'm sorry I can't promise anything more definite—"

"Oh, that's okay. Keep me in mind, will you? For one of the Formula jobs?"

He shook hands with Hauser, then went back up the steps to the terrace. There was no harm in trying, and you never knew; one of these days he might latch onto something good. If he ever did, he'd show 'em who was a hot pilot. In the meantime, it'd be just dirt stupid to go pushing things in some pig. He saw a girl standing alone at the end of the bar, and thought he recognized her. Linda? Sheila? Something with' an "a." Pamela, that was it; he'd had her last year after a wild shebang in Rheims; she was pretty damn good, as he recalled. He went down to the end of the bar.

"Hi, honey, where the hell you been hiding?" If she was by herself, they'd have some fun.

The first official qualifying was on Friday. Peter's times were not good. He could still complain about the steering a little (it understeered—tended to plow ahead in a straight line under hard cornering), but the car was much better than it had been when he'd first tried it, at Monteville. Most of the trouble was with him, and he knew it.

It had never before been a great handicap to him, this inability to go fast in practice, because in the States—in most of the club events—practice was simply practice, and starting positions were assigned on the basis of engine; size and past performance. After he'd begun winning, he'd been assured of a good place on the grid without having to exert himself prior to the race (a practical system for amateur events, contributing to safety by eliminating the handicap, for the better drivers, of having to catch and pass the slower ones). In Europe, the system was different. You earned your starting position before each race, and the privilege of starting near the front was considerable, if not decisive. To be well placed on the grid meant not only the chance of running the first few laps with a minimum of obstructions; it also meant saving the wear and tear on the machine of getting by slower cars. It is a matter of record that the most successful Grand Prix drivers have had the ability to drive their fastest lap— their absolute maximum—in practice, with no other cars around them, and it was precisely this skill that Peter had never had occasion to develop.

Saturday he went out again and again, using up more of the car than was justified, pushing himself closer and closer to the barrier of what he felt were his limits; achieving raggedness instead of speed. At last Lefevre stopped him, said, *"Assez, assez,"* and nothing else.

When the session came to a close, he was placed eleventh, and knew there were half a dozen machines ahead he should have beaten. Because the new car was fast, he could not deny it; whatever its shortcomings, it was a good car for Monza, and if Lefevre or Volanti had been certain it was reliable as well they would have taken the car away from him and given it to Kettering. It weighed almost a hundred pounds less than the team cars, had nearly fifty extra horsepower; the brakes were excellent, and there weren't many comers at Monza subtle enough to penalize its handling.

He was miserable about his performance so far, but it was too late to improve it, at least so far as starting positions were concerned. For, suddenly, it was Sunday. He'd thought he would get up, go out to the track, wait for the start—and hope for the best. Instead, the worst happened.

Sunday morning it began to rain.

On the 7th Day God Created the Chevrolet
a novel by Sylvia Wilkinson

Sylvia Wilkinson has tremendous powers of concentration. Imagine being in the pits during the 1984 Indy 500 doing timing and scoring for Bobby Rahal and here comes Gordon Johncock's March-Cosworth careening off the Turn Four wall headed in your direction at, oh, 170 mph. "My entire crew ran because they had been hit by a car once before, at Phoenix," says Wilkinson, who stayed put. "Johncock hit right at the base of my wall. I caught my printer with my foot and I got part of his fiberglass in my stand, and I just kept timing (laugh). I wrote his number down and put a circle around it, like he had pitted. Later, I saw the replay on television and I saw how close I came—it was a pretty shocking experience."

Wilkinson did timing and scoring for several years ("I just love it," she says) while writing <u>World of Racing</u>, *a 10-book series for Children's Press; four juvenile racing novels (as Eric Speed); five literary novels set in the South; and two non-fiction racing books:* <u>The Stainless Steel Carrot: An Auto Racing Odyssey</u> *(1973), and* <u>Dirt Tracks to Glory</u> *(1983), the latter a history of stock car racing.*

It was after writing <u>Dirt Tracks to Glory</u> *that she got the idea of writing a novel about stock car racing's early days. "I had a lot of stuff that I didn't use in that book, and I got to thinking, wouldn't it be kind of cool to do a novel about two brothers. I always liked the idea of brothers doing things together."*

It ended up being more work than Wilkinson ever dreamed. "The story was kind of burning to be written, and it about killed me getting it done, because I did it over so many times. In one of my revisions I wrote in the first person, from Zack's point of view. I wrote a hundred pages that I had to throw away."

The title was her editor's idea. "I never liked it," she says. "I called it 'Aqua Velva Man' and at one point I called it 'Lying Dog'."

The excerpt is from Chapter Ten. After a four year separation Zack Pate is reunited with his older brother Tom, who's been struggling to make it as a stock car driver.

One Friday night in June, after Zack and Cy cashed their paychecks and finished paying off their transmission parts for the Chevy, they went to pick up their dates. The Chevy had become one of those things in life that, after you've had it for a while, you can't imagine life without. For Zack it was like when his father had built two new rooms on the back of their house; afterwards it was hard to believe all six of them had lived in that little space that was the house before. For Cy, the Chevy was a practice race car on the back roads of Greenmont; he burned each set of its used tires down to the cord as fast as he could retrieve them from the trash pile behind Maurice's Pure Oil. And for both of them, it was a chance to go out with girls.

They were picking up Sue Ann and Hazel, two women they'd met at Auntie's Grill. Hazel, the plump one, worked at the cosmetics counter in Kress and had taken a liking to Zack because he looked intelligent with those glasses. When Zack met her, every time he got close enough to her to feel her warm skin, every flaw on her body, from the deep pores in her face to her saddlebag legs, evaporated. His brain airbrushed her body till it resembled the photos he'd bought from Sherwin Greenburg in eighth grade.

"I don't know about them women, Zack," Cy said on their way to pick them up. "We ain't even seen them in the light of day yet." He blew the horn in front of Sue Ann's house instead of going to the door.

Hazel had looked a lot better in the dark at the bar than she did now. She had covered the rough places on her face with pancake makeup; her skin was like a fender smoothed out with bondo, ready for sanding. Sue Ann, on the other hand, looked like she had experimented on her own hair with every new style and tint she learned at the Greenmont Beauty College until it looked like singed corn tassels. When she got into the car, she crossed her arms and looked straight ahead. "My daddy says he's heard you drive too fast. He almost didn't let me go out with you. You're reckless."

"Not me. Musta got me mixed up with somebody else," Cy replied.

"Well, I don't know what you think is so exciting about somebody who thinks they're a race car driver."

Without another word to her, Cy dropped the Chevy down a gear and gassed it; the tires screamed down Sue Ann's street. He headed up the hill behind Greenmont to Rolling Pen Road, turning the radio up and waiting for a song to begin before he floored the pedal. Both girls squealed and screamed for him to stop as the car began to whip through the switchbacks, the wheel sliding easy through Cy's hands.

Hazel jabbed her high heel into the top of Zack's foot, yanking his loafer off when Cy dropped the inside right wheel and sent a flurry of rocks into a Sweet Peach Snuff sign on a tobacco barn, sounding like a snare drum roll.

"Hang on, good buddy. Got a record run going this time!"

At the top of the hill Cy hit the hand brake for a bootleg turn. Sue Ann, grabbing for the dash, dumped off the seat onto the floor. Cy let the engine idle, waiting for Elvis to finish "Devil in Disguise." "All right! I beat it a bunch, Zack. He had to sing 'devil in his eyes' two more times before he was through."

"What?" Zack was confused.

"Elvis! 'You're the devil in his eyes.'"

"'Devil in disguise,' Cy. Not his eyes."

"Dis guys, dos guys, don't matter. I beat him."

"You're racing songs?" Zack shook his head. "How do you know they're all the same length?" Sue Ann climbed back onto the seat and straightened her skirt.

"Hey, good buddy. Ain't you ever seen a stack of records? They're all the same size. Hang on! I'm going to blow off old Martha and the Vandellas on the way down. *Heat wave!*" Sue Ann was thrown forward again onto the floor.

After another run up and down Rolling Pen, up to Peter, Paul and Mary singing "Blowing in the Wind" and down to Del Shannon's "From Me to You," Hazel sat stiff as a dummy, one set of fingernails digging into the seat, the other set into Zack's arm. Sue Ann rocked to her sobs as she cried, "I-wanna-go-home, I-wanna-go-home ..."

Cy zigzagged through the dirt roads to the back streets, finally pulling up in front of her house, sliding to a stop against the curb. The Chevy stopped so fast, Zack hit the back of the seat. As soon as the car was still, both girls jumped out and ran like cats dumped out of a sack. Cy dropped the Chevy in low and drove away as slowly as the middle car in a funeral procession. "As my old man would say," Cy drawled," 'Whiskey eyes, lies.'"

"How'd you get so choosy?" Zack complained, crawling over into the front seat. "Man, I'm hornier than a four-peckered goat."

"Hey, man, we've got a car. A car." Cy patted the seat. "A

Chevy. Remember that. We don't have to take the first two that come along. Hey! We can still get inside in time for practice!" Cy turned into the lot at Greenmont Raceway.

"How much are programs?" Zack asked Cy. Cy put his arm around the girl selling them, and smiled. She handed him a program, smiling back, as if that was the proper way to buy one. That program was the key to what Zack was looking for. On the third page he found it: a photo pasted into a collage, a weak shot, but clear enough for him to be sure. The driver dropped his arm out the window and looked straight at the camera. Number 7 was on the door. He wore a helmet with a leather chin strap that fit his head like a white bowl.

The track opened for hot lapping. Zack's eyes searched the moving cars. There was no number 7 on the track.

"Cy, this guy, do you know him?"

Cy squinted at the photo and shook his head. "Can you read what it says on the door?" Zack insisted. "Does it say Pole Cat?"

Cy shrugged. "Hell, I don't know. There used to be a Pole Cat Somebody."

Zack brightened. "How good was he?"

"Pretty good. Fast while he lasted. He only come once or twice last year that I was here, maybe four times at the most."

"What else?" Zack pressed.

"I never seen him win one. But I don't believe he had much of a car. Hard to remember. Why?"

"It might be my brother is why. Tom."

Zack pounded his fist on his knee, irritated with Cy for not knowing more. He watched the race anxiously, searching the pit area, cleaning his glasses and searching again. When the race was over, the two boys crossed the track into the infield, shoving into the crowd that tunneled through one small opening in the fence before heading across the now-dry track, its surface blackened and pounded as hard as asphalt.

A group of men stood in a circle. Others tried to squeeze through to see what they were laughing at. Zack felt a magnet pulling him towards that group. He climbed up on the roof of the concession stand; Cy followed him. When Zack looked down, he spotted the top of the man's head in the center of the group. Everyone was watching this man. His hair was blue black and thick.

"Do it, Pate, go ahead," a big red-headed man said.

Tom turned towards the man and laughed.

"Hey, give me a minute. This takes some concentration."

When Zack heard his voice, it was as if he had finally remembered the name of a song that had been driving him crazy. He started to call Tom's name, but something kept him quiet, like when he was a little kid and Tom would get mad if he interrupted him.

In Tom's left hand was a mousetrap. The spring was set and he was slowly sliding his index finger towards the release. It was a reflex game Tom and Zack used to play. Zack was always chicken because he knew what would happen to his finger. He would have taken pride in waiting for his smashed finger to heal up, but he just couldn't let it happen. At home Tom used a trap so old and rusty that sometimes even the old mouse beat it, stealing the cheese to boot. This trap was brand-new shiny metal.

The race track was so quiet he could hear Tom breathing. Zack's index finger ached as though the trap had already snapped shut. The wait was almost unbearable. Suddenly Tom's shoulder jerked. As the trap shut, Tom's finger lifted to point at the sky, no trap attached. A cheer went up, and a few men clapped. A young man started handing out money, paying off the bets. The red-headed man didn't get any money.

Just as Zack was getting ready to hop down, the red-headed man reached into his tool box, pulling out another trap, three times as big as the mousetrap.

"Okay, Pate. You've won the heat. Let's see how you do in the main event."

"Aw, come on, Daddy, that's a rattrap," said the young man who held the bets. "That mother will break your finger."

"Just take the bets, Allie," Red said.

"Burcham likes to separate the men from the boys," one man commented.

Red Burcham grinned at Tom, saying, "Or the mice from the rats."

Tom studied the trap while the bets were placed. His eyes hadn't moved from it since Red had produced it. He reached into a tool box for a screwdriver. When he set the trap and touched the release with the screwdriver, the trap sprang shut so violently, it flipped out of his hand.

Red Burcham picked it up, the screwdriver still in its

jaws, and laughed. "Look at that. Bent my best screwdriver."

"Take it back to Sears," one of them said.

They all looked back at Tom, waiting for an answer.

"Whatcha say, Pate? Met your match?"

Tom didn't answer. He took the trap back, then walked back over to the tool box. He released the spring and dropped the screwdriver back into the drawer. He shut the tool box lid and placed the trap at about waist level, pulling back the lever to set the spring. The men began to gather closer around him again.

"That guy is nuts," Cy whispered to Zack. He had forgotten Cy was on the roof with him. "But I think he's got the guts to try it."

Zack felt a gust of wind hit the side of his face, just like the day ten years before when the corncrib door had blown shut. A bad feeling ran through him. The men placed bets, but Zack already knew what the outcome would be. All of his excitement at finding Tom was replaced with a terrible sadness. He hated that red-headed man, and his rattrap.

Tom's shoulders moved and almost instantly, Zack heard him cry in pain. Tom dropped to his knees, moaning. His hand lay on the ground, two fingers caught in the giant trap. The red-headed man's son dropped the money and stooped beside Tom. He moaned once again, as Allie Burcham released the trap.

"It just got the tips of his fingers, Daddy," Allie said, holding up Tom's hand. "That ought to count for something."

"Give you a quarter change on that ten you just lost, boy."

Tom yanked his hand away, jumped up from the ground, and butted his way through the group, walking on the money and scattering the men who were collecting it from the ground. Two of them slapped him on the back and one said, "Bet that hurt like a sonavabitch."

"The guy's got some guts. I'll give him that."

"Shit for brains."

Zack jumped from the stand; it was too long a drop and he crumpled to the ground in the midst of the men. He jumped back up and ran to an open cooler where he fumbled for a handful of ice. Then he ran after Tom yelling, "Tom, wait!" Tom stopped and turned around. Zack's hands were cupped out in front of him. "I got you some ice," he said.

Tom winced as he stuck his fingers between the cubes. Zack's hands were aching so from the cold, he could barely keep them cupped.

"Thanks, buddy . . . sonavabitch." When Zack looked up at Tom's face, his brother shook his head and smiled. "How the hell did you find me? Hey, you didn't get much taller." Tom paused. "But those new glasses make you look smart instead of sissy," he added.

When they got to the parking area and Tom saw the Chevy, he said, "You already got a car."

"It's not mine, Tom. Belongs to Cy here. I helped him get it running is all."

"You been doing cars?"

"A little. Not as much as I'd like. How about you?"

"About the same for me." Then he was silent again.

When they reached the car Cy asked him, "Where you headed?"

"Home, I guess. I mean, nowhere really."

"Let's go get a beer or something," Cy suggested. "Celebrate Zack finding his long lost brother."

Cy jumped behind the wheel and started the car. Before they left, Tom's friend, Allie Burcham, ran up and asked if he could go along. Allie resembled the red-headed man only he appeared undeveloped, his skin and hair lacking color like a piglet that had been born too soon. As they left the track, Cy peeled a wheel on the pavement, the squeal floating over the racers in the parking lot. If they'd been in Summit, someone would have said, "Get one." Or "Get on it." Or "Do it." "So you laid Rubber, man. What's her sister's name?" No one inside the car said anything. Zack felt embarrassed, like Cy'd lit a cigar with a dollar bill in front of a bunch of millionaires.

He kept telling himself that this was his brother sitting beside him, the brother he had been waiting to see for four years. He was thankful for Cy, who was the reason Tom came with them. Here he was, really riding to get a beer with Tom, like it was anybody on any day of the year. Zack thought about punching Tom's leg to see if he was real.

"Your hand hurt pretty bad, Tom?" he asked.

"Hurts like a son of a bitch. I could have beaten that rat-trap. I just didn't get my concentration going good before I tried it. Should have held it in my other hand instead of putting it on that tool box. I'll get it next time."

"That's a hell of a act to practice," Allie Burcham laughed. "Like practicing sticking your head in a lion's mouth. Oughta ask my old man for his trap. He'd probably love to watch you practice. He's had it for two weeks." He turned to the boys. "Couldn't wait till he saw Pate. Said he'd let him drive one of our race cars if he beat it."

"I guess he's thinking of another way to rub my face in it tomorrow. He's never going to let me drive his damn car. Why don't you just quit screwing around with that car of yours and let me drive it, Burcham? You can't drive a nail in a snowbank."

"I'm getting better. I went half a second faster tonight."

"Yeah, in qualifying. Then you race like you got an anchor tied on your ass."

Cy pulled up in front of the Speedway Bar and Grill. When they got out of the car, Allie held his white palms up and teased, "Slap my hands, Pate." Zack recognized the hand-slap game that he and Tom used to play.

'Kiss my ass." Tom held his hurt hand against his side as if it were paralyzed. "I don't plan to be feeling any pain pretty soon."

All of Zack's nights of eating supper, then going right home to his room, and saving his money came to a halt as he put down dollar after dollar for beer after beer. The more Zack drank, the more he wanted to talk. Tom was the opposite. He was so quiet, Zack started worrying that maybe he wasn't his brother after all. Up until that moment, Zack had spent four years thinking about being with him; now he was here and he could see Tom like a person in a glass box, but he couldn't get to him.

"Remember when, we had storytelling contests, Tom?" Allie and Cy weren't listening; they were watching a blond who was dancing by herself. Zack couldn't wait for an answer from Tom. "That was the only contest I ever beat you at." Tom looked up, his back straightening a little, his chin lifting from his bottle. "Don't you remember the one I beat you with? I told you I could tell a story that would make you cry and you dared me to try. It was about an old dog. His master had left him behind because he thought he was too old to make the trip west, but the dog followed anyway, dragging his bum leg. The dog limped for days across the blistering desert. He finally made it to the house where the man lived."

Tom yawned and leaned back in his chair, but Zack continued, "The man's house had a new doghouse in front. While the old dog was heading up to check out the doghouse he thought was for him, a puppy ran out of the people house and into the doghouse." Tom took a swig of his beer, but still didn't speak. "A garbage truck sped around the corner," Zack went on, "and drove over the old dog and smashed him. And the garbage man threw him in the truck so the man never even knew the dog had followed him for two thousand miles. That was when I saw the tear. It rolled out the corner of your eye and you tried to wipe it away before I saw it, but I saw it. You knew I'd won."

"I don't remember that story," Tom said flatly. His eyes were glassy in the bar light. He had cried before, Zack was sure of it. Maybe he had changed. He tried to look at Tom through his brown beer bottle.

"Tom, do you remember the idea you had about a bottle that would turn back to sand if you busted it?" he blurted out.

Tom turned his beer bottle in his hand, staring at it like it was supposed to tell him the answer.

"We were down at the trash pile," Zack insisted, "and had busted a bunch of bottles shooting at them. You were afraid Daddy was going to see the glass and we'd have to lie and say somebody else did it."

Tom shook his head slowly, nothing appeared to snag on his brain. He absently tried to tap his cigarette pack with his hurt hand. He groaned and shook his hand, then stared at the cigarette stuck inside.

"The experiment," Zack urged. "Jigger Carmichael was always trying to turn some junk metal into gold and you told him what a dumbass he was because iron had never been gold. You were going to turn glass back to sand. You were going to sell the idea as a way to keep people from getting cut with broken glass." He tossed words until finally one caught. "Sand. Broken glass. The chemistry set."

"Chemistry set," Tom responded slowly, as if he were speaking his first words from a coma. "I wanted the deluxe set for Christmas."

"Right!" Zack said, too loud.

"Mama said it was too dangerous," Tom went on. "She was afraid I'd blow us all to pieces. She gave me an Erector Set instead. Typical Mama." Tom leaned back in his chair. "Wait until somebody lets me drive their car again. It'll drive her crazy," he said with a grin. Then he looked at Zack suspiciously. "What made you think of that bottle stuff?"

"I read where this guy came up with a bottle like that. To prevent litter. You smash it and it turns back to sand. Or maybe it was water."

"Damn," the old Tom filtered through. "He'll be a millionaire." Then he was quiet again.

"Speaking of smashing stuff, you aren't going to believe what we found at the trash pile, Tom. We found Daddy's lost wallet. Remember?"

"Yeah," Tom said. "He told me I stole it."

"It was in the commode. It must have come out of his overalls when he was taking a crap, and he flushed it."

Tom frowned. "How'd it get in the trash pile?"

"That's where he threw the commode because it kept plugging up and then I busted it open shooting."

Tom stared at his beer bottle, tipping his head from side to side.

"'You busted up a perfectly good commode, boy,'" Zack grunted in imitation of Hershel.

Tom began to laugh. Soon both of them were laughing so loudly that a man said, "Hey, buddy, that one's too good not to share." Tom wiped tears out of his eyes with the back of his good hand and laughed some more.

"Your family sounds as fucked as mine," Cy said to Zack.

Zack went to the bar to get another beer; he got one for Tom and paid for it. Tom didn't give him any money. Each time Zack got up to go to the men's room or for another beer, his body felt heavier and his head lighter. He was starting to veer off course and bang into things. He could hear his words and they were slurred. He couldn't remember what anyone said long enough to answer them. He reached into his pocket for a pencil and piece of paper when Tom told him where he lived. He didn't have a pencil or piece of paper. He was as drunk as he'd been the night that Hershel smashed his guitar. He was drunk enough to try to tell Tom the news he had been carrying for weeks. "Hey, Tom. Remember that Holly Lee?"

Tom frowned as though a hammer had tapped him between the eyes.

"Yeah, my girlfriend. What about her?"

Tom's words hit Zack hard, sobering him momentarily. "Uh, she married Buck Herndon," he answered, then quickly changed the subject. "Me and Cy here want to be your racing crew, Tom. We talked about it a lot. We'll work for nothing."

'Well, that sure as hell's a good thing, because I haven't got a dime," he said bitterly.

"Or a car," Allie added, his smile fading under Tom's stare. They sat in silence for a few minutes. Cy got up and went to the men's room.

When Cy got back, Allie said, "You better go tell that big guy over by the bar you're sorry or he's gonna kill you. That blond dancing by herself is his wife and he said he don't like the way you was looking at her."

Cy stumbled over to the bar and stood in front of the man, who was double his weight. They could hear the man's laugh boom across the room. "Allie, did you tell this asshole that whore was my wife?" he called.

Cy came back with a big grin on his face. "I owe you a big one, shithead."

Allie laughed so hard his eyes started to tear, then he sneezed. When he unfolded a perfectly ironed handkerchief, all three of them stared at it before he caught their glance and stuffed it quickly back into his pocket.

The lights started going off. Cy had been trying to outstare a cross-eyed drunk who was slumped in the corner. "Nine days of bad luck, if I don't," he told them. "See, I did it. He give up."

"He didn't give up," Allie replied, looking at the drunk, whose eyes were closed. "The fucker passed out."

"Bar's closing," Tom said, and stood up, steadying himself on the chair back before heading for the door. Allie followed like a pet dog.

Outside, Zack leaned against the car, trying to decide if he needed to pee again before he got in. He heard the engine start, so he crawled in. Cy gunned the motor and slid through the lot, kicking up gravel that bounced off the fence and the cars that were left.

"I think you just totaled the bartender's car," Allie sputtered. Cy laughed as the wheels whined onto the highway. Zack leaned back and looked at the roof. It dawned on him that he might get sick. The next thing he knew, the car was stopping on a bridge. Everyone got out and stood in a row and peed over the side.

"I'm writing my name," Allie said.

"Not me," Cy said. "I'm just pissing."

"Let's see you dot the *i* in Allie," Tom countered.

"I'm just going by Al tonight. That's my real name, Al."

"Your real name is Alfonzo."

"Is not. It's Al."

"It's Albert or Alton or something like that. Take a whole six pack to write it if it's Alexander," Tom argued. "Nobody's real name is Al."

"Well, you can tell my mama that because she named me Al and didn't even know it wasn't my real name." Allie looked over the edge, wobbling as his gaze tried to follow his stream to the water below. "Boy, it's sure a long way down there."

"Nah," Tom answered. "Not so far. Fifteen or twenty feet at the most."

"Have you ever dived that far?" Allie asked.

"Sure. Lots of times. The quarry is twenty-five feet up and a hundred feet deep."

"How deep is the river?"

Don't know. Why don't you jump in and find out?" Tom laughed.

"Dare me."

"I dare you," Zack said.

"Pay me."

"Bullshit," Tom replied.

There was a moment when no one talked. Zack stared down at the water and could see shiny spots where the moon looked back in broken pieces.

"Ten bucks says you won't do it," Cy said. He didn't have ten dollars to his name.

Suddenly they heard someone cry out, an exaggerated yell as if someone were pretending to fall. A dark object blocked the light from the moon, then scattered the pieces of light. A splash rose over the sound of the running water. Then everything went back like it was. Except for one thing: there were only three left on the bridge.

"Holy shit." Cy turned to Zack. Zack felt a rush of sobriety before his drunkenness came back. He gripped the cold metal post in the center of the bridge with both hands.

"He jumped," Zack said.

"The dumb fuck jumped," Tom echoed in disbelief.

They all turned and started moving. Cy and Zack tried to follow Tom down the riverbank, slipping on the rocks and banging on their backsides down to the edge of the water. Tom headed out into the water.

"He's walking on water," Cy said.

Zack slogged out into the knee-deep water behind Tom. Allie had dived headfirst into water two feet deep.

Tom found Allie. He tried to drag him out by the arm. Zack lifted his other arm and they tugged him towards the shore. Dragging Allie's limp body was as hard as pulling out a stump. When they got to the bank and let go of his arms, he fell face down into the mud, his feet still in the water.

Tom whispered to Zack, "I think he's dead."

Zack heard someone coming down the bank. They were silent until they saw it was Cy.

Cy looked down at Allie. "I went to see if he got back in the car. He wasn't there," he said dumbly.

"I think he's dead," Tom repeated.

"Oh, shit," Cy said. "He's dead. We better bury him fast." Cy began scooping up leaves and sticks and throwing them on Allie's back. Then he lost his balance and fell down. "I better go find a shovel," he sputtered.

"Get quiet. I hear a car,' Tom whispered.

Headlights flickered through the bridge railing, hesitating for a moment near their parked car, then moving forward slowly.

"You think they saw us?" Cy asked.

"Yeah, they saw us," Tom answered. "We've got to get him out of here fast."

They began to tug on Allie, dragging him back up the bank towards the car. When Zack pulled Allie's arm, he felt his shirt rip under his arm. Dragging Allie up the bank was like carrying a sack full of rocks that rolled and shifted in all the wrong directions.

Zack felt a sudden burst of strength. Inside his head this seemed like something he would wake up from, but his body knew it was real. Allie's weight was real, the slippery bank, his water-soaked shoes. Finally they shoved him into the car with Cy tugging from inside and Tom and Zack on the outside pushing, trying to get the doors closed before another car came by. Cy started the car. Zack felt the car start moving away from the bridge. His feet were on top of Allie, who was on the floor in the backseat. Tom was in front.

"Where are we going to dump him?" Cy asked. "We could leave him in a gas station."

"Dump him at his house," Tom answered.

That was the last thing that Zack remembered until he woke up when the sun came in the windows of the car. He looked over the front seat where Cy was stretched out asleep. Tom was gone. Then he looked under his feet in the backseat. Just sticks and mud and leaves. Allie was gone too.

Zack threw the car door open and started screaming Tom's name. He woke Cy up. Cy crawled out and grabbed his arm, shoving him back inside. A man on the sidewalk was staring. They were in a vacant lot in a place Zack had never seen before.

"Tom is gone again and I don't have any idea where he went" Hot tears hit Zack's face like spattering grease.

"Shut up and go back to sleep. Tom went home."

"Home?" Zack's voice was thin.

"Wherever he lives, that's where he went. You couldn't find the key to where you live, remember?" Cy dropped back inside the car, grabbing his head as the sun hit his face. "Shit, I don't see how my old man can stand feeling like this every day."

Hours later Zack and Cy went by Red Burcham's shop, where Tom worked. The ghost of Allie Burcham was using the drill press, his head tipped so he could see through a swollen-shut eye, his arms scraped red from the wrists to the elbows.

Tom had his back to them, pounding on something in a vise.

Permissions & Purchasing Information

Permissions

Purchasing Information

Several of the books excerpted in the Anthology are available for purchase.

"Stand On It" by Bill Neely & Bob Ottum is available from:
> Aztex Corporation
> Tucson, Arizon
> Telephone 520-882-4656
> www.aztexcorp.com
> webmaster@aztexcorp.com

"The Last Open Road" by Burt Levy is available from:
> Think Fast Ink
> 1010 Lake Street, Suite 103
> Oak Park, IL 60301
> Telephone 708-383-7203
> www.lastopenroad.com
> thinkfast@mindspring.com

"The Ragged Edge" by Richard Nisley is available from:
> www.racingfiction.com or
> www.Amazon.com

"LeMans 24" by Denne Bart Petitclerc is available from:
> www.Amazon.com

Printed in the United States
20336LVS00001B/232-279

9 781588 500489